Praise for *B*

A rapid-fire thriller filled with captivating characters, **Betrayed in the Bluegrass** ***is a must-read for all horse and horse racing lovers. Set on Keeneland's backstretch, with a brilliantly executed feature race, this action-packed whodunnit packs a punch that will keep you guessing till the end.*** **Betrayed** ***is a riveting addition to Slachman's Bluegrass horse racing series.***

Adrian Beaumont – Director of Racecourse Services for International Racing Bureau

Praise for *Blood in the Bluegrass*

"Slachman captures the essence of why devotees of Thoroughbred racing are enraptured by the majesty, courage, and sensitivity of the animal. An adrenaline-pumping mystery, highlighted by drugs, murder, love and family, and set against a backdrop of Bluegrass traditions, the book is hard to put down as it races headlong at full speed to the finish line."

Barry Irwin, CEO, Team Valor International

Betrayed in the Bluegrass

Virginia Slachman

ISBN: 978-1-950613-90-8

Cover photo: Ed Miller
Cover design: Chris Holmes

Taylor and Seale Publishing, LLC. Daytona Beach, Florida 32118

Acknowledgements

So many people helped bring this book into being. As always, my thanks go to Barry Irwin, who has been an invaluable friend over the years. In addition, this book would not exist without the help of Arian Beaumont, Director of Racecourse Services at International Racing Bureau, who advised me about the particulars of this manuscript from start to finish. Others in the horse racing industry, too, were remarkably generous with their time and advising, and are listed below. And I'd be remiss if I didn't mention the equine vets and other professionals caring for Thoroughbreds, who helped me make sure all the intricacies of equine physiology and health are accurate. And to my brother, heart surgeon Dr. Frank Slachman, thanks for your quotes and advice on Aubrey's injuries. And of course, to editor extraordinaire Veronica H. Hart, and my publisher, go my heartfelt thanks.

Special thanks to:

Barry Irwin, CEO Team Valor International
Adrian Beaumont, Director of Racecourse Services at International Racing Bureau
Shannon Huber
Dr. Frank Slachman
Todd Quast, General Manager/Trainer, Whisper Hill Farm
Dr. Olivia Rudolphi, DMV
Bruce Howard (Equine Medical Director), Kentucky Horse Racing Commission
John Hall
Cesar Terrazas, Yearling Manager, Taylor Made Farm
Jessica Berry, Clarity Thoroughbreds
Gary Priest, DVM, COO, Park Equine Hospital

Tom Riddle, DMV, Cofounder Rood and Riddle Equine Hospital
Jackie King, Indian Hills Thoroughbred Farm
Kelly Coffman, Keeneland Library
Shannon Luce, Director of Communications, The Jockey Club
Drew Smith
Kevin Keegan, DVM, MS, DACVS, Veterinary Health Center, U of Missouri, Columbia
Jim Billingsley, Pleasant Hill
Brenda J. Penzel
Philip Johnson—Mizzou BVSc, MS, MRCVS, DACVIM-Large Animal Internal Medicine, DECEIM
Carissa Wickens, PhD, PAS, Associate Professor Department of Animal Sciences, University of Florida
Karen Von Dollen, DVM, MS, DACT, Hagyard Equine Medical
Anne Nicholas

Cast of Characters

Harper Hill: Owner of Eden Hill Stud and wife of JD Cole
JD Cole: Police detective, husband of Harper
Marshall: Eden Hill's head trainer
Surrey: Marshall's wife
Aubrey Lowen: owner of Lowen Farms
Millie Lowen: wife of Aubrey Lowen
Henley Smythe: Head trainer for Lowen Farms, presently training at Keeneland's Barn 41
Stuart Minetti: New York art collector, friend of the Lowen's, and has financial interest in Lowen racehorses
Sophia Creighton: Friend of Millie Lowen's and owner of El Karta

Betrayed in the Bluegrass

Chapter 1

JD Cole walked through the swinging glass and paneled doors and into the police bullpen, moving fast. He'd gotten the call from his boss, Captain Al Walker, twenty minutes before. It was bad. And the victim was asking for him. JD passed an agitated hand over his auburn hair and made for his office amid siren sounds getting louder as they neared the station.

"He's in awful shape," Al Walker said, striding in and pursing his full red lips. "He literally crawled in asking for you. Keeps repeating your name over and over."

JD took off his jacket and vest, depositing both on the coat rack, dumped his keys on his desk and headed toward the make-shift infirmary they'd created in the break room. The detectives' unit had moved to the Lexington satellite location from East Main two years ago but were still setting things up.

Afghanistan had provided enough nightmarish scenes to last any two people a lifetime, so JD was prepared for what he saw. Nevertheless, it turned his stomach, as the results of torture always did.

JD called up the clinical, objective commander he'd been as the leader of an elite special operations force during the war. His alert green eyes surveyed every aspect of the surroundings, every aspect of the person before him in crystal clarity, searing it all in his mind and sealing it there to be retrieved as needed.

He went to the table, normally reserved for eating and taking a break from the darkness the police confronted day in and day out. The fluorescent lights cast a caustic glare over the dull green concrete block walls and over the scene where the bloody, beaten and apparently tortured Hispanic man lay prone. Two officers JD didn't know bent over him, pressing his wounds to staunch the bleeding.

He was dressed in blood-soaked, faded blue jeans, the right foot bent to the left at the ankle, which was shattered. His belt was worn and old. Someone had unzipped the blood and mud-covered canvas coat so it fell open to the shabby, stained shirt, punctured here and there and oozing blood. The man's face had been systematically and nearly totally destroyed with a shattered orbit bone at the one remaining eye, what looked like burn marks at the forehead, cheek and chin, and bruises so numerous it was difficult to try facial recognition to identify the man.

He moaned, and alternately screamed as the attendants attempted to provide aid, but the ministrations only seemed to prolong his agony. Still the two young officers bent to their work attempting to save a man well past that, the grimness of their toil apparent in each of their faces.

Then the tortured man lapsed into delirium, moaning due to the pain, and then mumbling, shaking his head slowly from one side to another. "JD Cole," he gasped, then lapsed into a dazed and frightened silence.

Al Walker came up beside JD, blanched as he had on helping carry the man in, and backed away from the table.

JD bent over the man's battered face, wincing at the protruding cheekbone and the black, blood-soaked hole where the man's left eye should have been.

"I'm JD," he said, staring into the remaining stark, staring brown eye.

The man seemed to have heard him and tried to move his arm which appeared to have compound fractures. He closed his remaining eye and made an attempt to turn on his side to better see JD, but lapsed back, gasping. JD took his hand, noticing that each finger was broken at the knuckle.

He'd seen this and worse in the war. The man would not survive.

The man's hoarse voice rasped out something unintelligible as he vainly attempted to raise himself. He'd clearly been beaten, broken, and left for dead.

JD looked into the man's eye. What he saw there was fear, yes, and a knowledge of his impending death, yet there was something else. A determination, as if he were willing JD to understand what his mind, battered by his beaten body, was trying to tell him. Sacrificing his life meant the stakes were high, and JD realized he was looking into the shattered mind of a man of remarkable integrity and strength. To have survived what he had, to have willed himself to the precinct, and to be now struggling to make JD understand something against all odds—that was a man to be respected.

But he had no idea what the man was trying to say.

"I'm here," JD said, still bending over the man, willing all emotion away, holding a hand that felt like a collection of small, hard pebbles, the result, JD knew of repeated blows with a flat-faced hammer.

JD waited, his eyes never wavering from the man. He did not revisit his time in Afghanistan, when so many like experiences had occurred, teaching him hard lessons, making him the hard man he was when that was needed. Emotion would not help this man, nor would it honor him. The man, though not yet dead, had given so much to bring something of importance to JD. The former special opps commander would not dishonor that by being human in this moment. What was needed was steel and JD brought that to bear in recording every detail of this encounter.

The man closed his eye and made another valiant effort to convey something to JD but gasped and lapsed into silence. JD impassively considered him, not at all sure what the man was attempting to tell him since the dying man's breath was coming in shallow, rattling spasms and this close to the end, he had lost the ability to speak.

The ambulance arrived then, and paramedics whisked in with abrupt efficiency, carrying the stretcher.

When JD turned back to the man, all he saw was a blank, empty, staring eye.

JD took a seat before his captain's desk. Behind Walker, a tow-headed family stared back at JD from various metal frames on the wood credenza, oblivious to all the horror that passed before them month after month.

Walker fiddled with the black lamp on his desk then leaned back in his chair and folded his arms over his stomach, his blue eyes searching JD's face. "You know the guy?"

"Never seen him before." JD said thinking, not for the first time, how different his boss' life was from his own.

Married to Harper Hill, he and his wife now managed their merged Lexington breeding and racing farms. Eden Hill and Hawk Ridge were proving a formidable pair, as, it was said, was the power couple who owned them. JD glanced at Walker's family. His own life seemed like something from Mars compared to his captain's.

The two officers sat in silence a while longer, each lost in his own thought, neither of them knowing where to go next.

JD's eyes narrowed as he went over the man's injuries in his mind. Someone knew what they were doing. He wondered if the perpetrator had gotten the information he had tried so hard to gain. It appeared not, or why go to lengths that would kill the man in that prolonged, painful way—that was not professional. It took a certain kind of evil to do what was done to the victim and a certain fortitude to survive long enough to reach the police station.

"He must have been tortured close, he couldn't have gotten far in that condition," JD said, rubbing the stubble on his cheek as he thought through the situation.

"Yeah," Walker agreed. "But why you? What did he want with you?"

JD thought about it. He was quiet a long time.

It could have something to do with the war. JD turned that thought over in his mind. That would be unusual but not out of the realm of possibility altogether. The guy dressed like he worked hard for pennies. . . JD tucked that away. The man was Hispanic, but JD couldn't place his accent any more than that, especially since the man speaking at all was nearly impossible through broken teeth and a battered mouth. He'd replay the scene in his mind later and see if it yielded more information on that. JD leaned forward and put his elbows on his thighs, staring at the floor in silence, continuing to process the scene. The torture was not random. It began with the hands since the damage there would not have affected the man's speech. The methodical assault was probably initiated in an attempt to send a message—provide the information or worse will come to you. The damage to the larger bones, the burns on the face, the missing eye . . . it seemed the perpetrator had moved from lesser to more serious injury in order to gain information that was not forthcoming. At some point, JD knew, the torturer would have crossed the line, inflicting increasing pain with the knowledge that the man would die. JD pondered that. It might mean that the perpetrator had originally hoped to gain information in a less-damaging way, allowing the man to live so that, perhaps, he could be put to some other use.

JD paused, reflecting on his lack of feeling. The war had taken something from him. This ability—to detach, to observe and record, to analyze and act—it was not something civilians knew how to do, nor should they. JD had turned a part of himself into something not wholly human. He had also learned to tuck that part of himself away to be retrieved only when needed. Like any muscle, it had to be exercised and he'd gotten plenty of that in Afghanistan.

He generally didn't discuss his cases outside of the precinct—not because it would cause him to relive a horrid experience, but because he did not want anyone to witness what part of him had become. He especially didn't want his wife Harper to see that, but that was the problem.

Many times, she was the only one he intuitively knew could help. She was as hard as he was in many ways. He'd seen that in her unrelenting will to bring her sister's killer to justice. She'd done that against all odds, even though the killer had damaged her beyond endurance in body and mind and heart.

And like JD, she'd had the will and strength to survive. He needed that part of her. He needed it yet he knew it came at a cost. It was a tension he carried with him through each day—his love for Harper set against his need for her unearthly strength.

Finally, JD looked up at Al Walker and sat back in the black wood chair.

Walker repeated himself, "Any idea why you?"

"None," JD said.

"Or what the hell he was trying to say?"

"No idea," JD said, putting aside thoughts of his wife and staring straight into his captain's clear blue eyes. "But I will get to the bottom of this."

Walker nodded. He had no doubt this was true.

Chapter 2

Aubrey Lowen was many things—a successful Thoroughbred stud farm owner, a savvy purveyor of horseflesh, and an art collector. One would have thought the walls of his enormous stucco mansion, inhabited by himself, his wife Millie, and assorted staff, would be laden with historic race paintings. This was true, but a closer look at the dimly lit study revealed some curious choices, ones that spoke to Aubrey's keen eye in things other than horseflesh. An early Franz Kline, a Karel Appel, two Motherwells, a deKooning, and assorted other abstract expressionists graced the walls of his private haunt. He was also a flamboyant presence in the Lexington horse racing world. His antics included holding seances to communicate with the Byerly Turk and the other two Thoroughbred foundation sires, as well as showing up at parties with his face painted like a Native American war chief and shouting at those he deemed competitors.

Yes, Aubrey Lowen was an unpredictable and idiosyncratic icon in Thoroughbred racing. Some said his innovative showmanship as the preeminent blueblood rule basher changed the industry. He was audacious, opinionated, generous, wildly successful, and generally correct. He'd made and lost fortunes, then made them back again. And at present, his broken and beaten body lay on the graveled shoulder just behind his 4-Horse, Featherlight, bumper pull slant horse trailer which, in the dead of night, still housed the runners he'd been transporting to his imported English trainer, Henley

Symthe, who had been nervously awaiting his arrival at Keeneland's Barn 41 and who had, half an hour ago, phoned in his concern to Detective JD Cole. Ten minutes after that, a motorist had placed a 911 call, having stopped to lend a hand, and now the detective was speeding his way to the crime scene.

In the cruiser's dim interior with siren wailing, JD punched in a call to home hoping Harper would pick up. His headlights bored twin holes in the highway as he wove his way to the scene. JD knew Aubrey well; he was Harper's second cousin on her father's side and had bought numerous paintings from her during Harper's days as a Manhattan art gallery owner. They were close and both knew more than most about art and about horse racing. Their connection was why Henley Smythe had called JD and why his boss wanted JD as far away from the scene as possible.

As usual, JD ignored Al Walker. And, as usual, Al Walker relented. JD was the best investigator he had. What JD wanted, JD generally got.

Drawing near the milepost noted by the motorist, JD slowed, pulled to the shoulder but left the kaleidoscopic blue and red lights whirling into the dark night. The motorist stood over the prone figure—JD assumed it was Aubrey on the gravel shoulder—lying unmoving behind the horse trailer. The paramedics would arrive soon by the sound of the wailing siren, mixing with the several police cars also dispatched to the scene.

JD strode to the man gazing at his cell phone looking dazed. He was short, dressed in gym clothes and a thick fleece sweatshirt, with a receding hairline and a short man bun perched low at his neck. His eyes held fear, and he squinted down at the phone, sending a text then glancing up at the detective.

JD held up his index finger asking for a moment and bent to Aubrey just as Harper pulled in back of the police cruiser with her horse trailer. She'd had enough presence of mind to know the horses needed transport to Keeneland as quickly as possible, and Eden Hill was close to the scene. Who knows how long the young racehorses had been trapped in that trailer?

Harper gathered her blond hair into a ponytail as she raced up, zipping her coat, and bent to her relative, concern showing in her blue-green eyes. She looked into her husband's face after seeing Aubrey's labored breathing and the fact that he was both bloody and unconscious. And quite badly beaten.

The horses were whinnying, stomping, and in need of getting the heck out of the vehicle.

"Doesn't look good," JD said, removing his fingers from Aubrey's throat and confirming Harper's fears. "His pulse is thready." JD donned plastic gloves, took Aubrey's phone from his jacket pocket, and slipped it in a plastic bag for later examination.

The paramedics arrived in tandem with the two police cruisers, and four officers jumped out with crime scene tape and evidence collection kits, hurriedly placing lights and cones to close the highway off to one lane at the far shoulder. The night suddenly lit up with a multitude of strobing red and blue lights with yellow caution lights flashing along the highway—all of it casting an eerie otherworldliness to the scene.

Harper stood and backed up a step as the paramedics rushed in to care for the fallen man. After a quick exam, they glanced at JD who raised an eyebrow.

"His BP is marginal—80 over 50—so we'll get Ringers solution into him pretty quick," said the paramedic hanging some IV bags as her partner expertly slipped a cervical collar around his neck. "We need to get him to the hospital pronto."

JD nodded and turned to the motorist.

"Mr. Pollard?" JD said, also standing and turning to the motorist. The man nodded as JD said, "Can you tell me what happened?" He handed the bagged phone to Officer Kane as she passed with the evidence collection kit. She nodded and moved along, intent on her job.

The man reported he'd seen the trailer and observed the open cab door as he'd passed, so pulled over and backed down the shoulder to see if there was a problem. "I was headed home after my workout and it just seemed the right thing to do," he said, glancing at the trailer as the horses pressed noses to the open window bars, snorting and pawing the trailer floor in agitation.

JD took down the man's statement, got his driver's license and contact information and sent him on his way. The man got into his Volvo, not turning back, and pulled onto the highway. Family man, thought JD noting the car then glancing down at Aubrey who was now on a stretcher with two bags hung at his side and a neck collar on. At the count of three, two paramedics hoisted Aubrey off the shoulder and into the ambulance. JD saw that he was still unconscious.

"Keep me posted on his status," he said as the doors closed, and the ambulance tore off into the night. He turned to Harper, reaching to pull her to him as the police officers called to one another, took photos, and inspected the inside of the cab, dusting and swabbing, and generally gathering any evidence that seemed remotely pertinent.

JD put a gentle hand on Harper's hair but didn't linger. He needed to do his job and get to the cab's interior before the officers made a mess of things.

He glanced to the woods strobed in deep green light, then blue, then red, then yellow, pulsing as if it possessed a beating heart. Overhead the stars were bullet holes in a dark and lifeless sky.

Harper and Aubrey were close, so JD took another minute and bent his head to her hair, whispering, "I'll call Marshall, get him to haul the horses to Keeneland when we're done." JD knew Eden Hill's longtime trainer would drop everything and come to Harper's aid. "You go on to the hospital. I'll tell Marshall to have Surrey come get you."

Harper pulled back and looked up into his eyes. "Those horses need out of that trailer now," she said.

"Let Marshall deal with it," JD said, glancing over to the cab, hearing the horses' agitation mounting. Harper was right, but the police had to do their work first. He caught Officer Kane's eye and circled his arm above his head, encouraging her to get moving and finish up the evidence collection. She tapped her partner on the shoulder as behind her, the other officers continued directing traffic. JD turned back to Harper. He knew Marshall's wife would arrive before the trainer did, so he said again, "Let Surrey take you. You need to be there."

Harper nodded and JD made the call on his way to the pickup, waving the police officers out of the way. His second call was the tough one, to Millie Lowen, Aubrey's wife.

Two days later, after sitting vigil at the hospital until dawn that first night and checking in every four hours the next day only to find Aubrey's condition deteriorating, Harper drove to Keeneland to check on the horses who'd managed not to hurt themselves too badly being stuck on the side of the road for a long, long while. A few scraped noses and leg scuffs, she'd heard, but nothing serious. Travel bandages and blankets, and closed-in slant gates helped, she thought. As did the hay nets.

Aubrey had lapsed from unconsciousness into a coma and the doctors were monitoring him, doing scans and tests, but there was no word yet on a prognosis. His condition was listed as "grave" and he languished in the ICU with tubes, beeping monitors, and bags streaming fluids into his arm. He was not yet stable enough to head to the OR, said the docs, adding that he didn't have a broken neck, but the CT scan showed a left-side fracture of ribs six through nine with associated blood in his left chest and a ruptured spleen.

"We put a chest tube in and drained nearly 1500 ccs of blood," Dr. Baxter had noted that first night, his stethoscope around his neck and hands in the pockets of his white coat. He was seated next to Harper, and peered over at Aubrey's wife, Millie, then back to Harper. Noticing her blanch at the number, he delivered more bad news. "It's the ruptured spleen I'm worried about along with possible closed head injury . . ." He trailed off to let Harper digest that.

"So what's the plan?" she asked the doctor as she turned to Millie who had sat in the waiting room by her side, silent as stone.

"Ideally, we'd do laparoscopy, but he's unconscious. The trauma surgeon advised monitoring the situation, so we'll go with that for now. I am sending him up for a CT of the head.

The good news is he doesn't appear to have brain swelling with herniation . . ."

"English please," Harper said, getting irritated with the doctor who seemed intent on intimidating her with jargon.

Around them, the waiting room was filled with low murmurs and the drone of a TV game show host's excited proclamations of an all-expense paid trip to Paris. Two children on the floor fitted together a puzzle of the world, working in serious silence on the African continent.

Dr. Baxter patted the chair arm and grabbed the stethoscope, his long face serious. "There's no evidence of brain injury—so that's good news—but we need to see what's going on under the hood." He stood, checked to see if there were questions, then turned to go.

"You'll update us?" Harper called after him, taking Millie's hand. The older woman seemed stunned, unable to process what had happened.

He turned back knitting his dark eyebrows. "Of course. When I know, you'll know." With that he left.

Harper fetched a blanket so Millie could rest her head on Harper's shoulder and maybe get some sleep. Wait and see, it seemed, was all they could do at the moment.

Harper slammed the Range Rover's door, exiting the vehicle at Keeneland's backstretch parking lot and inhaled deeply trying to put the hospital scene behind her, filling her lungs with the scent of hay, liniment, sweet grain, and the earthy, restorative scent of horses as she made her way into the barn. A few tufts of loose hay skittered along the concrete walkway in the early light. She put her hands in her back pockets and surveyed the clothesline hung with washed and drying whitish bandages punctuated every now and then by hanging baskets of newly planted bright red geraniums.

She glanced up at the sign, Barn 41, where Henley Smythe now worked his magic. Aubrey had called him to the U.S. from Lowen's Newmarket location four months ago. Henley's training system was working miracles on the European tracks, and Lowen U.S. seriously needed an infusion of that. And, unlike at Newmarket, Henley would train solely for Lowen Farms. Henley had agreed on one condition—that Aubrey import Aviragus, Henley's most accomplished 4-year-old colt. Aubrey had readily agreed, saying he had already planned on it.

Harper waded past the first row of stalls stretching off to her right, through the short, dark, packed and raked dirt entry aisle, emerging at the covered shedrow also lined with stalls. Ahead, hot walkers were circling the oval dirt track beneath a huge oak tree, cooling down several two-year-olds who'd just worked by the look of them. They filed by—tucked up, fit, gleaming, and with that oiled, hingey front shoulder walk and confident head nod that meant they'd loosened it all up on the training track and would soon be put in their stalls, their legs wrapped in white cotton stained with cayenne paste. No horse in Henley's care would tear off their stall wraps, that was for sure. Or at least, not after the first time they tried it.

A big, dappled gray strode by on the cool down track, his nostrils still flared, his hind end smooth-muscled. After another round, the Latina hot walker glanced under her charge and smiled at Harper, pointing to Henley's office to Harper's left, just as the trainer came out with a fistful of colored Sharpies and a penciled sheet of paper clutched in one hand. A goat trotted alongside on her leash. Henley stopped next to

Harper, nodding to her, and watched the six horses circle the budding out oak, inspecting each one and raising a flicking hand to their hot walkers. Move along, his signal indicated. He glanced beyond Harper to the wash station where a bay on the smaller side was getting his bath.

Henley glanced at Harper who stood quietly, taking in the horses. The trainer had arrived four months ago, but he was still ungodly uncomfortable in Harper's presence. They'd met soon after the trainer's arrival, Aubrey touting Harper's racing expertise and advising Henley to take advantage of it. He'd snorted at that one. Still, those eyes, Henley thought, taking her measure, they saw too damned much.

He fidgeted, thinking of it, tapping the fistful of markers and scribbled paper on his pants leg as Minerva, the goat, stood by and stared at Harper, her leash swinging to and fro. What the hell did Harper want, anyway, Henley wondered. He tapped and alternately lifted his hat off his head, settling it on his bald pate, then glancing down the shedrow to where his whiteboard was. He needed to get the training regimen updated. Tap, tap, tap.

He stroked his substantial beard with odd affection. It calmed him. All the while Harper stood quietly by his side, watching the colts and one filly pass round and round before them. She seemed to have all the time in the world. What the hell does she want, he wondered again.

"How's Aubrey doing?" he asked finally, more interested—if he was honest—about his job than his boss, though he and Aubrey had been close friends for many years. In fact, their friendship and the fix Aubrey had got himself in, was the reason Henley had agreed to come to the States in the first place. He wiped his bald head with a meaty hand. Abandoning his career now looked like a blasted stupid mistake. He shuddered to think what would happen if Aubrey's loon of a wife Millie ended up in charge.

Harper didn't glance his way. "Still in a coma. It's wait and see at this point." She said it without emotion, avoiding the seriousness of his condition.

Henley nodded and tapped his pant leg with the fist of markers. The soft strains of Latin music washed over them.

God knows, Henley thought, Aubrey better not die, there was too much at stake and they were right in the middle of it.

His mind drifted. It did that under stress . . . back to Newmarket, where in a pique of self-absorption, he'd begun shaving his head. He was going bald anyway, so why not. It was fashionable. And he was nearly sixty-three, so who cared anyway. But the beard. The beard was another story altogether.

"The doctors have concerns," Harper said, her eyes trained on the runners. A nicely made chestnut colt gazed longingly at the grass just beyond the track then swung his head back and continued his slow, circling walk. "About Aubrey's condition" she said.

The trainer nodded soberly then smiled to himself, remembering the days when he could call the shots. Not like the States, with Aubrey and Minetti hovering around. No, back in Newmarket he had the freedom to flaunt conventions, to do as he wished. He stroked his beard—case in point. One did not train at Newmarket and sport such a beard. Unless one wanted to call attention to oneself. And unless such a person could, having had a thirty-year training record, first on The Curragh and then for twenty years at Newmarket.

Then, smirked Henley, one could do whatever the bloody hell one pleased.

Harper pointed to a large bay with arched neck and regal bearing, turning to Henley and raising an eyebrow. "Who's that?"

Henley presented a studied nonchalance, trying to hide his pride. "Aviragus," he said, as if that was enough. He loved that colt, harboring a feeling for him he'd never felt before for any living creature, even his first ex-wife for whom he'd felt some small amount of sincere affection. But nothing like the colt. Not even close.

Staring straight ahead, he cleared his throat and tugged on Minerva's leash in agitation. The goat lowered her head to butt the trainer.

He stole a look at Harper and cleared his throat again. Maybe, blast her, she'd stop staring at the runners and say the bloody hell why she'd come.

Henley sighed. He should definitely have stayed in Newmarket. But when Aubrey crooked his finger, he'd come along as placidly as Minerva on her leash, knowing, of course, he was expected to toe the line. And do Aubrey's other bidding.

He wondered how much longer Aubrey would be around to call the shots. That was a concerning notion.

Henley considered Harper. Yeah, she was a steely one. Never gave away anything, this one. She was a looker, too, Henley thought, catching himself just after. No need to go there. Much too complicated.

The trainer bent to stoke Minerva's head and the goat bleated and backed away. Harper wouldn't give him trouble, he thought, when she learned the lay of the land. After all, Aubrey was her relative and they were thick as thieves. He grinned at his small joke, but sobered thinking of Harper and that husband of hers. JD Cole; he'd be staying away from that one.

Blast the woman, he thought. When she focused on something, it was like she could see right through it. And we can't have that, he thought, now can we?

He'd just have to suck it up while Aubrey was laid up, that's all there was to it. Harper was not about to mess things up for him. He wanted to say if she knew what was good for her, but well, he'd prefer not to go there, either.

Harper finally spoke, looking squarely into Henley's squinty eyes. "Came to check on those horses who were with Aubrey the other night," she said, glancing at her phone to see if anyone at the hospital had texted her. Nothing. Poor Aubrey, she thought, sending him good thoughts. He'd looked bad at the side of the road, so pale. Not like the vibrant powerbroker he normally was, especially back in her father's day. He'd lit up the Lexington hierarchy like nobody before or since. She fervently hoped he woke soon—they needed to get to the bottom of whoever had done this.

Harper stole a glance at Henley. Still pretentious, she thought, just as she had when he'd first arrived. She glanced again. Well, he was entitled.

They both agreed on his entitlement. At least there was that between them.

She stayed quiet, torturing him with her silence. She felt bad about that, but just for a minute. Pretentious twit.

Under her gaze, Henley agitated in place. Harper enjoyed his discomfort a little too much. Idly, she wondered what might be up Henley's sleeve. He seemed unaccountably nervous in her presence. But then, he'd been that way since arriving.

He waved her down the shedrow toward the new arrivals, and turned to walk Minerva that way, heading for the whiteboard. "They're okay," he commented. "Not like Aubrey," he finished, frowning.

"No," agreed Harper, "not like Aubrey."

Henley pointed to the last stalls and told Harper they'd put the colts down there, away from the hubbub till they got used to things. "No worse for wear," he said to no one since Harper had moved on ahead, stopping at Fleet Light's stall. Henley kept his mouth shut as he passed her since she seemed intent on stroking the bay colt's white blaze and the horse moved his head up and down, enjoying the attention.

As she felt the trainer pass behind her, Harper wondered if what seemed Henley's continual state of agitation had anything to do with Aubrey's assault. Well, she considered, it could be her presence. She hadn't noticed he was that way with Aubrey or Millie or any of the staff. Just her. She was curious about that.

She'd like to have a look around his office, see what was what. She glanced down the shedrow to where he stood, marking up his whiteboard.

Real soon, she thought.

Chapter 3

The pair rode out early the next morning. They rode in silence, having argued the night before about Harper's interest in sticking her nose in Henley Smythe's business, a potentially dangerous place to be, her husband had noted. And, as usual, Harper had ignored him. JD had fumed, oblivious to the fact that this was exactly the feeling Al Walker had several times a week. Harper had not appreciated his smoldering objection, even though he'd kept quiet about it as they'd gone to sleep.

JD settled into the saddle, leaned forward, and patted Zydeco's long, chestnut neck. Beside him, Harper and Memphis walked out in sustained silence, the big, black colt seeming to take up all the air in the surrounding county, bouncing and shaking his head, ready to run now that the late March weather had broken winter's hold for good.

Around them the pines, having held forth the promise of life during the freezing season, were surrounded by budded out oaks, paw paws, and elms, and down by the river, some sycamores. The world was coming to life and the young colt was feeling it. That, and scenting on some mares in full heat.

"You talk to Marshall about racing that guy?" asked JD, attempting to break the ice. Perhaps Harper would remember that the colt had been a wedding gift from him. He handled the reins in one hand and moved at ease astride Zeke in the big western saddle. Harper remained focused on the path around the pasture. And silent.

"He's what, four now?"

"Yep," Harper said, finally, smiling at Memphis. The colt was like a coiled spring ready to explode beneath her. His good manners prevented that. They'd taken this route many times and Memphis knew they weren't out for a fast workout, just an easy tour along and maybe through the woods. "I'm not sure I want to put him through that," she said, letting her husband off the hook for the moment.

"Yeah, well, he's clearly up for it," JD said.

"We might have other plans," Harper replied, thinking about how intuitive the big colt was. Not to mention fast and athletic. There was another path for him, she was just waiting to see what he wanted to do.

"I'm gonna let him out," Harper announced, rising into a three-point in her English saddle and giving the colt his head. "Meet you at the rescues," she called over her shoulder as Memphis shot forward, lengthening his stride, and tossing his head in delight. Harper stayed still above the colt, sinking her heels. She wasn't riding short, but then early jockeys rode with long stirrups and her heels and hands kept her balanced as Memphis switched leads around the pasture's right turn and they made toward the rescues Harper had taken in from her friend Mariel, who rehabbed ex-racehorses, training them for new careers. If the horses weren't too injured. Down the line, Harper could see twenty or so eating the round bales set out in their enclosure. As soon as their large pasture grew up enough, they'd be turned out, much to their delight.

Behind them, JD let Zydeco move into a canter, then a gallop as the gelding tried his best to catch up to Memphis. But the colt was having none of it, holding his head up, ears pricked forward, and gathering in the cushiony grass expanse along the pasture, not paying any attention at all to Zeke doing his best to close the distance.

When JD finally met up with Harper and Memphis, Zeke was puffing hard but Memphis was zeroing in on the mares just over the fence, his neck arching and tail flared.

"Best not spend too much time here," laughed Harper, sensing the colt's stud instincts kicking in. "Just wanted to make sure they were doing okay." They all seemed fine, quiet and content, no squabbling that she could see.

Harper nodded to JD, wheeled Memphis to get his mind off the girls in the rescue herd and held him to a trot as Zydeco came along at a slower pace.

"Maybe cut back a little on the alfalfa for the big man—he's gonna run away with you," JD said when the two caught up with Harper.

Harper snorted. "Not likely."

She turned toward the creek, intending to cross it and wander up to the hay pasture beyond the woods, maybe let the horses graze a little. She wasn't dropping the conversation from the night before. Aubrey wasn't just a relative, he was her friend. She was intent on finding out what happened to him.

They crossed the creek, waded through the greening woods, and headed up the steep rise to the pasture's edge, wandering over to the towering maple beneath which John Henry had placed a bench for just these occasions.

The two dismounted and JD switched out the bridles for the halters he'd looped around his saddle horn and their horses bent to munch the sweet new grass side by side. Harper took off her helmet, then sat beside JD, watching their horses as Zeke raised his head to gaze over Memphis' bent neck and then went back to eating himself.

Harper settled and watched the contented pair, listening to their occasional snorts and the low chirping sounds the birds made above them. The greening pasture before them held high promise of a strong alfalfa and orchard grass crop as the short new growth stood up to the gentle breeze in the pale early light. She often rode Memphis around the hayfield, cantering along its edge beside the enormous trees, settling into the calm presence of the colt, so at one with his world. She reveled in whatever greeted them—a red-tailed hawk wheeling over them or deer stepping daintily through the meadow ahead. The silence, the leaves turning in the breeze, the azure sky overhead . . .a wholly natural world. A world wanting nothing of her but to offer its solace, its beauty, its peace.

As she sat beside her husband, her mind's eye traveled the path she and Memphis often took, heading down through shoulder-high Queen Anne's lace, from sunlight into the sudden dimness of the deep woods, down to the creek. Memphis' big, warm body beneath her was a comfort. Sometimes she felt the trees breathing. Sometimes she understood the music of the creek. He'd paw the water, playing with the minnows, then they'd cross and ride up the steep hill to the farther pasture and, in high summer, skirt the alfalfa waving in the dense pasture.

She glanced at JD and sighed. They were so far from those indulgences at the moment.

JD crossed his legs and laid his arm along the bench's back as Harper leaned into it. They were quiet for a time, then Harper broke the silence.

"Find anything on Aubrey's phone?"

JD leaned forward and put his elbows on his knees, his auburn hair catching the sun's early rays. He had held off telling Harper anything about the case. She didn't need any incentive to poke around. But after their argument, he figured he might as well confide in her, she wasn't going to let up.

"Yeah, Millie gave me the password." He pulled Zeke's head away from the colt—not smart to invade Memphis' territory. "There is one thing," he began, turning his clear green eyes on Harper and sitting back, letting Zydeco have a bit more lead as he moved away from Memphis to graze. "The victim I told you about, the one who came to the station asking for me?"

"The one who died."

"Yeah, that one. Aubrey's phone included a text--himself, Henley Smythe, and the victim. The guy's name was Miguel Figarosa and he was an exercise rider, though both Henley's and Aubrey's text comments made it clear he was also a groom and a hot walker. From the looks of it, Henley seems short-handed."

Which was odd, thought Harper. Lowen Farms was wealthy enough to afford adequate help.

"They're all connected then," Harper said, going quiet inside. She turned to her husband. "And it seems Figarosa knew something and knew it would matter somehow to you."

JD nodded. "What that is, though . . . still not clear."

JD had kept all this information to himself, not telling anyone at the station, until all the other evidence from Aubrey's assault came in. But Aubrey having the guy's phone number was not a good sign. One dead, the other one nearly so.

JD stretched his back, his broad shoulders pulling the Hawk Ridge parka. He ran a hand along his jaw and over his high cheekbones. "And there were a few more interesting texts including a horse connection, but supposedly the guy knew Aubrey from the art world."

"Oh, who?" Harper asked. That had been her world for many years and at one time she knew nearly all the major players in the New York art scene.

"Some guy named Stuart Minetti."

Harper frowned. She knew him. Or knew of him. The rumors about Minetti had flown around New York for years . . . mob connected, some said. Dealt in forgeries . . . He was an art collector of some stature and at one time was even implicated in the Isabella Stewart Gardiner Museum robbery. And yes, Harper recalled, he played the ponies. He played them a lot. So it made sense there was a racing connection.

Harper was thoughtful for a moment. Odd that Henley had not mentioned Minetti to her, given her knowledge of the New York art world.

"You know him?" JD said, seeing the frown.

"Yeah, but he's really not someone you want to know too well." Harper turned to JD, their eyes locking. "So Aubrey is somehow connected to Minetti, who may be mob connected, reportedly. No evidence, of course, but that's the rumor. One of the rumors. He's as shady as they come, though nobody's ever pinned anything on him." Harper was concerned. If Henley didn't know Minetti was a bad actor, the results could be catastrophic.

Memphis moved toward a new spurt of growth pulling Harper off the bench. "Hey," she said and tugged on the lead rope. Memphis' head rose and he gave Harper a surprised look. "Yeah, buddy, I'm still here," Harper reminded him. Memphis walked a few steps toward her and lowered his head. Zeke had not missed a beat woofing down the short, new grass. Harper tugged on Memphis for emphasis, thinking she might have to reinstitute the stud chain. She sat down, resuming her train of thought, and vowing to get into Henley's office as soon as she could. Something was definitely not right about the whole situation. She glanced at her husband. She'd keep that piece of information to herself.

JD waited until she was reseated. "It's odd. . .," JD said, somewhat to himself. "Minetti's interest in art and racehorses."

Harper looked at him to see if he was joking. He wasn't.

"And that you know him," he finished, catching his wife's glare.

Harper responded flatly. "Art and racehorses, huh?" She scooted back on the bench and crossed one leg over the other. "It's the same interest your wife has." She didn't look at JD.

He sighed. Hot water. Again.

Harper elaborated. "It's not so odd, actually. Collectors on the scale of Minetti—or Aubrey for that matter—they're attracted to gambling. They gamble a little-known artist will make the bigtime. They gamble that a painting they buy for a pittance will be a winner, appreciate beyond conception. It's all about return on investment . . ."

JD nodded, yeah that should have been obvious. "Okay, I get it. Racehorses share that, for sure."

"And the art world, especially in the City, is a small one. Somebody like Minetti sticks out, so it's not at all odd that I know him. Well," she said, revising herself, "I don't really know him. We've met a few times, but I never did business with him. I know him more by reputation."

The wind picked up and four deer came out of the woods to their left, jumping in graceful arcs, heading for the hay field. The horses shied in unison, and each got a gentle tug on their leads. They shook their heads and resumed grazing. The new grass was like candy.

Harper returned to the case. "So now a glorified groom is dead. And Aubrey's beaten to within an inch of his life. And

Minetti has shown up." Plus, she added silently, Aubrey's trainer is acting squirrely.

"Yes, that's the situation," JD said, attempting to put his free arm around his wife, a move that received a chilly reception. Oh well, he thought, might as well say it. Again. "And it's a police matter," JD stressed, his eyes narrowing and knowing the remark would receive as cold a reception as his affectionate gesture had. "The way this is shaping up," he added," it's not something I want you involved in."

Harper pursed her lips. That again.

"It's dangerous."

Harper frowned. "Paris' murderer was dangerous," she said, her blue eyes hard. "And I handled him."

JD sighed and pulled her to him with his free arm. This time more strongly. She stiffened, then relented, relaxing into his embrace. "You did handle him," JD murmured. "But he almost killed you."

Harper laid her head on her husband's shoulder. Yes, she would certainly be paying Henley's office a visit very soon.

Harper and JD parted once back at the house, he to the precinct and Harper to attend to farm business. Late in the day she made her way back to the hospital. Millie had called and said the doctor would meet with her at 4:00. She requested Harper's presence to "translate."

Millie was dozing as Harper entered the private room Aubrey had been moved to. He was still hooked up to monitors and bags and seemed to sleep on serenely in his comatose state.

Millie sat off to the right in a chair, and Harper turned at Millie's sharp intake of air and subsequent heavy expulsion, then she shuddered awake looking confused. She patted her pockets, likely looking for her pack of cigarettes. At this point in the day she'd be on her second pack. Harper gazed at the thin haze of bleached and dried out reddish orange hair that floated like a cotton candy halo around Millie's head. Everything about Millie, thought Harper, was round. It was as if someone had inflated a blow-up doll a decade ago and then forgot to deflate it, leaving Millie to traverse her universe with arms akimbo and a pronounced waddle to her step.

"Well?" Millie spat out, realizing where she was. And why. "Where the hell is the great god in the white coat?" Millie was in her usual combative form, thought Harper, and also no doubt missing her ubiquitous martini—dry and dirty. It was that time of the day.

She sighed. This was going to be an ordeal. Harper heard the door slide open behind her and in walked Dr. Baxter with his long face, still with the stethoscope around his neck. And hanging onto it, Harper thought, glancing at Millie.

"Mrs. Lowen, Mrs. . . . Cole?" he said.

"Hill," Harper replied, and the doctor nodded.

"Let's talk for a moment," he said, and he waved Harper to a chair next to Millie. She sat, while he remained standing, in the "doctor-as-god" position.

Dr. Baxter became focused as he glanced at Aubrey, then from woman to woman. He directed his speech to Millie. "Your husband has sustained a number of injuries, and as I mentioned the first night, only time will tell if he will recover. We'll need to monitor his neurologic function and watch for ongoing bleeding from his ruptured spleen." He looked at Harper to see if this was registering with both of them. He nodded then went on, turning back to Millie. "I don't want to pull any punches here, so you need to know that infections, respiratory problems, and permanent brain injury are all possible." He paused again to let that sink in.

Millie looked stunned and Harper felt her heart sink. Permanent brain damage. She hadn't considered that. The word "permanent" bored into her like a drill. She glanced at Aubrey, noting his head wrapped in white gauze. He looked smaller somehow, his normal vibrancy and presence gone, the sagging jowl even more pronounced, the pale, sunken look he had not offering much hope. Harper now wondered if a normal life would be possible at all, even if he did wake up. She turned back as Dr. Baxter continued.

"We plan to provide full support including broad spectrum antibiotics and nutrition while we are waiting for recovery of his neurologic function. We'll do everything possible to support his recovery."

Millie stirred from her stupor, turned to Harper, and blurted, "What the hell does he mean, permanent brain injury?"

Dr. Baxter pulled at his chin and then folded his hands, the picture of patience and simulated empathy. "We won't know much for a while, Mrs. Lowen. Let's not jump to any conclusions just yet."

"The ole coot . . ." Millie murmured dejectedly, staring at her husband surrounded by beeping machines.

The doctor then chatted blandly about the remote possibility of Aubrey's condition deteriorating, asked if he had advanced directives, or had signed a donor card. But when he brought up what Aubrey's "Code Status" was, should his condition deteriorate and his heart stop, that sent Millie over the edge. She hefted herself out of the chair, scowling, and faced the doctor square on.

Harper thought, Oh no, here it comes, just as Millie spread her arms wide and began.

"I don't want to hear any more about codes or donor cards, or advanced God-damned directives, whatever the hell they are!" she yelled, poking a finger in the doctor's chest. "You don't know my husband! You don't know me! We're fighters, so just shut your damned mouth and do your damned job. Get my husband back on his feet!" She threw her meaty hands back as if dismissing the entire scene, her halo of fried orange hair set aquiver.

Harper rose quickly and put an arm around the angry woman.

"And get us the hell out of here!" she hissed, looking angrily from right to left, then staring a hole through the doctor.

Dr. Baxter's expression didn't change an iota through Millie's tirade. His countenance retained an impersonal benevolence as the monitors beeped on—obviously the mask he wore in and out of patient rooms as routinely as he tied his shoes. He nodded at Harper, paused a beat to nod to Millie, and without a word, he left.

Millie deflated as he exited, and waddled over to the bed, taking Aubrey's pale hand in one of her own, the blue fingernails of her other hand tracing a pattern on his forearm.

"DNR my ass," she said.

Then Harper saw her back stiffen. Not a good sign with Millie. The woman was gearing up for another onslaught and Harper was the only other conscious person left in the room. Well, thought Harper, at least she's got her fight back.

Harper fiddled with her ponytail in anticipation. She glanced at Aubrey. Sleep on through this one, good friend, she thought.

Millie turned to Harper, still holding onto her husband. "The man wore Indian headdresses all over the house, for Christ's sake," she muttered. Millie then glared at Harper, waving her long blue fingernails in Harper's direction, her mood escalating. "The man claimed he was Crazy Horse reincarnated!" she bellowed. She narrowed her eyes at Harper. "You have no idea how challenging it is to service the ole coot with all them feathers to contend with." Millie huffed, then continued, "But if it's one thing I'm damned good at, it's servicing." She turned thoughtful momentarily. "That's how I made my money, after all . . . after my music left me due to them damned cancer sticks."

Harper had seen this coming, so she merely nodded and kept her mouth zipped. Always the best plan with Millie.

"For Christ's sake," Millie continued, her anger rising again. "Do you know what he said about that damned Arviragus?" She glared at Harper. "Minute the ole coot laid eyes on that colt he announces they'd been together in the Holy Wars. And a course in the Indian Wars, and who knows where the hell else . . ." Millie paused to catch her breath. "Crazy Horse my ass. . . "

Harper glanced back to make sure Dr. Baxter had closed the sliding glass door. She watched nurses and doctors pass without a glance in their direction. She turned back to Millie who stared at Harper, the bags under her protruding hazel eyes looking like two caterpillars had taken up residence under her skin.

Harper knew Millie was trying to cope with the doctor's dire predictions. The woman had little reserves, so lashing out in any direction was her best option for feeling anything other than terror. Harper got that. She tried to appear sympathetic and gave Millie all the attention she could muster. There was little else you could do about Millie's moods but endure them. Look on silently and wait. Anything you said might send her off on a tangent and who knew where that might lead.

Millie's eyes again flashed at Harper. "And what about the sales! Did he not wear warpaint, whoopin' it up in the barn showing off them babies?" She looked tenderly at her husband, lowering her voice and bending over his forehead. "You ole coot."

Poor Aubrey, thought Harper, happy he wasn't aware of Millie's tantrum, the likes of which he'd probably witnessed many times before. Their relationship had always been. . . well, colorful, thought Harper. As colorful as Aubrey himself. In his heyday, the horseman had been flamboyant, there was no doubt about that. He claimed in a newspaper interview to be able to communicate with Man o' War, Count Fleet, Lexington—and the rest of the big stallions who'd passed to the way beyond. He said they told him who to buy at the sales.

Harper gazed sympathetically at Aubrey's still presence, his chest softly rising and falling, the rhythmic blips from his heartbeat monitor regular and hopeful. She missed him. He was an odd bird, but a great and loyal friend. Not beyond cutting corners, she knew, or pulling a fast one now and then, but he was family. And he had a great eye for art as well as the horses.

"Charming, don't you think," spat out Millie, her brows narrowing at her husband. "You speak to them dead horses all the dang time, now dontcha?" She shrugged at Harper, her hands wide. "That psychic put him up to it. Channeling, she said. . . Channeling my ass," she repeated, glowering.

Harper thought back to the stories. Her father had said that Aubrey's flamboyance was in part concealment. Yes, he was the consummate Bluegrass carnival barker, but he was astute enough to buy good broodmares first not the flashy colts and stallions. Breed to the best and hope for the best, was his motto and he'd built a small empire doing it. Then he got into studs and sold off many of the broodmares, focusing on racing and booking his studs. Made a fortune doing it. Then lost it. Then made it back. And now that he'd brought over Arviragus, the farm's racing prospects looked bright again, as bright as their breeding future.

And now what's going to happen? she wondered, looking from Millie to Aubrey.

"Millie, let's go grab a coffee," Harper said. "I think we both need a break."

Millie bent and stared at her husband a moment, then gave the gauze covering over his forehead a light kiss. He didn't stir, so Millie turned to Harper and nodded then marched into the hallway, murmuring, "Do they serve martinis?"

Harper smiled and shook her head as Millie pulled out her phone.

"Then I'm gonna call Harold and take a damned break from all this," she said, staring at her phone but waving an arm. "Harold!" she yelled into the phone. "Get your ass over here." She glanced up at Harper and smiled for the first time since Aubrey had been attacked. "Yes, now, you twit. And bring the you-know-whats and the you-know-what," she said, glancing surreptitiously around.

Harper could read her mind: cigarettes and martini. And if past is prelude, she'd be having more than one of each.

A few minutes later, she stood at the curb with Millie as Harold drove up in the Lowen's black limo. Harold popped out and handed Millie into the back seat where she immediately snatched up her pack and unscrewed the cap on her traveling martini glass.

Harold smiled at Harper and shrugged. Harper mustered up a small grin in return.

"Cheers," Millie mouthed through the window holding her martini aloft then lighting up. She turned to the driver's seat and gave it a good whack sending Harold heading toward the hospital exit and beating a path for home.

Chapter 4

There are a number of undetectable ways to kill a horse, though some do show up in a necropsy. Ping pong balls up the nose will suffocate a horse to death. Then there are the overdoses—calcium, potassium, insulin—or give the wrong penicillin to a foal. Or Chlorhexidine. Tim Bradford, Eden Hill's vet, had seemed startled she'd asked.

"Or, of course, the old-fashioned way," Harper said glumly, "you could just break his legs."

Tim stood up in the barn isle after injecting a block into the lame mare's hock and signaled the groom to walk her up the raked aisle. Around them mares in foal wandered in and out of their stalls, free to roam their paddocks if they liked or come in for hay or a drink of water. Tim nodded at Harper's comment, then looked down. "Yeah, that's true." He stole a glance at Harper who tugged at her Eden Hill ball cap, hooking her thumbs in her back pockets, and watching the mare approach at a trot. Tim turned back to the mare approaching them.

"Looks good, Jose, that'll do it," Tim said, and the groom halted her in front of the vet. Tim bent and opened his x-ray machine and Harper squatted down to hold it at the right angle so he could get a shot of the hock as the groom held her still. After studying the image, he stood.

"That's fine, Jose, thanks." With that, Harper stood and handed the equipment to Tim and Jose put the mare back in her stall.

"That's more or less what they said about Alydar," Harper commented, turning to Tim as he stood. "Broke his leg for the insurance money."

Tim shook his head. "Naw, that's not what happened." He folded up his equipment as he spoke." I know a vet was on that case. Alydar broke his rear cannon bone on a weird gap in the stall." He looked at Harper. "Why are you asking about all this?" He motioned them to walk on and exited the barn. "I'm headed over to the stallion barn, my car's over there. Come with." As they jumped into the 'Gator, Tim turned to Harper. "Your mare will be good on stall rest. I'll check on her. Just have Jose hand walk her after today."

"She better be okay, she's got an expensive baby in that belly," murmured Harper, a bit of concern in her voice.

Tim grinned, his warm brown eyes filled with assurance. "She'll be fine."

Once at the stallion barn, Harper's phone rang. She saw it was Millie and a flood of fear coursed through her. She ran out of the barn and into the sun. "Is Aubrey okay?"

"Yeah, he's the same," Millie said, voicing a slight exasperation. "The great White Coat said every day he doesn't do worse means he's doing better." Harper heard her prolonged inhale.

Cigarette. So she wasn't at the hospital.

"Millie where are you?" Harper asked.

Millie snorted. "Well, I'm headed over to Keeneland to check on that Henley character. Somebody's gotta keep this outfit running." Harper heard the car door slam and Millie's heaving sigh as her large body sank into the limo seat. "Jesus

Christ, would you look at that? Harold! My damned drink!" Evidently Millie had spilled her martini. "Stop patting me, Harold! Get on the damned road!"

"Millie," Harper said, trying to get her attention. "I'll meet you over there." She wanted to check out the head trainer again herself. Might as well do it when she could keep an eye on Millie, to boot.

Millie inhaled a deep drag before replying. "Yes, that's exactly what I was calling for. Who the hell knows what that Brit is up to? You're Aubrey's kin, so it's up to you to figure out if that crackpot he brought over here is screwing us or not." She exhaled loudly. "You can tell if he's doing his damned job or not. I sure the hell can't."

"All right, Millie, just give me a few minutes. I've got the vet here. But I'll be there."

"Damned straight," cut in Millie, then changed the subject. "You got that handsome Tim Bradford over there? Glory, girl, you got 'em comin' and goin'."

"I'll be there as soon as I can, Millie."

"Comin' and goin'," Harper heard, and then a click as Millie hung up.

Jesus, thought Harper, that woman.

Harper turned back into the barn, heading past Nico, just as the South African stallion manager, Lucas, strode by with a wheelbarrow full of square bales.

"Hey," he called, smiling, heading down the aisle. He greeted Tim as they neared Sugarland's stall. "You here to check on your patient?"

Tim looked at Harper and then Lucas. "Former patient," Tim said, smiling. Sugarland had a condylar fracture the year before and under Tim's care was right back to racing form.

"Gotta keep tabs on this guy. Been following Sugar since he started racing again, he's looking good out there."

"Yeah, he got a bad draw there in the last race," Harper said. "Drew the number one and liked to get squeezed right out of the gate."

Tim nodded.

"He's a big boy now," Tim said, stroking Sugar's chestnut head. "Didn't panic, I saw that. Came from behind and did a nice job."

Harper smiled. "Yep, brought a check home, as usual." She moved over one stall to her big black colt. Both she and Tim grinned at Deacon, their bad-ass barnstormer.

"Marshall calls him Devil Boy Deacon," Harper said. John Henry, the groom, Deacon's jockey Cassandra, and Harper were the only ones Deacon let near him. At least without a pitchfork. Or a fight.

"You got a Dr. Fager on your hands with this one," Tim said, mentioning the legendary mean machine, as Deacon raised his head and peered down at the vet.

"After we had to scratch him from the Derby, he won everything. Not a place, not a show. And he savaged a couple down the stretch who tried to come up on him."

"Dr. Fager," Tim said, nodding. "Reincarnated."

Harper moved to Deacon and he lowered his head so she could stroke his big stallion jaw. "He sure races like him," she said. "No one stands up to him, and he knows it," she said smiling and planting a kiss on his cheek. "He's done pretty good in his turf workouts, too—Marshall's thinking about maybe pointing him to the Bourbon Classic on Derby Day."

Tim shook his head. "Yeah, that's a cool million. He'd intimidate the hell out of the older horses. Why not, if he can handle the turf." Deacon stuck his head out, ears pinned, and

Tim stepped back. Behind them Lucas passed laughing. "I think he objected to your use of 'if.' He's a piece of work, that one."

"Hey, Tim," Harper said, glancing at her watch. She didn't want Millie arriving at Barn 41 before she did. "I gotta head out, sorry. Meeting someone."

"No problem." Tim smiled.

"Thanks for checking that mare and keeping track of Sugar."

"Happy to," Tim said. "But you still didn't answer my question. Why did you want to know about killing horses?"

Harper glanced back as she exited. "No, I guess I didn't answer that, did I." She made her way to the 'Gator and took off for the house where her Range Rover was parked. She hadn't wanted to open up that conversation with Tim. With Minetti lurking in the shadows, some intuition told her the information might just come in handy.

Fifteen minutes later, Millie disembarked from her limo at the training barns on Keeneland's backstretch, climbed out, slammed her empty martini glass into Harold's stomach and waddled forward, looking around for Harper. Where was that child? No doubt chatting up her vet and swooning over that mean son-of-a bitch colt of hers. He'd hit Aubrey's runners hard—never had a horse pass him in the stretch. Monster horse. Swoon away, Millie thought, pulling gloves out of her short, boiled wool jacket. Whatever, the girl needed to just get over herself. She ground her cigarette under her scuffed boot and slipped on the gloves.

Harper's Range Rover pulled in a few minutes later. As she disembarked, Millie leaned on her limo and popped her big sunglasses back on her formidable nose, and then lumbered forward to greet her. Smiling broadly and shaking what she considered her shining orange tresses then curving them behind her ears like an ingenue, she embraced Harper and put a peck on either cheek. Noticing Harper's wince, Millie considered she might have chewed a mint before getting in the limo. She removed her sunglasses, took a step back and held Harper at arm's length.

"Well my my my," Millie said, acting if she hadn't just seen Harper the day before. "I see married life to that hunk of a man done you good. You look fat and happy as seven figure mare in foal."

Harper grimaced.

"There was a time they'd a said that about me," Millie began, oblivious to Harper's reaction. For a few moments she was quiet, lost in long-ago memories. She glanced up at Harper as a wave of sadness washed over her.

"I know you're worried about Aubrey," Harper said, her eyes softening. "I'll be over tomorrow and spell you a bit if I can."

Millie nodded, as the weight of Harper's words sank in. She was in a damned fix, that was for sure. And it damned well wasn't her fault. Not by a long shot.

"Oh, Jesus Christ, Harper!" Millie cried, arms on her hips, suddenly exasperated. "Of course I'm worried about the ole coot. But he is inconveniently indisposed at the moment, now isn't he? And I'm left with all this . . . all this." She shook her frazzled cloud of dried out tresses and fell silent, at a loss for words. They stood there like that for a minute and then Millie woke up. Well, hell, business was business. Better get to it.

"I called that Henley character this morning and set up this meet. Let's see what he's up to, shall we?" she said matter-of-factly. She turned to Harold, plucked off her gloves and stuck out her hand, tapping her boot impatiently. He reached in the limo, brought out a glass, and stuck the martini into Millie's waiting hands. She held the stem daintily between her thumb and finger, leaned forward a bit so as to not spill any on her Hillary Clinton royal blue pantsuit and sipped. "Let's walk," she said, once finished. She handed the empty glass to Harold, then they passed into Barn 41, Millie wobbling a bit more than usual.

Harper sighed. Millie had never been what you might call "stable," but Aubrey's condition had sent her into head-spinning mood swings. Still, she was glad she'd asked her to come to the barn. With Miguel Figarosa gone and Aubrey's three-way text, it was obvious Henley was even more short-staffed than he had been. She aimed to offer her services—there wasn't much she couldn't do on the backstretch, from exercise riding to leg wraps to hot walking or meds, and of course mucking out stalls. Being at the training barn would give her a chance to keep an eye on things, maybe figure out Minetti's role in all this and why Henley seemed so damned nervous. She figured Millie would agree to it since it would save her trips to the barn, giving her more time with Aubrey. And more time with her martinis.

Henley was instructing one of the grooms to graze the big, dappled gray Harper had seen on her previous visit as they walked out toward the dirt circle where a few grooms were hand-walking the horses that hadn't worked that day.

The trainer turned and scowled, obviously surprised to see them, then put on a bright smile. Harper noticed his teeth were somewhat bucked and crooked. Henley pulled at his beard. Minerva the goat bleated plaintively on the end of her leash.

"You've still got that stinking goat?" Millie said by way of greeting.

The groom hastily eased the dappled gray to the right and into the grass where he seemed intent on inspecting every aspect of his charge and avoiding the small gathering.

Henley opened his arms in greeting, pulling the goat to him in the process. "Let me put her in her filly's stall," he said, trotting off with Minerva reluctantly following. "I'll return in a moment."

Harper watched him walk away and turned to the rest of the stalls, casting her eyes down the way to Fleet Light's. She'd taken a liking to him on her earlier visit and wondered how the bay colt was settling in.

Millie waved her hand in Harper's face and leaned in close. "So here's what I had in mind," she whispered, sneaking a peek the way Henley had gone. Two young fillies stuck their heads out of stalls secured at chest height by covered, crossed chains, and munched their hay contentedly.

"I want you to keep an eye on Henley," Millie said, leaning back and widening her hazel eyes at Harper, nodding for emphasis. "We'll get him to take you on. You'll work here for the duration."

Harper opened her mouth to reply, but Millie cut in, raising a palm and looking down as if to deflect the coming objection. "I know, I know, you've got business. . .Eden Hill to run, and JD's Hawk Ridge to run, and syndicates, booking the stallions." Millie glanced up. "You sendin' any south this year?"

she asked, completely off topic, referring to the Southern hemisphere breeding option.

"I try to avoid that," Harper said.

Millie nodded knowingly. "You were never the greedy type, honey. I did always like that about you."

Harper blinked. Head-spinning, she thought again, wondering who-knows-what realm Millie's thought had trailed off into.

She glanced in the direction Henley had gone, wishing they could wrap up this conversation before he returned. Her heart sank as she saw him round the far barn aisle and head their way, but he veered off and darted into his office at the last moment. Harper turned to Millie who was scuffing her toe on the cool down track and trying not to lose her balance.

"I have things pretty much under control at the Eden Hill, at least for the moment," she said and Millie looked up, her hands coming together in a prayerful pose, the sagging flesh on her upper arms wobbling under the wool jacket. She looked ridiculously hopeful.

"I'd be happy to help out around here for a short time," finished Harper just as Henley exited his office with a folder and headed their way. "But only for a short time." Marshall could handle most everything and would be glad to, she knew, but his duties were training not overseeing the operations at Eden Hill and Hawk Ridge. If she couldn't get to the bottom of what was going on in short order, she'd have to get back to her real job. She looked at Millie. She at least owed Aubrey her best effort to find out who had attacked him.

Millie resumed her alcoholic attempt at an "all business" face as Henley approached and handed her a fat file folder. The Latina hot walker who had directed Harper to

Henley's office the other day passed them and smiled shyly at Harper.

Harper sketched a wave and smiled back at her, then turned to Henley.

"Aubrey wanted to see everything printed out--all the horses we have and their training schedules, plus the other particulars." He tapped the folder. "And there's suggested races. . .it's a spreadsheet. It's all there, all four U.S. strings."

Millie looked perplexed. But then she looked perplexed quite often, thought Harper. She turned to Harper and handed her the folder.

"Look here, Mr. Smythe," Millie began.

"I've told you, it's Henley," he said and lifted his Lowen ballcap in a salute of sorts, resettling it, and pulling on his beard. His mouth was drawn in a rather tight smile.

"Henley," Millie repeated, grinning, for no apparent reason.

A tall, lanky groom with a chestnut filly walked toward them, then seeing the confab turned on the cool down track and headed toward the stalls. Along the row, several young Thoroughbreds gazed longingly out at the grass.

"Don't forget her supplements," called Henley after the groom, "she's on for tomorrow, so get her ready for the big track early." The groom nodded without expression and passed to the filly's stall. "And check the schedule, I just updated it. Make sure Mariosa knows." He turned back to the two women. "Got to stay on top of them every minute. And we're a bit short at the moment."

Harper chimed in. "That's what we're here for," she began, her blue eyes sharp as the trainer turned her way. "I can spare some time right now, so I'd be happy to come help out."

Henley scowled. That's odd, Harper mused, he was obviously short-handed and needed the help. She watched as he glanced nervously from Millie—his boss, given present circumstances—to the oval cool down track, and back to the stalls. His nervousness only confirmed her interest in looking into the goings on at Barn 41. In the next moment, the trainer tugged at his beard as above it his cheeks flushed deep red.

Yes, thought Harper. I'm definitely getting on board one way or another.

She took the band off her ponytail and shook out her wavy blond hair, pressing the point, "I know how tough it is to keep a training program going," she said, trying her best to look authoritative and appealing at the same time. "I helped my dad. I pitch in with Marshall now and then. I'd be happy to help."

Millie nodded. "I proposed it to Harper, a course, and she agreed." Her stare bored into Henley, driving the "I am your boss" point home.

Henley blanched then smiled, his lips quivering a bit. He stroked his beard in a way that made Harper wince. There was something quite strange about the man's affection for his beard.

"Thank you, so generous," he said, finally, choking a bit on the words. He glanced around with disdain. Harper followed his gaze, from the wheelbarrow full of manure parked outside the stalls to the grooms huddled at the edge of the shedrow, talking in low tones. Henley shook his head and Harper imagined he was convincing himself that taking her on might get his crew in line. Whatever worked, she thought, smiling into his troubled eyes

"No charge, of course," Harper added, inwardly pleased—that should do it. She glanced at Millie, who fidgeted, then pulled a cigarette out of her pantsuit pocket. Harper glared at her and shook her head emphatically—Millie knew better than to light up around a barn.

Millie snorted then tapped the cigarette back in the pack.

Henley glanced toward the stalls, his eyes troubled. "If you're sure," he said, spitting the words out as if choking on them.

Harper noticed his unease and again smiled her reassurance. "Of course, I'm sure. Aubrey is not only a cousin, he's a good friend. If I can help out, I'd be very grateful to you."

Bloody hell, thought Henley, what a turn of events. As if he didn't have enough work already—now he had to manage this. Well, he mused trying to come up with some way to swallow this new development, if she was such a great friend of Aubrey's maybe he could keep things on the "down low" as they said in the States—an incredibly stupid phrase—or if not, convince her that it was in Aubrey's best interest to keep her damned mouth shut. He glanced at Millie, thinking she would not be a problem.

"I'd be just as grateful to have you," he lied, stumbling again over the words, turning to Harper and snatching the folder from his new employee's fingers. Can't have her perusing that. He nodded to Millie and conveyed his best wishes for Aubrey's quick recovery then turned and made a beeline to his office, studying the folder's contents.

Harper watched him beat a retreat then gazed at Millie who surveyed the dull white barns stretching off toward the smaller training track. Harper followed her gaze over the tall, newly budding trees, the white fences, the lime green grass.

"Let's get out of here," Millie said, closing her eyes, her posture slumping. She had abruptly sobered and the convivial, combative mood had faded.

Harper felt her sadness. She and Aubrey had spent many years on the backstretch, in the sales pavilion, and of course watching their racehorses, some of whom came close to making history a time or two. Her sadness, thought Harper, was earned.

As they walked past the two fillies at the end of the shedrow, Millie stopped for a moment to peer into a stall, her bloodshot eyes sad and brimming. The filly lay in her deep straw bedding, drowsing.

"Sleep well, princess," Millie said, looking suddenly old, and Harper took her elbow to lead her to the limo. When they arrived, Millie signaled Harold to hold off a minute, so he got into the Mercedes and shut the door. Millie turned to Harper.

"Listen, honey," she said, looking like a deflated balloon. "I know I'm a little off my game these days." Her voice trailed off as she gazed at the drying bandages swaying in the cool breeze. "I apologize." She looked at the dirt. "I didn't used to be this a-way," she said wistfully. "Back in the day." A slight smile played over her lips and she looked up at Harper. "Me and Aubrey spent our good years right here . . ." She sighed, looking around again. Harper had the feeling she was wondering if that was all coming to an abrupt end, and soon. "I never regretted one minute of it." She pulled out a cigarette and flicked the lighter with her long, blue fingernails. She took a deep drag and dropped her arm.

"And before that . . . up on that stage in Harlem with the band. Oh them black sons a bitches could play . . ." She again grew silent and looked out beyond the back of the limo where a used Snickers wrapper mixed with tufts of hay had skittered across the drive. "Me and Aubrey, we was somethin' back then." She tapped her cigarette, thoughtful. "I'm just sorry things turned out this way, sorry I leaned on you so hard."

Harper took her free hand and looked into her blurry hazel eyes. "It's okay, Millie, don't apologize. You haven't leaned on me at all. And none of us is handling this situation all that well." Notwithstanding her previous outbursts, Harper's heart went out to the aging woman. Her whole life was collapsing around her.

"Did you know that's where I met Aubrey? Up there in New York City, at them Harlem clubs I sang at? He was as dashing as they come back then." She nodded. "Hard to believe, I know, but he was. Took my breath right away." She let go of Harper's hand and leaned on her black limo. "The ole coot. . .Took me for the grandest ride I ever have had." She looked at Harper and tucked a stray frizzled curl behind her ear. "And I guess I just don't want it to end." She smiled wanly and looked away. "Not just yet, anyway. Not just yet."

Harper signaled Harold and he got out of the limo. Together he and Harper got Millie situated in the back seat, and Harold eased the door shut, got in the driver's side and pulled away.

As Harper watched them go, she, too, sobered. Yes, Millie cut an enormous and rather ridiculous figure at times. But though Millie might seem a parody of a dimwit--a woman you'd dismiss without thought--she wasn't. She was a shrewd businesswoman and knew as much about the racing game as

Aubrey. Which is why it was a bit odd that she'd enlisted Harper's help to figure out whether Henley was on the up and up. If Aubrey had been the showman with an eye for talent, Millie had been as much the brains behind the business as her husband. She could have reviewed the training and racing schedules, scoped out the runners and his training "system" just as well as Harper.

She mulled over Millie asking Harper to help out on the backstretch. Harper had her own reasons for doing so, but what were Millie's? No, Millie had not lost her shrewdness, no matter the picture she often presented, or how sincere her sadness was.

Harper gazed after the Mercedes and wondered whether or not Millie was playing a game Harper was not even dimly aware of.

Chapter 5

The reason Marshall bit his tongue and stayed silent at the edge of the training track as Milton jogged by on the Byrnes Mill colt was that Milton was already in trouble—the bay had his ears pinned and was bouncing all over on a big, bunched hind end. There was nothing to do, really, about Milton. He'd been around for a few months and hadn't performed worth a darn.

Eden Hill's head trainer frowned. He let a long breath out that immediately frosted up in the late March morning. Dawn was just breaking over the rolling hills beyond the track and the woods beyond the far pasture lit up in ethereal light. Marshall loved this time of day—the wind's bite with a taste of full spring on the way—in that, he was unlike most head trainers. A new day, he always thought, and who knows what might happen.

Too bad, though, about Milton. He liked the kid, as he liked most of the riders he sent out on Eden Hill's training track. Marshall was a softy, but he tried hard to keep that from people.

Actually, it wasn't a secret. Everyone knew he loved the horses, and the exercise riders, and the jockeys, and the grooms . . . but most of all, he loved Harper and had loved her sister Paris. He'd been head trainer at Eden Hill since before they were born and, since their parents' deaths, had been more or less a father to them.

"Hey, Cap," called Milton, pointing a finger at Marshall as he walked the colt toward his cool down. It seemed he wanted to show Marshall he had gotten him under control.

Marshall smiled. Well, he thought, the kid was too big anyway and didn't have the hands. It wasn't his first choice, but he'd given Milton as many tries as anyone deserved. The trainer held his Eden Hill ballcap in his hand and planned when he'd have the conversation. Needed to be today. Best get it over with.

Marshall's smile fled as Milton again began bouncing, unbalanced over the colt, his eyes flicking to Marshall then back to the two-year-old, who had realized he was headed for rest and maybe some grazing and so had picked up the pace.

Ah hell, thought Marshall, the kid was nervous to boot.

Marshall had come up with the rest of the older trainers around town over at Keeneland. Some of them learned their trade and some didn't. Like with the old gal. Miss Henrietta had been around for a thousand years breeding and training, first at Santa Anita, then she'd moved her outfit to Lexington and showed up at Keeneland. She'd been a terror in her younger days, and a darned good rider, but when she hit 65 and still thought she could ride two-year-olds on the training track, well, that's when things got dangerous even with helmets and what little protective gear they used back then. She was a disaster waiting to happen and nobody said a damned word.

He'd stood next to Brookfield's trainer the day it happened. Clay was a good ole boy even back then, who brought his babies along slow and if they needed an x-ray, he got it. Not like some. His daddy started riding at thirteen down in Juarez in the wild days and had run into Pancho Villa storming the villages. That was a heady time for a young kid and you either learned to fight—both on and off the track—or you folded your cards and went home. Clay came up with his no-nonsense daddy and had enough horse sense even in those early days to make everybody else seem worth less than dirt.

"The old dame better get offa them colts," Clay said. He looked away as Miss Henrietta rode past and obligingly nodded to them. "She's gonna get herself or somebody else kilt," he whispered and, lifting his head, gave her a slight nod.

To their left, Adriano Batista, an Argentinian trainer whose family had been in racing since the 1800s held forth, splattering his opinion over kowtowing sycophants, as usual. He squinted into the new sun's glare just mounting the horizon and gestured with the leather stick in his hand, talking a hole in the wind which was what he was best at, holding forth until his horses came down the path from the backstretch barns.

"She's an idiot," Clay said to Marshall, his eye on Miss Henrietta. He shook his head, all that red hair falling over his face like he wished for a curtain so as not to see the pile-up.

Marshall patted him on the back and pulled at his black mustache.

Adriano was today conducting a tutorial on the subject "horses that don't win." Because, of course, his string was having a dull time of it.

"I no want my babies win first time out," he asserted imperiously, waving his stick to the right and left of his pot belly. "Owners no like that. The babies, they need go to school—listen to the rider, get mud in your face, you go—yes—into the gate . . ." He gestured trackside and then to the stands, holding court. "You break good, you change the lead, you learn trust—the babies need trust." He bobbed his head at his little group, emphasizing how wise were his observations. "Go slow." He closed his eyes a moment, nodding sagely and then glanced briefly at Marshall and Clay. "You understand this, no?"

"Geez I love it when the sun comes up," Clay said, ignoring Adriano to the Argentinian trainer's embarrassment which he tried to hide with a disdainful snort, just as Miss Henrietta's bay colt curvetted and bolted into the breeze lane by the far rail. It took about three seconds, and she wasn't ready for it. Of course she wasn't ready. She was ancient.

She flew, wide-eyed as a cartoon character, up and over, off the colt's back end, turning and tumbling to land under the feet of a very fast bay who had come up pounding hard, trampling her then just kept going, never mind his rider doing his best to pull the colt up. Miss Henrietta's trainer had the ambulance on speed dial and hit the button before she hit the ground.

Around them in the dawning light, the horses lined up awaiting their turn began snorting, crow hopping, and side-stepping as the exercise riders did their best to hold them all in check.

Adriano surveyed the broken woman lying prone by the far rail. He gasped, clutched his chest in anguish, sank into the grandstand seat, and glancing around at his equally horrified small gathering, murmured, "Miss Henrietta, my little sparrow, my darling." His bowed his head, a stricken look on his face.

She'd spent the race season in traction and never went to the track again.

Marshall blinked and sipped his coffee, gazing at the runners now completing their workouts on Eden Hill's sand

and dirt track. Well, what the hell could anyone have said to her, anyway? he thought.

They'd all talked like that for a few weeks after it happened. Even Adriano. Then Miss Henrietta slipped into the past and nobody much mentioned her after that. Nobody wanted to jinx their string by mentioning what bad luck she'd run into. Bad luck that could so easily rub off on them.

Bad luck of her own making, thought Marshall, which was why he always fired the ones he knew wouldn't make it right off the bat. Rip the Band-Aid off, that had become his motto.

"Hey, Marci," he called to one of his best riders, the one up on Meadow Flower, their new hot prospect. She pulled the filly to a halt, perpendicular to the track, to wait their turn. The filly was compact and fierce. "Tell Milton to see me once ya'll are done."

Her ball-topped knit cap nodded once as she rubbed the filly's neck with her stick. "Sure thing." She had eyes, she knew the score.

Marshall turned to see JD striding up. The cold breeze picked up and ruffled what hair the police department allowed. Not for the first time, Marshall noted how much he looked like his mother, though his strong jaw was a nod to his father, Red Cole.

JD approached, hands in his pockets, his big frame relaxing the closer he got to the track. Marshall was glad to see him. JD generally came to workouts when he could before heading to the police station. The Thoroughbreds seemed to soothe him. And why not, he'd grown up on one of the best broodmare farms in Lexington. With his father out of the picture, and JD's marriage to Harper, they'd merged the two farms and it appeared their plan was working out better than anyone had expected. Breeding Eden Hill's premier studs to Hawk Ridge's Argentinian and Brazilian broodmares had been a stroke of genius and it looked like the early babies were going to add a lot of black type to Eden Hill's pedigrees.

JD shrugged inside his Hawk Ridge parka and pulled his gloves on. The two men were about the same height, but Marshall noticed—and not for the first time--that JD had those wide shoulders, muscled out arms, and the hard body that evidenced time put in at the police station gym, keeping his military service body in shape to chase the bad guys.

Marshall's hand unconsciously went to his stomach. He had been known in the confines of his bedroom to exercise a slight streak of vanity, standing sideways to the mirror, taking stock of the slight paunch he'd developed and blamed on his wife, Surrey. A blame, he knew, she deserved—she was a great cook. Still, he didn't like the paunch.

The trainer glanced from his runners to JD, bringing his cup up to his lips.

"So," JD said, holding Marshall's gaze, "how they look?"

"Mostly good. Comin' along," Marshall said, focusing on the two-year-olds striding by. He set his coffee cup on the rail and stuffed his hands in his jacket pockets.

JD smiled, his eyes lively. "No promises, right."

Marshall learned that lesson the hard way—never get out ahead of yourself, it took you right out of the game when things went wrong. And they did. They did go wrong. Stay in the moment. No looking too far ahead, especially with the precocious two-year-olds.

Take Deacon, the closest to a "sure thing" he'd ever trained. Look what happened to him . . . But not getting out ahead of the moment had paid off, and now, well, now who had any idea what the son-of-a-bitch black colt with the bad attitude might do.

"Well, there's Deacon," Marshall said, saying it all in three words. The fractious colt was the gift every trainer hopes will come along. That is, as long as the trainer stayed away from the business end of the colt. He smiled. "It's always the bad asses . . ."

They both paused, watching a while in silence, then gazing out over the track as the workout wound down and the exercise riders headed their mounts to their cool down. Some were still raised off the tiny saddle in a riding perch, knees in, even at the walk. Marci nodded at Marshall as she passed with another bay and two black colts—she'd taken Meadow out on a solid jog just as Marshall had asked. Around her, the riders jabbered about grabbing a beer later.

"Seems Harper's headed over to Keeneland. Said she's gonna help Aubrey out on the backstretch for a while," Marshall said, bringing up what he knew was a sore subject with JD. He pulled his hands out of the jacket and leaned on the rail, gazing at JD. Harper hadn't shared too much with him, but the trainer had known her since birth. She had that look in her eyes. Marshall couldn't imagine JD was happy about it. The trainer got quiet, and JD dropped his gaze to the track.

"Yeah," he said. "Think you could talk some sense into her for me?" He smiled and shook his head.

Marshall grinned, picked up his coffee and sipped the steaming liquid. "Right," he said, sucking his salt and pepper mustache and thinking how alike they were. When either one got a notion, there was no talking sense into them. "I'll get right on that."

The conversation died as the pair watched the last few muscled out horses walk by, two by two or singly. They shook their heads, full of spirit, attitude, and the energy of bodies fit for the bright future spread out before them. Marshall vowed to do his best to see they achieved that future safely. After their juvenile year, after they'd gained knowledge and tactics on the racetrack, they were poised to take on the campaign of their next year. By then, they'd settled into a fine nobility and the joy of bodies that did not impede them. He toasted the last of the horses, those under his care and charge, with his Styrofoam cup. A few tried to break into a trot, anxious to get back, but settled under their riders' cues. They were learning at this stage. Let them learn well, wished Marshall. As their hooves kicked up little whorls of dirt, Marshall thought there wasn't anything more beautiful on earth than a fit, sound, barely contained racehorse—in body and in mind. So he focused on fitness. To keep them safe and give each of them the best shot at reaching their potential. He watched the babies depart and inhaled the comforting scent of two-year-olds he loved then turned to JD.

"How's work?" he said, forcing his mind into another channel, knowing JD had seemed a bit frustrated lately.

"Caught a bad one just before Aubrey was attacked. Not great timing." JD sighed and pushed off the rail. Conversation over.

Marshall nodded, not surprised JD had cut the discussion off. He wasn't one to talk about his cases, even when prodded.

"Gotta go," JD said. "We'll catch up later. You coming for dinner?"

"Surrey and I'll be there at six," Marshall said. "You know Surrey. You'll have enough food to last you a month."

JD patted the rail and left.

Harper glanced out the kitchen window to Buck's Creek and then over it to the barn her Grandpa had built when he'd founded the stud over a hundred years ago. Harper and Paris had, more or less, grown up in that barn working with their grandpa, mucking out stalls and doing whatever else was needed to take care of the horses. Harper stared at the windows a few moments, hoping to see Memphis' fine black head appear, then turned back to her task. She set the tip of the chef's knife down on the cutting board and scissored the handle up and down, moving the length of the carrot, scooping the even circles up on the blade and dropping them into the salad bowl. Then she picked up the celery and did the same, thinking about what she might find at Henley's barn—she was due there bright and early the next morning.

Well, no sense anticipating, she'd just have to allow things to unfold and wait for developments. Worst case scenario, she'd get into Henley's office after hours. She had her racing license so being on the backstretch late wouldn't be an issue or even an oddity, though getting past JD might be a different story. She set the knife down a moment and peered up at the sky, thinking they could use some rain. Resuming her task, her thoughts went back to Barn 41. She needed a look at the folder Henley had snatched out of her hands, the one containing information about the horses-in-training. He'd studied it with an odd intensity after grabbing it back, making Harper wonder what he might be trying to hide. And, of course, there was Minetti and how he figured into all of it.

She forced herself to stop thinking about the backstretch, refocusing on the task at hand, making sure she moved the celery evenly under her blade. Time enough for Henley and whatever he was up to in the morning.

She chopped as she'd been taught by Jung Hee, an old Asian man in the City, though he used a different sort of knife. It was not how his relatives sliced vegetables, he said, but he was in New York now, so he'd "adjusted."

She paused and again looked out the window to Grandpa's barn, the softening light at the end of day portending a full spring. She had been "adjusting," too—back in Lexington, married, running the stud. She smiled as Memphis stuck his finely featured black head out of the stall window and looked her way. She lingered there, indulging in her affection for him and his uncanny intuition. It wouldn't be the first time he'd read her mind.

She resumed chopping, needing to finish up her tasks. She glanced at the clock. Marshall and Surrey would arrive soon, and JD was due home anytime. She'd also invited Millie, thinking she could use a break from the hospital and some company. Millie was bringing along her friend Sophia Creighton who had recently put a horse in training with Henley—a favor, apparently, Millie and Aubrey had bestowed upon her. She must be a very good friend, thought Harper. As he'd mentioned, Henley had horses in training scattered across the country under the watchful eye of Lowen's assistant trainers, but Sophia's horse was at Keeneland. Unless things had changed there, that would be quite a favor.

Sure enough, a few minutes later and right on time, the door opened and Marshall's deep voice announced his and Surrey's arrival. Harper's golden retriever, Kelso, trotted in before them, his nails clicking against the polished wood floor and heading for the fireplace to plop and snooze in front of it.

She waved her knife at Kelso and sent him "behave yourself" messages then glanced out the window, but Memphis had gone. Likely John Henry was making his rounds for the evening feeding.

Harper's cell phone rang. Tim Bradford, their vet. She picked up. He'd been due out that day to check on the rest of the mares they had in foal but hadn't showed up.

"Hey," she said, and heard Bradford sigh. Not good news, then.

"I got a call from Stella, the Lowen's broodmare manager this afternoon. Two of their mares in foal needed looking at, so I didn't get over like I thought."

"No problem," Harper said.

"Their regular vet is out of town so she called the back up, then me. Sorry it took so long."

"How'd they do?" asked Harper.

"Lost the best one's fetus, the other one's okay," Bradford said. "I'll be over in the morning to check on your girls."

Harper frowned. More bad news for Millie. Harper set the knife down as Surrey and Marshall headed in from the foyer. Could be just bad luck. Breeding and foaling season never went as you planned. Her heart went out to Millie. It's never easy.

Harper picked up her knife. But still . . . too much bad luck for one farm.

"Okay, missy," chirped Surrey, interrupting Harper's thoughts as her short, portly frame bustled in. As usual, she was grinning, numerous bags hanging from her arm. Marshall trailed behind with the covered dishes. "Just scoot yourself on over," she ordered, winking. The kitchen had always been Surrey's domain. Her shoulder-length white pageboy shifted as she gave Marshall his orders. "The pies go in the refrigerator," and then back to Harper, her brown eyes dancing, "Why don't you go poke that fire up, sweetie, and I'll get the rest of this going."

Marshall gave Harper a shrug and twitched his salt and pepper mustache, which Harper thought made him appear rather walrus-like. She popped the hors d'oeuvres into the oven and headed to the fire.

"Get to work you two, I'm just going to heat up the pot roast a bit, and we'll be ready." Marshall dutifully plodded into the great room and popped the cork on a nice Pinot Noir he'd brought. "Where's that husband of yours?" he said to Harper who was toeing Kelso off his spot in front of the fire.

Harper poked the already roaring fire, and closed the large, wrought iron decorated glass doors. "He'll be here, he said. But we can eat and he'll catch up if he's late." She patted Kelso's head and he rose from his sit and again curled up in front of the fire.

Surrey popped the potatoes au gratin and marinated green beans into the second oven, then lit the flame under the pot roast. Marshall and Harper gazed her way and gave her a thumbs up. The already cooked beef gave off a savory, rosemary-scent that made their mouths water.

Harper took the goblet Marshall handed her and they clinked glasses. Harper crouched to pet Kelso and stared through the pass-through fireplace into the formal dining room. The table glittered under the contemporary chandelier—Harper's addition—her mother's silver, china, and faceted glasses creating a special occasion when there really wasn't one to celebrate.

"Looking forward to getting the last of the foals on the ground," Marshall said. They'd had a good foaling season so far, with no mishaps for their own or their clients' foals. "Cody's done darned good job and it hasn't been an easy go with a couple."

They'd bred Hawk Ridge mares to a few of their studs. Mary Edvers did the nicking along with JD. Harper put the Lowen's fetus loss aside and rehearsed the nicking negotiations, which made her grin—it had been quite the tussle to get JD to agree to work with their bloodstock agent. Mary was not the easiest person to get along with, but she knew her business and had been with Eden Hill since Harper's father had been alive. She could read a pedigree and performance record like no one else and had developed an instinct for productive breeding pairs. "Here's what my daddy said back in the '20s," she'd intone, "Fair Play crossed with Rock Sand and you got yourself a winner. And here's what I say. To hell with breeding twigs for legs—get some international bloodlines in our runners or the game's goin' to hell. Take it or leave it." To say Mary had her "own opinion" was an understatement, but JD was right in her league. Harper had been glad to be far from the fireworks of that working relationship. And, Harper thought, better JD to deal with her than me. "You owe me bigtime," was JD's comment on the agreement.

Marshall plopped down on the leather sofa in front of the fire. "Couple more to go. I think Quillon's gonna foal here next . . ." Marshall looked up and patted the forest green cushion. "Come, sit," he said.

Harper sat and stared at the fire. "Got a call from Tim just now," she said finally, sipping her wine. "Did you hear from him?" She settled into the soothing sound of a crackling fire and the equally comforting presence of Marshall.

"Yeah, I heard. Tough to lose a potentially great foal," Marshall said. "They're doing a necropsy."

Harper nodded. That was standard. The insurance company wouldn't pay off without it.

"Something didn't sit right with Tim," Marshall said, frowning. "Lot of insurance money involved with that Lowen mare, and she was bred well . . . so some bucks at stake."

Harper looked at Marshall. Tim Bradford had incredible instincts. He'd saved their friend Gray Burke's farm a few years back and came on board a year later when Eden Hill had come close to being destroyed.

"What'd he say?" she asked.

Marshall stared straight ahead. "He didn't. Waiting on Rood and Riddle to do the necropsy. With Aubrey down, I'm glad Stella called Tim."

They sat in silence for a while, listening to Surrey hum. She checked her pots, glanced up to the two on the couch then rounded the granite countertop to switch on the lights in the great room. "No sense sitting in the dark," she murmured then whisked back to her pots and pans, clattering about from island to stovetop.

Marshall finally broke the silence, turning a bit to Harper. "I think we got a couple a fillies and at least three colts look good for the season," he said, reporting on the training of their two-year-olds.

Harper nodded, meeting his gaze. She'd wait with the rest of them to hear about the Lowen mare.

"JD said the same thing. Said you have one filly there might contend with the boys, too." She squinted a bit at Marshall, her eyebrow raised in question. It would be great to have a budding Rachel Alexandra on their hands.

"Yep," Marshall said, "Meadow Flower, she's not the biggest girl out there, but she's a tightly wound package."

Harper nodded.

"Inside and out. I'm gonna put Cassandra on her for the first baby race—fire meets fire and see what happens."

Cassandra Maloney, one of the nation's premier jockeys, had become their "go to" rider the previous year. They'd had an impossible time finding a jockey who could ride Deacon but had settled on Cassandra with good results. She'd somehow had enough strength to ride the biggest colt she'd ever sat. But it wasn't physical strength that made Cassandra successful with Deacon. She had the connection. She also had the hands, the head, the heart, the vision, the aggressiveness, and the guts to back it up, and the stillness. She knew when to check him and when to turn him loose. It was the connection, though, aside from what you saw with your eyes, that made Deacon listen to her.

Simply put, she'd earned his respect. And not many had.

Harper smiled. Putting her up on Meadow made sense. "Hopefully we'll get fireworks of the right kind."

"And Meadow, she's smart as a whip. She's small, but we'll see if she gives the boys a run for their money," Marshall said. "I'm looking forward to her first juvenile race."

The door slammed and in strode JD, taking his navy-blue jacket off and laying it on the couch back. He walked over to Harper, bent, looked in her eyes, and kissed her, cupping a big hand softly on her cheek, then went to the fire and leaned on the mantle, propping a foot up on the marble fireplace plate. He bent and ruffled Kelso's big head.

"How was work?" she asked. She knew JD had been trying to piece together the Minetti, Lowen, Miguel Figarosa connection. And, like JD, he hadn't talked about it much after the conversation they'd had by the hayfield.

JD stood and shook his head, his auburn hair catching the deep red tones in the firelight. "Not great, I'm afraid," he said. He looked at Marshall and then at Harper, his green eyes focused and unreadable. "Not the discussion to have around a family dinner."

The doorbell rang and Kelso popped up and trotted to the door, followed by Harper. She opened the door on Millie and a willowy, dark-haired Sophia Creighton who stepped in, Sophia with a bouquet of flowers and Millie with a cigarette. Harper shook her head. Millie sighed and flicked the live butt into the gravel in the turnaround.

"Please go put that out," Harper said, but Millie made a face and lumbered by Harper, while Sophia smiled and went to extinguish the cigarette.

Typical, thought Harper, thanking Sophia and escorting the elegantly dressed woman into the foyer.

Sophia turned her gray, appraising eyes on Harper. "Thanks so much for including me," she said, extending her hand gracefully and introducing herself. Harper took her hand but not before noticing the rock and the 18-carat gold, emerald-studded bangle she wore. "Loaded" was the message. She took the bouquet of tulips and smiled her thanks.

After introductions all around, Harper put the flowers in a cut-crystal vase, then hearing the convection oven ding, she pulled the hors d'oeuvres out and set them on a serving plate. Marshall uncorked another bottle and they all sat before the fire to chat while the roast finished heating.

"Quite the feast," noted Millie, raising her glass to all, sinking more and more into the cushiony chair, as she plucked a bacon-wrapped shrimp from the plate Harper offered.

Marshall turned to Millie. "Sorry to hear about your mare," he said and she shrugged, the gesture suggesting she had more serious issues to contend with.

Marshall changed tactics, nodding to Sophia. "So how did you two meet?" he said. Everyone seemed curious about that. Sophia's obvious refinement and her quiet graciousness was a sharp contrast to Millie. Harper guessed her age to be mid-fifties, but she'd obviously had some high-dollar work done, so who knew.

Sophia smiled. "Our families were acquainted, so it was natural . . ."

Millie interrupted. "My mom cleaned the Creighton's house, if you could call it that. More of a mansion, if you ask me." She looked at Sophia. "No sense sugar-coatin' it, honey. That's the truth."

A small, good-humored chuckle came from Sophia. "Okay, that's right. But," she added, looking around, her gray eyes shining, "Millie and I did become friends."

"It was the horses, a course," chimed in Millie. Harper noticed her lipstick had strayed a bit out of the lip line, perhaps a misapplication due to some earlier lubrication.

JD shifted at the fireplace, and replenished Sophia's glass. Surrey leaned forward, all ears, and Marshall nodded, indicating he'd like to hear more. They all would, so Harper was quiet.

Kelso got up and trotted over to plop next to Sophia. She let her hand stroke his head, finding the spot behind his ear he loved to have massaged. His big eyes lowered in delight.

"They had a dang big ole barn, is what it was," Millie said, cutting to the chase. "And a course Sophia had all the lessons, the half-a-mil European jumper, and she was all the rage on the eventing circuit." Millie toasted her friend with her wine.

"But you had the hands, Millie. You had the heart," Sophia said, looking around the group. "You should have seen how the horses took to her, they melted in her hands. She rode like a queen." Sophia finished and toasted Millie back.

Marshall stifled a guffaw. Harper blinked doubtfully.

The fire crackled. The shrimp lay ignored. The roast might well burn but nobody moved. Only Kelso's golden head moved from person to person sensing something unusual in the air, then tucked it under Sophia's hand for more rubbing.

Sophia resumed stroking Kelso and smiled at the group's reaction, turning tenderly to her longtime friend. "But she had another gift," she said. "A voice like an angel." She took a small sip of wine. "When she sang the blues, the heavens wept."

Harper glanced at Millie. It looked as if she might weep, too. Harper moved to stand behind the woman whose life was crumbling and laid a supportive hand on her shoulder.

The room was quiet. There was a sort of reverence in the silence, as perhaps tribute to a past Millie had left behind for the love of a man who lay just as silent, just as still, in a coma on the other side of town.

Harper thought to move the conversation along and perhaps get Millie's mind off her husband, at least for a moment or two.

"Where do you live now?" she asked Sophia.

Sophia sipped her wine. "I'm on the upper east side in Manhattan. Wanted to be close enough to the Met to walk."

"Oh," Harper said, "so you enjoy art?" She looked at Millie, who stared at her wine.

"It is one of my passions," Sophia said, smiling, her gray eyes alight. "Aubrey and I have had many conversations." She glanced at Millie. "He has a wonderful collection of abstract expressionists. A collection I envy," she said, seeming to stress that last comment. Harper wondered what that was all about.

Millie looked at her and frowned momentarily, then gulped her wine.

Surrey, as usual, brought everyone back to earth. She slapped her hands on her thighs and said "Well, we better eat or it's all gonna burn up," then rose to bustle around in the kitchen getting the buffet set up along the granite-topped island.

JD stood at the fireplace, his big frame commanding the room though he said nothing. Then, as Surrey and Marshall got busy setting everything out, JD posed a question to Sophia. "What made you send your horse into training with Aubrey and Millie? Send your colt—or is it a filly?—now, as opposed to last year or next?"

Sophia was thoughtful a moment, took a small sip of wine, then seemed eager to respond. "It was Henley and that incredible training system he put in place at Newmarket. Gosh, he turns out winners like no one I've ever seen." She looked from Millie, who seemed skeptical, to Harper and back to JD. "I just couldn't pass it up when Aubrey offered. Of course," she said, "I'm paying a premium." She glanced at Millie. "Which I'm very happy to do—Henley taking on a non-Lowen-syndicate colt . . . I'm very grateful. I know that is not what the trainer signed up for."

Harper looked at Millie who squirmed in her seat. "Actually, that whole dang barn is filled with client horses.

Aubrey got a hair this year when everybody started calling after they heard that Henley character was coming. We only got Aviragus over there at Keeneland. Had to move our horses other places."

Millie's tone soured. "If you want my two cents, I told the ole coot, it was a bad idea. Especially didn't want your colt in on Aubrey's little 'experiment,'" she said. "But me and Sophia, we're old friends," Millie said morosely, looking away. "So Aubrey insisted."

"And I really couldn't be more grateful," Sophia said, looking a bit perplexed then nodding to seal the point. "Very happy. I can't tell you how I absolutely adore El Karta. He has *absolutely* captured my heart. And every indication is, he could be an incredible racehorse." She looked from face to face. "Under the right training, of course, which—to answer your question, JD—is precisely why now, why here, and why Henley. He's a proven commodity and I wouldn't trust my beloved El Karta to anyone else. The trainer told me he was out of a 'blue hen mare' and he looked forward to training him." She looked perplexed, so Marshall chimed in from the kitchen.

"He was telling you that El Karta's dam had produced proven winners on the track. He must have some fine breeding in him," he finished, extending the compliment, watching the smile spread across Sophia's face.

At that, Millie rose and headed toward the kitchen. Sophia looked after her and said to the group, "Excuse me." Rising, she followed Millie saying, "I feel very fortunate. Very grateful to you, Millie, and to Aubrey."

For whatever reason, Millie acted as though she hadn't heard her. They arrived at the counter and began to fill their plates in silence. Only Sophia seemed oblivious to the undercurrent of unease that had spread through the room.

Chapter 6

The next morning Harper's alarm went off at four o'clock. She turned to face JD who slept on. She gently lifted the blanket and prepared herself to step lightly out of bed when JD shifted, turned onto his back and gathered her under his left arm. His warmth was intoxicating as was his scent. Harper snuggled her naked body next to his, resting her hand on his chest and throwing a leg over his thigh. A minute, she told herself. She closed her eyes, indulging in just a moment of drowsy pleasure. Then JD, still half-asleep, turned to her, nuzzling her neck just above the clavicle. She sighed, and as JD rose over her, she found herself not too sorry to be late for her first day of work.

A while later, after a shower, a protein smoothie, and a carafe of coffee to go, she glanced at the clock and cringed—it was nearly 5:15—the training tracks would open in fifteen minutes. Without doubt, she'd be late for work.

Thank the stars, she thought once on the road, for light traffic. Still, it would take her some time to reach Keeneland, she might well miss the first set. She sped up impatiently and after a time spied Keeneland's Gate 1 and rushing through it, headed toward the backstretch. She passed the track kitchen, and once at the barns, she hopped out and sprinted through and into Barn 41. Henley had just given a leg-up to the last exercise rider and the horses began to make their way to the Polytrack—the small track closest to the barn.

Ah, good, she thought. He's not heading for the big track for the next set. She trotted toward him just as he turned.

"Well, good to see you could make it," Henley said in his crisp British accent, fingering his stopwatch, "on your first day."

"Sorry," Harper said and gulped her coffee. His normally bald head looked a bit fuzzed. He was in need of a shave. "Happy to do whatever. Just point me in the direction."

"I'd like you to accompany me, please. I have three colts I would like you to observe."

And with that, he and the Hispanic riders atop their charges continued their walk down the dirt and white fence-lined path in the early light down to the Polytrack for training. The riders chatted amicably among themselves, while Henley gazed at his phone, checking messages. He pulled out a ballcap and covered the fuzz.

Out ahead of them the sun rose higher off to the east, changing the sky from gray to vivid pink as rays began to hit the white fencing and poles, dispersing the drifting mist. As they neared the Polytrack, Harper could hear the horses, the air moving in and out of lungs and hooves hitting the track as the few riders crouched above their Thoroughbreds close to the far rail breezed their mounts.

Harper hoofed along behind the horses, gulping her coffee and cursing the magnetism of the husband she loved to distraction. As she passed a trainer at the rail watching a two-year-old colt, he glanced at his stopwatch muttering, "A piece of junk from day one."

Henley glanced up from his phone and motioned Harper over to the rail to watch with him, leaning on it as the earlier set wound down their workout. He nodded to his timer down the way and pocketed his stopwatch. A group of bays and one deep black filly, all with long legs and smooth muscles, came to a walk as the new riders headed up the rail and the ones finishing up their jogs and gallops headed past going the right way. The track was crowded, but orderly.

Along the rail a last bay finished up his breeze, the rider off the colt's back, quiet and steady above a young horse obviously enjoying a bit of freedom.

Harper saw a group of five other young horses and their riders approach along the dirt path from another barn, the riders in black helmets and chest protectors, the horses done up in the navy and gold colors of their trainer. The Thoroughbreds swung their heads and moved into an easy, loose walk as they all entered the track gate and headed up to await their turn. A few broke into a bouncy trot, then they all lined up perpendicular to the track on the other side of Henley's group.

"I have three out today I am quite keen on. I would like to hear what you think," Henley said. He stroked his beard.

You are a cagey one, Harper thought. Henley wanted to see what sort of horse sense she had. He didn't need her opinion.

She'd watched Fleet Light's exercise rider get a leg up, so she was interested to see how he moved out there. It was curious that Henley had pointed him out as one of the "good ones," since he'd so recently arrived. Unless he was clearly a wonder, it was too early to know if that was the case. From what she'd briefly seen, she had some questions anyway about whether Fleet Light fit the bill. He was well made, yes, but the sweet disposition and soft eyes she'd picked up from him sometimes translated to not much heart on the track. Sometimes, she corrected herself, but certainly not always. And he was a bit on the smaller side. It took a whole package to make a star—heart, breeding, the right training, the physical chops, desire, a head for it . . . and luck.

She pulled out her phone, prepared to video anything she found of interest. Or concern.

Henley unzipped his jacket a notch and pointed to two other colts he had out there along with Fleet Light and a couple of others. "I'd like your opinion on Aviragus," he said, pointing to the seventeen-hand bay colt with a jagged white blaze and two white socks.

Right, she thought, that's the colt he and Aubrey had imported when Henley came to the States, the one she'd noticed on her previous visit.

"He's four now?" she asked, knowing he'd raced in England and Europe, making a name for himself on the continent. He was the same age as Deacon. Harper would definitely video tape him for Marshall. The two would no doubt be meeting each other head-to-head.

Henley nodded then continued. "And over there you have El Karta, a close friend of the Lowen's' owns him."

Sophia's colt. Harper gazed at the black colt, not quite as big as Aviragus, but he still stood over a lot of ground and had a racy appearance. He swung his head their way and Harper caught the small white star between his dark eyes.

"They're doing gallops?" she asked as the colts trotted out after the previous horses had exited.

"I have the babies at the gallop, the rest we have jogging, but yes, I'm not pressing any today at the rail."

"I paired Aviragus and El Karta," Henley continued, pointing to the pair, and turning Harper's attention there. "El Karta is ready to work. I would like to see what he's got in here." The trainer tapped his chest. "They'll go out together."

So Henley wanted to see how they reacted to a partner with talent—this was a workout about heart, about desire, about what her grandpa called "the look of eagles." Deacon had it in spades. Did Aviragus? Harper was glad Henley'd insisted she come watch.

She turned her attention down the track along the center lane where the colts had finished their trots and now moved into an easy gallop. She raised her phone to record the three. As they came along the far stretch and headed for the last turn, she saw Fleet Light surge ahead of his small pack, then be pulled back by his rider. Ahead of them, Aviragus and El Karta, both with long strides, looked like they were anxious to run, pulling on the bit and rolling their eyes at each other, on the muscle. As they rounded the turn, Harper heard their hooves drum the track, and their breathing. She'd been videotaping the two and had gotten Fleet Light's brief surge, but it looked like the pair coming toward them were locked in a battle with each other and with their riders. Then Aviragus ignored it all and took off, bucking at the rider's attempt to check him. El Karta kicked into action, too, elongating his head and busting out after Aviragus. The riders quickly got both colts under control but not before Harper saw what she needed to.

Sophia had reason to be excited. El Karta had a mind of his own. But he was a baby so he'd learn, that's what two-year-old training was about—putting the precocious babies through "how to be a racehorse" school.

But Aviragus. Harper smiled. He'd been to school and appeared to have dropped out. Just like another racehorse Harper knew. Deacon, she thought, had perhaps met his match.

Once the entire set had finished, Henley nodded at each of the riders as they came by, the Thoroughbreds lazily bobbing their heads and the riders quiet, their sticks tucked into breeches and blue jeans, sticking up behind their backs. Henley asked each rider how their horse had felt and each gave a thumbs up as they passed.

Harper watched El Karta bringing up the rear and narrowed her eyes. The colt seemed a tad off on his left front leg. She glanced at Henley, but his attention was elsewhere.

Harper moved off to take a look at the set from further up the track, passing Henley's clocker who headed toward the trainer and began a flurry of Spanish. He pointed to notes he'd made on a small pad, then handed them both to Henley and left. Henley's face gave away nothing. Harper couldn't tell if he was pleased, surprised, dismayed, or had heard just what he'd expected.

Harper turned her attention back to the track. Fleet Light seemed frustrated, playing with his bit, sidestepping, then jumping into a trot. Maybe she'd misjudged him. She'd have to wait and see. She wondered, too, if she knew anyone in his syndicate. She glanced at Henley who was occupied with checking the horses over. She'd ask about that later.

Separately, first El Karta walked by looking superior and a bit haughty, though still ever-so-slightly off. The attitude was okay, he'd earned it. He was followed a horse length behind by Aviragus, who was snorting and still looked pumped to run. As he exited the track, Henley grinned and got in step with the big colt as they walked back up the path to their baths and cool downs.

Harper hurried up to catch Fleet Light and quietly walked by his side until he was at the cool down track.

"I'll cool him out," Harper called to Henley. She liked the colt and, anyway, she was there to do some work.

Henley nodded. She untacked Fleet Light and put on his thick leather halter and stud chain. Close up, Fleet Light seemed to gain in size, which happened with some horses. They don't look like much, but the closer you get, the bigger they seem. She took his measure. He had a nice laid-back shoulder which helped his front-end action; tight, straight legs, and his front and back end were nicely weighted. He was a well-made colt, thought Harper. No wonder his prospects looked bright.

She glanced over at El Karta's glistening black coat, and then at Aviragus, both ready for a bath. She'd check on Sophia's horse later.

After she'd hot walked Fleet Light, she was heading to his stall when Henley motioned her into his office. She handed him off to Aliana, the Venezuelan groom she'd met on her first visit, thinking she'd like to talk to her privately. Aliana smiled and nodded, taking Fleet Light's lead and talking to the colt as she led him toward the shedrow.

Harper meandered down the aisle, past feed buckets, cinder block walls, and stalls hung with full hay nets. She paused a moment, inhaling the scent of warm horses, green hay, sweat, and dirt. There was nothing like the smell of a barn. The big tree in the center of the cool down track towered over the dirt circle, budded out, promising a bit of shade in a short while. As the sun rose, a soft glow tinted the sky a hazy blue.

She entered Henley's office, closing door behind her, and sat in the metal chair in front of a gray metal desk. It was dim inside the office, with only the early, weak light coming from a filthy window behind the trainer, whose desk held a laptop, liniment, and hoof treatment, along with a dirty coffee cup, a stiff coat brush, a pencil holder, a water bottle, and a few files. Henley laid his stopwatch and the scribbled pad to the side of the computer and pulled on his beard, staring at her. In the power chair, Harper saw he was trying his best to intimidate her, which made her inwardly smile. Bring it on, buddy.

The parts of the desk she could see were covered in dust. In contrast, the walls held shiny brass chifney and snaffle bits, well-oiled leather tack, and to Harper's left, a file cabinet. Though the desk and cabinets were dirty, Henley did appear a stickler about his tack.

The file cabinet had a lock on it, and it appeared engaged. She'd need the key. And a password for the computer. Harper trusted her instincts. The groom's torture and death, and then Aubrey's attack . . . it all led back to Barn 41. And it all led back to Henley. She needed to see those files as soon as possible. She smiled politely.

"So how was your first day?" Henley said, breaking the silence which hadn't worked as he'd apparently hoped.

She offered not a squirm, not a frown or fidget.

"Good, good," Harper said, nodding and brushing off her breeches. "I can see why you wanted to bring Aviragus over. El Karta is no slouch, either, though he seemed to favor that left front a bit." She raised an eyebrow, asking for some comment.

Henley smiled, ignoring her question about the young colt. "Yes, Aviragus will set the States on fire. And Sophia will be pleased with the progress El Karta will make. He's young, he's learning. But quite talented, obviously."

Henley shifted in his chair, changing the subject. "I would like to see you up on one of the three I had out there today."

No doubt, Henley wanted to judge how competitive Harper was, not just his three colts.

"Fleet Light has a little fire in the belly, too," she said, not responding to Henley directly. Tit for tat. She smiled. She'd enjoy taking Fleet Light out.

Around them dust swirled a bit in the shafts of light as the day came on in earnest. The silence lengthened.

"Yes, we will have you up on Fleet Light first, then," Henley finally said. "I will pencil you in. Perhaps you could rotate?"

So, Henley wanted to see what she would do on the big colts. She'd ridden Deacon, not telling Marshall or JD of course, but she'd taken him out for a two-minute lick a few times—she had a good clock in her head. She'd be okay on either one of them, or both.

"Sounds great," she said, her blue eyes staring a hole through Henley.

Henley averted his eyes, sighed, and picked out a pencil to fiddle with. When she didn't move, he smiled and stared at her, the look chilling as he said, "You will, of course, be very careful. You know . . . accidents do happen. Bones can break."

Chapter 7

Baby races were as fun as they could be exasperating, Harper thought, fiddling with her Daily Racing Form, especially this early in the season. April races were short sprints, a bit like an extended workout or schooling, with the races increasing in distance half a furlong as the season went along. Oh well, she sighed, it's good see what's out there. She always went to the baby races to scope out the competition if nothing else. And in that she was like most of the other spectators at Keeneland that fine day.

Harper emerged from the short walkway onto the grandstand aisle just at the finish line. She paused, drew a long breath, and surveyed the infield's huge screen where Keeneland races were shown to racegoers wanting to see every moment, including the backstretch. Beyond, the lovely white fencing, green grass, the Keeneland expanse stretched out before her under a blue sky she was thankful for in the early April rainy season.

The stands weren't packed, of course, just the serious race lovers, trainers, owners, and assorted other connections, showed up for the babies. The two-year-old juveniles were the future, and serious players wanted to survey the crop as soon as possible.

Harper turned to smile at Surrey who came alongside, corralling her white pageboy as the wind picked up. She and Harper both paused to admire the track, glancing up at the "Keeneland Green" stadium. They'd all spent many years watching races unfold on the dirt or turf before them. Sophia soon joined them, looking very springlike in her flowered dress and sweater, her eyes glowing. They mounted the grandstand steps and excused themselves along the second row, seating themselves in the stadium chairs. "Best view in the house," Harper's mother always contended, normally avoiding the members only clubhouse, and over the years, Harper had come to agree.

Surrey surveyed the track while beside her Harper nervously fiddled with her binoculars. She knew she wouldn't have time to really see anything through them. The babies were going four and a half furlongs, a race that would be over in the blink of an eye. Sophia gazed around, grinning from ear to ear. She'd come to watch El Karta, while Harper had come to watch Meadow Flower, Eden Hill's prized filly, as well as El Karta and Fleet Light who were both scheduled a few races after Meadow and would go the same distance.

Meadow Flower and her group were up first in the maiden special weight for two-year-old fillies so Marshall and Cassandra were over in the saddling area, getting the filly ready to walk out in her first post parade ponied by a steady older horse.

"Here they come," Surrey said, patting Harper's arm and pointing to the group of fillies, jockeys aboard, march in, one by one. "There she is." Surrey pointed to the five horse in a seven filly field.

Harper grinned, peering through her binoculars, watching Meadow's wide eyes taking it all in. She side-stepped at the big Palomino, but the gelding was good at plodding ahead while Meadow's eyes swept the track, the stands, and the other horses. This was her first race. First of many, Harper hoped.

She looked from Surrey to Sophia, wishing the circumstances were different and Millie could be present. Mille had begged off saying she was exhausted and thanked Harper for taking Sophia to the races.

One by one the assistant starters loaded the juveniles into the starting gate. The three horse reared as her jockey leaned forward and soothed her neck once all four feet were on the ground. The starting gate amid all the other commotion was new to all the babies.

Meadow went in like an old pro, then the other two, and quick as a wink, the starting gate banged open and seven new racehorses charged onto the track. The scene looked a bit chaotic as the outside post horse tried to angle in and nearly bumped the filly trying to take the lead. But Harper only had eyes for Meadow, who took the first two jumps fine, stayed out of the chaos, and obeyed Cassandra who checked her just a moment, waiting for a hole as the babies crowded together. In short order a hole opened, and Cassandra let Meadow surge through and into the lead, changing leads smoothly into the turn.

Harper admired how well Cassandra read the filly as well as the field.

The other babies around Meadow became slightly distracted, running greenly—a few had bobbled out of the gate and one gray filly bolted wide. But Meadow stayed steady under Cassandra's hands and once through the turn flew straight up the course. She lengthened her stride as the stretch unfolded before her. Two fillies came up on her and the leaders ran three wide, with Meadow—the smallest of the three—in the center and in the lead by a head.

Harper watched the filly fight for a bigger lead as Cassandra urged her forward with her arms and the wire loomed. Meadow pinned her ears, didn't look right or left and with tail flying, hooves furiously pounding the dirt, the filly bore down on the wire. It was as if the focus of her short life had pointed to this moment and there was not one ounce of back down in her. Meadow crossed half a length ahead and still charging, then as Cassandra slapped her neck, Meadow galloped out as proud as she could be for beating back the bigger girls. Cassandra bent over her and slapped her neck again, agreeing with the game effort the filly had put in.

"She's got heart, that's for sure!" shouted Sophia, over the crowd's happy cries. Harper high-fived her and turned to accept Surrey's hug of congratulations. Up the stairs pounded Marshall, beaming, his arms wide. "Told ya!" he said to Harper, once he scootched past fans in the row behind her. He was grinning and shaking his head. "Came out firing early, and she's just getting started!"

Harper laughed. Marshall seemed a bit like a proud father.

They all hopped down to the winner's circle and Harper watched Cassandra look straight into Meadow's eyes, thinking the diminutive Cassandra and the small Thoroughbred might feel they were looking into a mirror. Then Cassandra turned to Marshall and said, "She's a fierce one!" to which Marshall replied, "Takes one to know one . . ." and they both laughed.

It was easy to feel jubilant. Meadow had lived up to all expectations, and she had speed and stamina in her lines so who knew what the future might hold. Privately, though, Harper wondered if she could, in fact, prevail against the colts. She had a fast turn-of-foot, yes, and kicked away before the wire like a demon, but she might need a bigger body to handle the boys. She smiled as she thought about Marshall. He tried so hard not to put blinders on when it came to their runners, evaluate realistically, not get ahead of himself, but it seemed Meadow had lit a flame in a little piece of his heart. Well, she thought, they'd just have to see what else the filly's fire might ignite.

She took a moment, turning to scan the stands, thinking about how many people had sat in those seats or stood at the rail, how many had bred and trained and raced Thoroughbreds here, hoping for a moment exactly like this one. She glanced at Marshall, still beaming, as he hugged Cassandra who barely came to his shoulder.

After a time enjoying the win, Surrey gathered them all into a chatty group and they made their way for a snack and a drink. Harper glanced over the crowd wondering if Henley was attending to El Karta and Fleet Light. She surveyed the milling fans, looking for Stuart Minetti or any of Lowen's other connections but didn't see any of them. Harper excused herself as the group talked affably and called JD to fill him in on Meadow's win. He didn't pick up so she left a message.

Surrey corralled everyone and they headed back to their seats for the colts' race, the crowd around them standing and chatting or heading to their seats while studying their racing forms. As they settled in, the colts made their entrance.

El Karta looked nervous coming along with the pony and behind him two other horses followed, keyed up and bouncing. They all sensed the atmosphere and knew something special was about to happen. Fleet Light followed soon after and simply seemed curious. As they neared the gate, El Karta crow hopped a bit then settled. Around them six other two-year-old colts also approached the starting gate, the assistant trainers on the alert for a reluctant baby. They found him in the two horse, a big bay who took one look at the gate and shied. The assistant trainer up front tried to lead him to the gate and got him closer, but the colt was having none of it. His jockey stayed put, as two assistants got behind the colt, hooked arms, and pushed the horse into the starting gate, slamming the doors. The rest of the field loaded without incident.

Sophia watched El Karta through binoculars, taking in his every step and squirming a little in her seat as he approached the starting gate at post position four. Surrey leaned over Harper as he entered the starting gate and whispered, "He looks fantastic," to which Sophia nodded enthusiastically.

Surrey was right. El Karta's black coat gleamed with health and his big muscles lay smooth and fit at the shoulder and hindquarters. Harper crossed her fingers that he'd recovered from the slight hesitation in his gait during training.

In front of Harper, the spectators watched in anticipation, realizing there was some class in the race. Fleet Light was the number seven horse, so in a minute he, too, was loaded.

"And they're off!" cried Marshall a moment later, still bubbling over Meadow's win. Surrey slapped his arm and exhaled a slightly exasperated sigh then turned to him, smiling. Marshall put his big arm around her, pulled on his Stetson with the other and kept his eyes on the track.

The colts all broke alertly, but El Karta had a huge jump out of the gate, great for a big horse, and took the lead. Fleet Light settled in off the pace behind the leaders.

"Let's see if El Karta can get comfortable on the lead," Marshall murmured.

It wasn't a long race, so tactics weren't at issue. Speed was the name of the game.

The colts jostled for position, and Fleet Light got squeezed back. Harper shook her head, knowing it wasn't easy to regain momentum in such a short race. Then Fleet Light surprised them all and went wide approaching the turn. That was likely not the plan his jockey had in mind and going into the turn he angled the colt toward the rail and then barreled straight ahead, saving ground.

Fleet Light bore down on El Karta. The big black colt sensed it and pinned his ears. Three other horses came up on the two leaders, their jockeys bent over them using their sticks. All the colts seemed to let any thought of losing fall away as they dug in and extended their necks. The crowd was on its feet, yelling and whooping.

As the pack neared the wire, Fleet Light came alongside El Karta and glanced at the big colt. Even though El Karta's size was intimidating, Fleet Light dug deep, extended his stride, and stretched out, his eyes on fire. All five horses hit the wire nearly simultaneously, but both Fleet Light and El Karta were a nose in front of the rest.

And that's how El Karta won it, by a bob of his black nose at the wire.

Harper, Marshall, Surrey, and Sophia jumped up and down with the rest of the stands, yelling and laughing.

"Now that's a crop of two-year-old colts!" screamed the man in front of Harper to whomever was in earshot. "They were rockin' and rollin' down the stretch!" He turned to his left, palm up, looking for agreement and got a big high five from the guy next to him.

Sophia could hardly contain herself. "Did you see that? Did you see that?" she exclaimed over and over, her gray eyes dancing. Harper patted her on the back and Sophia gave her a huge bear hug, then turned and raised her arms in the air in victory.

Harper kept her eye on the big colt as he slowed to a trot, then a walk, relieved to see he seemed okay. But she knew that could be a post-race high. She was pretty far away, as well, and he'd only seemed slightly off on the leg. She'd check on him at the barn later.

Marshall scooted past Surrey and Harper, his mustache twitching with good humor, and took Sophia by the arm. "I think you're wanted in the winner's circle," he said jovially, and they all rushed down the stairs for the second time that day.

Harper caught a glimpse of Fleet Light's wet bay coat as he went past. He'd put in a valiant effort, galloped out well and looked like a champ to Harper. She couldn't wait to hop aboard him on the training track and get a real feel for him. She laughed to herself. They had three powder kegs in the works—two colts and one darned hot filly.

Her mood sobered momentarily as she thought about the colts and Henley. She'd do her best to see they stayed safe in the care of a trainer she didn't trust as far as she could throw him.

Chapter 8

Over the next week and a half, Harper kept her eye on the horses and looked for an opportunity to get into Henley's office but didn't find one. She was increasingly worried about Sophia's colt, El Karta, who after his race seemed a bit sour and wasn't coming out of his stall eagerly to train. El Karta was exhibiting signs of something bothering him. She'd taken a phone photo of Henley's whiteboard and showed it to Marshall, adding in the little she'd found on Equibase about El Karta's recent workouts—sure enough he'd dropped off in performance.

"Looks like Henley drills them," Marshall said with concern, looking over the papers Harper had printed out from Equibase. He glanced up at her. "I checked with a friend across the Pond. Henley has a reputation all right. Report is he sends some of his babies home in body bags." He pursed his lips in disgust, handing Harper back her phone and the papers. "And you're right to be concerned about El Karta. Best talk to Tim."

Marshall had confirmed Harper's suspicions. Training two-year-olds was an art requiring a delicate balance building the needed bone density by concussive workouts and making sure each juvenile got just enough to do that, but not break down. It seemed more and more clear that Henley wasn't concerned with the art, only the outcome.

Harper showed up right on time the next morning and was given the task of mucking out the stalls of horses being worked on the Polytrack first, followed by the others. She wondered if Henley thought she'd consider the work beneath her. It was obvious that he didn't want her around—she knew he was trying to get her to quit.

As she hefted the wheelbarrow filled with the end stalls' droppings and soiled wheat straw bedding, she picked up the sharp smell of urine and loamy manure, reminded again that even the most mundane aspects of taking care of racehorses were just fine with her. As the time passed, she made her way from stall to stall, wondering who owned all the runners. She read a few stall plates: Dame Falona—"noseband," "blinkers (to breeze)" and next to her: Tamerett—"draw reins," "shadow roll," "earplugs." Just the horse's name and training gear. She'd need the files Henley had snatched to learn anything more about them.

She glanced around in the early morning's hazy peach light. A few horses not training today were being led out to hand-walk in the oval circle, their easy stride and calmness brought on mainly by grooms who expressed the same. Beyond them, a few racehorses grazed in the white-fenced green pasture. The patter of convivial Spanish mixed with quiet strains of Latin music washed over the barn.

Harper headed down the shedrow to dump her load then continued working her way down from stall to stall, emptying and refilling them with fresh, deep bedding. The sun rose and the runners headed out and came back from the big track for their cool down. The backstretch routine was as soothing as a massage.

Pretty soon Aliana, the friendly Latina groom, showed up with the hose, there to wash out and refill the stall buckets.

She smiled as she pulled the hose along from the other end of the shedrow and Harper waved. She glanced beyond her as the set walked up the hill but didn't see Henley and wondered if his assistant, Manuel, had handled the last workout. She kept an eye out for him. If Henley would be gone long enough, this was her chance to get into his office.

"Hola," she called as she approached Aliana. The young woman nodded, smiling, working her hose. She had caramel-colored, flawless skin, dark hair, a round face, and short legs. She spoke English and seemed about twenty-five years old.

"You handle the babies well," Harper said, referring to how Aliana efficiently sprayed down the young racehorses post-workout. They could be a handful, even after a workout. Sometimes, especially so.

Aliana beamed. "Gracias, gracias," she said and looked down a little embarrassed at the compliment.

Harper glanced around and spied Manuel heading to Henley's office and unlocking the door. So he had a key. Useful information. She turned back and noticed Aliana gazing in the direction of Manuel. It seemed the young woman had a bit of interest in the assistant trainer. Harper smiled at her.

"He's quite handsome," she said, not taking her eyes off Manuel's slight, wiry build.

Aliana again looked embarrassed. "Sí, he is very good trainer." She nodded. "He good with the babies."

Manuel exited Henley's office and, flipping a keyring around his fingers, headed their way talking on his cellphone. Aliana looked in his direction, then back to Harper. "I no talk more," she said, her expression darkening. Harper noticed the groom seemed a bit frightened as she glanced back at Manuel and moved on to her next stall.

Harper followed her and asked for her cellphone, wanting to know more about the young woman's sudden change of mood. Aliana mutely handed it over and Harper entered her contact information. She handed it back and said, "If you ever want to talk, please call me."

Aliana nodded, her face serious, and turned to her work.

Manuel drew near Harper, listening intently, his dark eyes narrowed, the flipping more agitated. He pocketed the keyring in his khakis, nodded briefly in Harper's direction, his worried eyes downcast as he passed down the row toward Fleet Light's stall.

"Si, Si, I will give, yes," he said, "you not worry." He hung up and Harper watched him walk past Fleet Light's stall and enter El Karta's, raising a hand to move the colt back out of sight.

Curious, Harper walked that way with her wheelbarrow, passing a few grooms squatting beside their horses, wrapping white stall wraps as the juveniles looked out the stall doors and grabbed hay from their hay nets. The grooms murmured to their horses. A slight scent of liniment rose from the stalls as she passed.

Manuel was just rising from El Karta's leg when she arrived. He deposited something in his pocket and the black colt stuck his head out of the stall to nuzzle her upturned palm. "No peppermints, buddy," she said, laying her hand on his small white star and casting an eye at Manuel who was rubbing the colt's neck. That's what Harper did after an injection. El Karta turned and nipped at the trainer, who softly flicked the colt's nose with his finger.

Manuel smiled. "He a good boy," he said, patting the black colt's neck, his eyes searching hers. "Very nice." He seemed to genuinely like the colt.

Harper lightly rubbed El Karta's tiny star. Though he appeared to have an attitude on the track, he was a surprisingly gentle colt and at present, not acting like himself. Harper recalled Sophia mentioning how she adored the two-year-old—always risky business to let a horse steal your heart. "Yes," she said, agreeing with Manuel, El Karta seemed a very good boy. She waited a moment, studying the colt's finely made head. "Everything okay with him? I noticed the shot," she said innocently.

Manuel dark eyes looked confused for a moment. Then he smiled and fumbled in his pocket, pulling out two tubes—a needled syringe and an oral medication tube.

He hastily repocketed the one with the needle and held up the tube, which Harper readily recognized. Phenylbutazone. Bute . . . a ubiquitous anti-inflammatory that Harper had used on her own runners.

"No, no, he fine. Just little bit sore." He rubbed the colt's shoulder and neck again, not meeting Harper's gaze.

Bute was given to alleviate pain and to reduce swelling, so Manuel's comment made sense and distressed Harper further. They wouldn't be giving him bute if something wasn't inflamed and painful. But what about the shot? What was that all about? Whatever was going on, the colt should not be training right now. The track was ripe with the fruit of ignoring slight injuries, from promising racehorse careers cut short to something far worse—catastrophic fractures resulting in death.

"Left front?" she asked? Babies sometimes got injured there because they're trained counterclockwise, and the left leg absorbs more of the concussive pounding. That's where El Karta had seemed slightly off.

"Sí," Manuel said, still not meeting her eye.

She nodded. She'd get a peek for herself once Manuel was out of range. She would talk to Tim Bradford about it, too, after she took a look at El Karta's leg. She trusted Tim's vet skills. And his instincts. Harper had one more question. "You pointing him to another race?"

She hoped not. That would mean he'd not get a layoff he obviously needed.

Manuel didn't look at her. "Is maybe yes," he said, his voice so faint Harper nearly missed his reply.

She nodded, not wanting to push the issue. So, another thing she'd be looking into. She smiled, patted El Karta's head and said, "That's good. He's a fine-looking colt, I would like to see him run again." She changed the subject. "Do you know when Henley will be back?"

The trainer eyed her. "Is at the kitchen then maybe he back." Manuel seemed conflicted, both agitated and, Harper thought, a little sad. The assistant glanced behind her and signaled the grazing grooms to get their charges back to their stalls.

Harper nodded. So Henley might be gone a while. . . she'd see about getting into his office.

As she turned to go, she watched Manuel glance in her direction, a look of concern on his face.

She went back and hefted her cart, heading to clean the remaining stalls and when she was done, she caught up with Aliana winding the hose after finishing with the workout horses. She pulled off her gloves and leant Aliana a hand. The groom glanced at Harper then seemed intent on finishing up. Her ready smile had fled.

Harper dove in anyway. She felt that Aliana might be the only one to talk to about Figarosa, the tortured and murdered groom. "Aliana, did you know Miguel very well?" she said.

Behind her the horses snorted and shuffled their new bedding around. The air warmed around them.

Aliana looked up, her round face flushed. "Yes, I know him."

"Do you have any idea what happened to him?" Harper glanced around to see if Manuel was watching.

Aliana shook her head no and refused to look at Harper, concentrating on finishing with the hose. Harper got the message—she didn't have more to say on the subject. Harper was convinced the young groom knew something.

Harper gave her a friendly smile and as she turned to go, she spied Manuel heading for Henley's office. Seeing her chance, she followed, arriving, and pushing the door open then entering into the dim interior. He'd flipped open the computer and was bent over it, clicking through files. Finding what he wanted, he bent to study it, then sent it to the printer.

"I'm finished for now," Harper said, startling Manuel. His head flew up and he flipped the computer closed. "With the stalls . . . Happy to graze one of the horses, if you like."

The assistant attempted a smile and plucked the sheet out of the printer as he rounded the desk. "Yes, maybe Miss Somers, she go?"

Manuel hurried to the door and Harper followed, allowing Manuel to exit first then pulling the door almost shut. She watched him head to his truck, studying the printout, and speed away.

Harper checked the time, glanced around, and not seeing anyone, re-entered the office, shutting and locking the door. She moved to the computer, glad to see Manuel had been too startled to log out. She opened a few emails from the vet, found nothing, then sorted through the desktop folders, locating what she wanted in short order—El Karta's radiograph. She studied it but didn't see anything pronounced. She searched for a date to know when it was taken, but that was absent. She printed it out, and flipped through additional files on the desktop, finding other x-ray results, which she also sent to the printer.

She heard talking outside the door and stood still, her heart pounding. Motes of dust turned lazily in the few shafts of light coming through the dirty window as she stood stock still. The voices were not Manuel or Henley, so she shook off the fear and bent to her tasks, working swiftly through files and closing the computer. She walked to the file cabinet and found it locked. But on the desk was a thick folder. Harper opened it and began taking photos, not pausing to read, just getting through as many as she could. She'd review them later, hoping they were the papers Henley had grabbed from her that first day.

She checked the time and took a last look around before exiting the office and shutting the door. She hurried to the Range Rover and threw the papers in, then shut the door and went to find Miss Somers.

The diminutive bay filly was all too happy to munch the short grass, but Harper was careful not to overload her system and after half an hour, pulled Miss Somers' head up and headed to her stall, only to stop dead in her tracks at the far side of the cool down track. Walking through the barn aisle, two figures emerged into the light.

The man with Henley was Stuart Minetti and the two rounded the stalls to the right, heading down the shedrow,

Henley looking none too happy. The trainer paused at Aviragus' stall and said a few words to Minetti. The big colt stuck his head out and pinned his ears at Henley who took a step back. He turned to Minetti, shook his head vigorously and glared at the man. Minetti looked on coolly and made a low comment. They seemed to be arguing as Henley pulled on his beard in agitation. The conversation seemed inconclusive, though Minetti seemed like the one in control.

Presently, they trod on, Henley angrily jerking a thumb at a groom seated on a square bale checking his phone. The groom hopped up and scurried away as the pair made their way to Fleet Light's stall, Minetti glancing around, his gaze passing over Harper who had turned away, her head down. What was he doing at Fleet Light's stall? she wondered, thinking at the same time it was good he hadn't recognized her.

She moved toward the filly's stall, deposited her and went to inspect the hay net a few stalls up from Fleet Light. She looked in to see the horse circle his straw and lay down. She'd top off his hay and maybe overhear a few words between the two men. She grabbed a flake from the open square bale and set about her work.

"He will go next week with the black colt. Then Aviragus on Friday." Henley said and Minetti stood impassive, his head swiveling and his dead eyes again surveying the barn.

Next week. There were more juvenile races upcoming at Keeneland, so that's presumably where Fleet Light and El Karta were running. They had a few of Eden Hill's two-year-olds entered that day. And Friday was the Grade 1 Maker's Mark, a mile race on turf that Marshall had entered Deacon in. His turf workouts had been great and he'd posted a bullet in his last outing, so Marshall said why not give it a go on home turf? Aviragus had done well on the European turf, so that's most probably where he was pointed. At $300,000, the purse attracted a lot of accomplished turf runners. It would be Deacon's first race on grass, and everyone at Eden Hill would be watching.

So, it seemed possible that Aviragus and Deacon would go head-to-head in a battle of wills sooner than she'd expected.

Harper returned to her work, surreptitiously studying Minetti. She shuddered. The man was an imposing, menacing figure with his tall, patrician bearing, hooked nose and hooded eyes. There was something ominous and predatory about him. In the next moment, she realized he wouldn't be looking over Fleet Light so closely if he didn't have an interest in the colt, likely a financial one. That didn't make her happy. A man like that with a nice colt didn't augur well for the two-year-old's future.

Then there were the races. Harper gazed at the bay colt contentedly laying in the straw. The three of them—Aviragus, El Karta, and Fleet Light—they were all entered in races. She'd have to figure out how badly El Karta was injured by then. It could be not-so-serious, maybe a slightly strained muscle as Manuel had suggested. Or it could be something else altogether. But Manuel's syringe and his uncomfortable responses were concerning. She'd have to take a look at the radiograph and get a closer look at the horse's leg. She'd also scope out his training schedule for the rest of the week.

She finished with the hay and got out a broom to sweep up, hoping to stay long enough for Henley and Minetti to leave. Sure enough, once finished with Fleet Light, the two of them headed for Henley's office. She again kept her head down as they passed and neither took notice of her.

She swept her way down the shedrow to El Karta's stall and went in. The colt stood with his head down, drowsing. He hadn't finished his feed and she'd seen one of the grooms tugging at the colt that morning to come out of his stall for training. Harper frowned. That and his sourness . . . all signs that he wasn't feeling well. She murmured "Good boy," to him so he wouldn't be startled and bent to his left front leg, undid the stained leg wrap and felt along the back of the cannon bone. Sure enough, there was some heat and it was sensitive. But no horse likes his suspensory fooled with so she'd ignore the sensitivity for now.

El Karta had come fully awake and stepped away the moment she palpated the back of his cannon bone below the knee. She took her hand away. And there was a bit of swelling, too. Harper frowned. High suspensory injuries were common among two-year olds and hard to diagnose since often mild lameness was the only symptom. She stood up, getting his stud halter and lead from the hook outside his stall. She stuck her head out and glanced around to see who was about, then down to Henley's door. Still shut. She led the colt out to the cool down track and walked him. He favored his left front leg a bit, just as she'd seen earlier, so he didn't appear to be doing all that well, even on the bute. She sighed. Looked like it could be more than a slight muscle strain after all. She'd show Tim the radiograph. He'd be able to tell if it was a high suspensory ligament issue and whether or not it had already progressed to a slight fracture. She returned El Karta to his stall. Unfortunately, just as she opened the stall door, the tall, lanky groom exited the filly's stall down the shedrow. He frowned at her then turned away.

So, she'd been seen.

She couldn't worry about that now. She headed down to the whiteboard and shuddered to see El Karta was scheduled for regular workouts pointing to the race Manuel had indicated. She thought about how to get him out of that. She sure didn't want him injured further. A conversation with Tim Bradford was certainly in order.

She looked again at Henley's closed door, not at all liking this turn of events. Her duties finished, she hurried down to the feed room and grabbed her backpack. A lot of darkness at Barn 41 churned below the surface. Then there was Aubrey. And the dead groom, Miguel Figarosa. What had he discovered, Harper asked herself, climbing into the Range Rover, that had gotten him killed?

Chapter 9

She'd intended to look at the information from Henley's office as soon as she got to her own at Eden Hill. Once through the building's doors, she attempted to pass Pepper and head straight to her review, but the receptionist laughed and handed over a fistful of return calls to make. Harper sighed, gave her a rueful thumbs up, and headed through the lobby to her office, shutting the door and seating herself behind the black desk. She placed the pile of papers she'd printed out beside her computer. Shuffling through the calls and consulting her calendar, she got to work first on farm business which took much longer than she'd anticipated.

It was late afternoon by the time she finished. She put in a call to JD and Marshall, asking them both to meet her in the office to go over the documents and photos from Henley's office. She texted Tim Bradford to see if he was available, but he was tied up the rest of the day and said he'd get back to her if he could swing by. Marshall said he'd be right over, and JD said she'd caught him at a good time and he'd be there in fifteen minutes but could only stay a short while as he was following up on Figarosa's death. A few leads seemed promising. Harper asked about Aubrey's case. There was nothing, JD reported. The scene was clean—no prints, no fibers, no witnesses to the attack. And Aubrey, of course, wasn't able to provide an ounce of information. He hoped the leads on Figarosa would break something open he could use on Aubrey's case. He agreed they had to be connected.

A few minutes later Marshall trudged in, his big black Stetson in hand. He sank into the leather chair in front of Harper and set his hat on the chair to his right.

"Got the last of the foals on the ground last night," he murmured, running a hand over his eyes and yawning. "Middle of the night, of course. Wasn't an easy one, so Cody called."

Harper nodded. "Quillon?"

"Yep, turned out fine. Little colt, wobbly but doing fine." Marshall gazed at the door. "JD coming?"

Harper's cell phone rang, and she glanced at it, nodding to Marshall. Dr. Baxter. She looked at Marshall, mouthing "the hospital" and he nodded. She answered.

It wasn't the news she'd hoped to hear.

Harper gazed unseeing at Marshall as Dr. Baxter delivered the news. Aubrey, he said, had passed away a short time before. He'd never regained consciousness. Harper listened numbly as the doctor droned on, trying to take in the news, to focus. Both attempts failed. Her eyes roved Marshall's face and he got up, taking the phone, and spoke to the doctor. Harper stared at the far wall. Aubrey, dead? The news—delivered so abruptly, so . . . out of the blue—loomed over all other thoughts and triggered a wound that still lay deep inside her. That other phone call, the one with news of her sister's death, came flooding back, overwhelming her capacity to think. She sat unmoving, her breathing shallow. In her mind's eye, her New York apartment rose, starkly vivid—the scene she'd stared at just as blankly trying to absorb that her sister had died. Like a photograph, that image was all she saw for a full minute, and she was unable to bring herself back to the present moment.

She felt Marshall's hand on her shoulder, yet still she couldn't move.

She vaguely heard Marshall thank the doctor and hang up the phone just as JD came through the door. She stared at him numbly. JD ran a hand through his hair and pulled her up, kissing the top of her head gently. He looked over at Marshall who shook his head, his expression full of concern and grief. Harper took a long, ragged breath and tried again to take in the news, laying her head on her husband's chest, listening to his heartbeat. Nobody spoke.

Marshall murmured the news to JD. Though not totally unexpected, the news seemed impossible for any of them to process. Harper pushed away from her husband, feeling confused. Aubrey . . . gone. She sank back down into her chair, still and blank, staring again at the office wall.

JD gave her space and glanced at Marshall who pursed his lips and fiddled with his hat, not knowing what to do.

The phone rang again and brought Harper back with a jolt. JD reached for the phone, but she took a deep breath and answered it, hearing Harold's voice. She motioned JD to the leather chair but he remained standing beside her.

Harold reported the doctor had called a while ago with the news and Millie was stunned and despondent, refusing to leave the house. And the lawyer called but Millie wouldn't speak to her. Could Harper help?

Harper hung up and rolled her neck, took a long breath, and sat back in her chair. She took a few minutes, looking from Marshall to JD and back again. Finally, she was able to focus and stumbling through the words, filled the two men in.

JD asked for Harper's phone, noted the lawyer's number she'd scribbled, and returned her call. The lawyer was insistent that speaking with the family was of paramount importance and suggested a meeting the next morning. JD said he'd call her back within the hour. He filled Harper and Marshall in, but the two still seemed stunned.

Pepper appeared at the door with a few papers for Harper to sign but left without comment when Harper shook her head.

She looked at Marshall who stifled a yawn, realizing he'd been up all night foaling and needed some sleep. She told him to go home—clearly, they weren't going to get to the conversation she'd planned. JD took a seat and the two sat there after Marshall left, not saying anything for a long time. Finally, JD mentioned food and Harper shook her head. Nevertheless, he got his wife on her feet and took her home, heading them both to the kitchen, and rustling up an early dinner. They needed to eat. It had been a long few days, and it looked like the future held more of the same. JD flipped on the news. Aubrey's death had set the family back, and the Thoroughbred racing community as well. There was a large story on the local news recounting Aubrey's legendary nonsense as well as his influence. One reporter called him a legend and his passing the end of an era. Not an original description, but an apt one.

Harper sighed and focused. It would fall to her to make funeral arrangements since it seemed unlikely Millie would be able to surmount her grief. The pills and martinis would do little to help. The duty brought back memories of her sister's murder and how intimate that service had been. This would be different. The Lexington folks would expect some sort of affair befitting the showmanship of the man they were bidding farewell to.

JD mentioned the morning meeting in the lawyer's office. Harper was torn. If she was going to find out what had happened to Aubrey—she shuddered, realizing it was murder now—she needed to be at Barn 41. But whatever the lawyer wanted was also pressing, she'd not have insisted on a meeting otherwise.

Harper agreed to the one-hour, morning meeting, stressing to JD that she needed to bring Millie along. JD made the calls.

Then, Harper promised herself, she'd review the material from Henley's office and get herself back to Barn 41.

And see to the funeral arrangements.

The pair passed the evening speaking of mundane things, not mentioning Aubrey, Henley, or the issues at Keeneland or Lowen Farms. They all needed attention, but for the rest of the night, JD and Harper focused only on each other and that was enough.

Chapter 10

"I'm coming with you," JD said the next morning over coffee.

"You need to find out who did this," Harper said. "I can handle the lawyer. And Millie."

JD looked at the time. "The lawyer's at nine and I'll be at work by ten-thirty, so I'm going." He finished buttoning his blue oxford shirt then picked up his coffee.

Harper sighed and munched a piece of toast. JD's sharp eyes took her in. "Look, this isn't easy for any of us, but especially you." He moved around the island and took Harper in his arms, kissing her tenderly. "I love you and I will get us both through this."

Harper looked up into his clear eyes and sank into his strength. "I love you, too," she said, though her voice was tinged with sadness.

The news about Aubrey had triggered all her feelings about her sister's murder, and last night had not been easy. Her "go to" was to steel herself up and just get through things, do what needed to be done, and JD knew that. He knew it because he was exactly the same. She felt his strength surround her and, just for a moment, allowed herself to take it in.

"Okay," she whispered, "come."

JD went back around the island and lifted his coffee cup to his lips, keeping an eye on Harper. "So . . . What's going on over at Keeneland? What did you want to go over yesterday?"

She knew what he was doing; he'd changed the subject, prodding her to talk about what else was percolating in her, too often, very private world.

He leaned on the kitchen island's granite countertop. "You've been pretty quiet about it."

She'd been mute, actually.

Harper hedged. She didn't want JD knowing how bad things seemed to be shaping up at Henley's barn, but she needed his help, his advice. She also knew if she confided in him, he'd just harass her more to get her nose out of things. She shook out her long hair and inspected a few split ends.

"Harper," said JD more sternly. "Spill."

Harper looked up. "You share, I'll share," she said, her sass coming out.

JD's shoulders dropped slightly, indicating he was relieved at her response.

"That's always been the deal," she finished, flipping her hair behind her shoulder. She turned to the sink, setting her coffee cup in it, glancing out the window and over the creek to the barn but didn't see Memphis. Well, she thought, she wouldn't blame him if he never showed his face again. She'd been neglecting him. She vowed to do better.

JD pulled on his navy-blue jacket. "Sure, why not. You go first." They both knew they worked better together than each on their own and since it was clear he was not going to keep her from investigating what now amounted to Aubrey's murder, they might as well share.

Harper turned back to her husband and stared at him for a few moments. His face had taken on an impenetrable, flat, impassive look. His presence was utterly still. He stared a hole through her with those green cop eyes above high cheekbones. He saw everything, remembered everything, and had a brain that put it all together with uncanny speed. She told him what she knew and what she suspected. And about the files and photos they still needed to review—she just hadn't been able to deal with it the previous evening.

When she was finished, JD nodded. They'd set up a time to go over all the material from Henley's office as soon as Harper felt ready. JD then went over what he knew . . . Minetti was, as Harper had indicated, a bad actor who had never been officially convicted of anything but had been suspected in various schemes, owned numerous clubs in New York where he purportedly laundered money, and seemed capable of almost anything. Interestingly, JD also learned that Aubrey had not paid a number of bills, including some very large vet bills, and had stiffed his previous trainer who, unlike the story Aubrey had told, had quit, and not been fired.

Harper thought that over. It wasn't like Aubrey to not pay his bills. She wondered what sort of scrape his outlandish behavior had gotten him into. It wouldn't be the first time. And she had a strong suspicion that Minetti had to be involved somehow.

"We'll see what the lawyer has to say," JD said. "And we need to get the books from Millie."

Harper nodded, troubled. She turned to the window, longing to head to Grandpa's barn and Memphis' comforting presence. She took a shuddering breath. That would have to wait. She looked at her husband, wishing she could wake up from what increasingly felt like a bad dream. One she'd been through before when her sister had died.

"I'll try to follow up on the Figarosa leads later today," JD said, finishing up and reaching a hand over the counter to touch Harper's cheek. She closed her eyes a moment, nodding, trying to process it all.

Aubrey dead, Minetti's presence, and now a bunch of debts.

She opened her eyes and touched JD's hand, grateful for him and again able to focus. She'd been around the game a long time. She knew how much pressure financial straits put on an owner. No wonder he'd brought Henley over. She also considered that was no doubt why he had changed course and accepted client two-year-olds in training. Henley's training fees would not be cheap and as a Lowen employee, his portion of any purse winnings, or some percentage depending on what they'd negotiated, would go to the farm. And Aubrey sorely needed money.

In order to get the money, Lowen Farms needed to produce winners. She thought about El Karta.

But at what cost?

Promptly at nine a.m., JD, Millie, and Harper entered the lawyer's office and sat down in the chairs arrayed around the barrister's formidable desk.

"I ain't sellin' if that's why you're so all-fired bent on us bein' here," Millie said before the lawyer could open her mouth. "So just get that thought right outta your head." Millie huffed and sank back in her chair. She folded her arms over the purse in her lap and fell back into despondency, though with a defiant set to her jaw.

They sat across from the Lowen's lawyer, a small woman, whose response to Millie's comment was to sit back as well and straighten her suit coat lapels. She had short arms, a thin face, a perpetually furrowed brow, and looked somewhat like a doll in the big, black leather chair. Around them were bookcases filled with law books and oriental ceramics. The walls were deep violet and hung with Asian block prints. The lawyer looked from Harper to JD. Her expression conveyed hope they'd talk sense into Millie.

She then concisely laid out the substantial debt Aubrey had run up at Lowen Farms. Millie's defiant look increased with every word the small woman uttered.

JD spoke up, gazing at Millie. "How about you let us talk to the vet and your previous trainer—see if we can work out a settlement or a payment plan."

The lawyer nodded her head in agreement. Lowen Farms had racked up a ton of debt, in the millions. Everyone's eyes turned to Millie.

"That trainer ain't worth two dead flies," she spat at JD, her eyes fiery. "I ain't sellin' and I ain't payin' that good-for-nothing loser." She patted her orange tresses then poked a finger at the lawyer. "You fix this," she said. "That's what we pay you for. So do it."

Harper sighed and looked down at her hands. "How about we talk this over with Millie and get back in touch?" she said, wiping her hands along the top of her jeans, looking up at the lawyer who seemed relieved to be rid of them all.

"That's a good idea," she said, then stressed to Millie, "But as the sole owner of the business, you're going to have to come up with some plan to satisfy these debts, Millie. You can't get around that."

Millie pulled out her pack and plucked a cigarette from it, defiantly waving it in the lawyer's face. "I heard you the first time," she said, flicking her lighter.

With that, JD and Harper rose and escorted Millie from the office.

Harper glared at Millie and plucked the unlit cigarette from her fingers.

"Yeah, yeah," Millie said on the way down the elevator.

Once at the curb, JD trotted away to fetch the car and Millie snatched her smoke from Harper's fingers, lit it, and took a deep drag. "That didn't solve a damned thing, now did it?" she said, exhaling around the cigarette hanging from her lips. She rummaged around in her oversized handbag for her "nerve pills." "Don't start with me," she muttered to Harper.

"How long did you know?" Harper said. "About the debts?"

Millie snorted. "All along, a course. Aubrey was plannin' on that Henley character saving our bacon after he got rid of Rawley."

Harper nodded, recalling JD had mentioned the trainer had quit, not been fired.

Millie took a drag and looked down at the sidewalk. "Course he cut me outta any say so," she said, her voice tinged with sadness. She looked up and gazed off, seeming to go someplace else for a moment. "Not like it was before," she said, staring into the distance. Around them cars honked and sped by, but they didn't disturb Millie. "We was always in it together, back then," she murmured, taking another drag, "back when things was good." She exhaled and then shook herself out of her reverie.

"We got Aviragus over here. Aubrey called him his 'kingmaker.'" She pulled out her pill bottle. "Get it?" she said, sarcastically.

Harper had no idea what she was talking about.

"The name, dummy." She unscrewed the cap, pulled her cigarette from her lips, and popped a couple of pills in her mouth. "Supposedly, Aviragus was some long, lost English king

. . . I say, 'Who gives a damn?' Just so he wins." Her mood had gone from sadness to all-business in the blink of an eye.

JD drove up and they got in. As they sped away, JD said "I'll talk to the veterinary hospital." He and Harper exchanged glances. "And contact the trainer—it was Rawley Stevens, right?"

Harper twisted around to watch Millie's reaction. Millie's pouting face turned to the window.

"He dug us a big ole hole, Aubrey did," Millie said, looking at the rearview mirror where she could see JD's reflection. "Wasn't the first time. Not by a long shot," she muttered. "I think he might've borrowed a bunch even before we got into this mess, counted on Rawley to bail us out with some big winners." She huffed. "You seen how that worked out."

JD and Harper again exchanged a quick look. So there could be more debt than just the vet and trainer. Debt that had happened before Henley had gotten to the States. Cars and trucks buzzed by. The day was overcast, just as the mood. JD pulled into the right lane to slow down, letting them all pass.

"Where did that money come from?" Harper said, swiveling around in her seat as best as the seat belt would let her. "The money before these debts? And how much was it?"

And how come the lawyer hadn't mentioned that money, that debt?

"Then the ole coot ran up more bills with them vets and such."

"There's more than one vet?"

Millie nodded morosely.

"Who was the original lender, Millie? Maybe we should talk to them as well," Harper said, trying to get Millie's attention. Millie kept puffing on her cigarette and blowing it out the crack in the window, gazing out to the green blur shifting by beyond the cars and trucks.

Millie glared at Harper. "You don't give that Rawley Stevens one damn cent! He was a bag a hot air. I told Aubrey as much. Rawley kept promising winners here, winners there—stakes races, mind you—not them flim-flam sorry-ass cheap races. No," said Millie spreading her arms wide and inflating her large chest. "No, we was gonna win the *big* races." Her hands fell in her lap. "Nothin' of the sort happened." She looked at Harper who extended a hand that Millie batted away. "I'm not sellin' so you can just get your mind straight on that," she spat. "Both of you," she finished, leaning forward and poking JD's shoulder.

Millie sat back and again looked out the window, ignoring them both.

JD turned to Harper, frowning. The situation was worse than either of them had thought. "I'll deal with the vets and Rawley," he said, their eyes meeting.

Right, and Harper would get Marshall and Tim together. They needed to go over what she'd found at the barn as soon as possible.

Chapter 11

Marshall had Deacon poised on a knife's edge for the big race on Friday of the following week. Deacon was a badass, yes. But Marshall's genius was that he knew each horse and trained each one as he or she needed to be trained. Eden Hill had a lot of horses in training each year, but it wasn't a commercial operation, so he had the luxury of individualizing every horse's workout to make the most of his string and bring along the babies slowly. He kept a close eye on them. He'd learned long ago that the horses will always tell you what they need, so he listened, and backed off or pushed them as they were ready. He trained the whole horse—the mind and the body. You had to build cardio and bones and muscles but if you left out the mind, you had nothing but junk.

With Deacon it was different—what he needed was always the same, and also was what he wanted. And with Deacon that was training hard.

The horse simply lived to run and had the body to do it. And while he had tried to savage a few horses down the stretch in a couple of races, primarily his reason for being was to get to the finish line first and that's what he set his entire body and soul to do every time he ran, the rest of the field be damned. And to Deacon, "every time he ran" meant every time he ran, period. The training track to him was no different from the dirt unspooling before him out of the starting gate.

He was coal black, huge as a freight train, with a hind end that drove like one and a front end big enough to balance it out. His chest was enormous, his legs four arrows, his girth deep, and his shoulder existed only to move his two long front legs forward as fast as possible. He stood a bit over 17.1, had a fast turn of foot for a big horse, and there was not a four-year-old to match him.

But though a physical freak, it was his eyes that made other horses quiver and back down, eyes that looked right through any groom, jockey, or other horse that ventured near. Eyes that melted the soul of man or beast, full of steel and an otherworldly determination. In fact, Marshall was convinced the colt existed in a universe entirely his own and in which he was the sole inhabitant—and Deacon aimed to keep it that way.

So Marshall trained him hard and told Lucas, the stallion manager, to let the colt do whatever the hell he pleased. Didn't want to be turned out? No problem. Wanted to be fed first? So be it. Didn't take to being groomed? Let the dirt stay a while.

He gazed at Deacon as he strode past on the training track. The rest of the set kicked up dust as they went by and the sun sent its rosy hues over the far greening pastures. Deacon majestically made his way after his workout at his own pace and all by himself. He didn't need anyone or any other horse—he knew his worth and was utterly self-contained.

Cassandra, as usual, would be up on him Friday when he faced the Continent's phenom, Aviragus. It was as if the two had waited until the planets aligned and decided now was the time.

They'd meet for the first of at least two major races, and Marshall was anxious to see how Deacon did on turf. And against what might end up being his archrival.

It had all the makings of an Alydar-Affirmed match-up, and Marshall could hardly wait till the starting gate opened.

He tipped his ballcap as the colt stopped before him and peered down from the vast universe he inhabited to take the trainer's measure. Jesus, thought Marshall, I swear that colt can read minds.

Across town, Harper made her way down Barn 41's stall line filling the water buckets after the horses finished their morning workout. She'd made arrangements with JD, Marshall, and Tim to meet in her office after her barn chores were finished to review the radiographs and other evidence she'd gotten from Henley's office. She'd set up funeral arrangements with Pepper's help and was trying her best not to give in to the deep pit of sadness attempting to suck her in.

Henley stood just outside the shedrow overhang gazing out over the white fences, Minerva at his side, and seemed startled when his cell phone rang.

"Mrs. Hawthorne, yes, thank you for returning my call so quickly," he said, a clearly manufactured smile plastered on his face. He bent his head and ran his hand along Minerva's curved horn. "Yes, that's right. We had the vet out yesterday." He nodded as Mrs. Hawthorne presumably had some things to say.

Around them, the hot walkers murmured to their horses and the soft clop sounded comfortingly across the shedrow expanse.

"Please, Mrs. Hawthorne," Henley said, his voice carrying, "there is no need to be alarmed." More from Mrs. Hawthorne, and Henley began tapping his foot. A little agitation. The horses stuck their noses out of their stalls, a few snorted, a few swung their heads from side to side, picking up the unease in the air. "No, let me assure you, it is a small chip." He listened. He stroked his beard with the hand holding Minerva's leash, pulling it taut. She glared up at him and bleated. "Yes, that is correct. Rood and Riddle can easily remove it, this is not a problem." Harper saw Henley's shoulders visibly relax. Minerva started off in the direction of the cool down track, and Henley tugged on her leash, shaking his head at her.

Behind Harper, a horse whinnied and another blew and snorted, then churned in his bedding and flopped down with a loud groan. Harper glanced at the filly in the stall she was working on. Pretty girl, she thought, with a refined head and deep bay coat.

Henley nodded at the equine masseur as he passed, and then batted a hand at his office manager waving a handful of papers from the office door.

"Mrs. Hawthorne, please. One moment. I have another issue to discuss." He again looked down, a scowl crossing his face as he was interrupted. "Yes, Procietta is quite a fine filly. She trains well, she's well made . . ." He nodded and kicked at the track. He glanced up and scowled at the hot walker leading a colt and checking his phone messages, shaking a finger at him. There ensued a space of more time during which Mrs. Hawthorne apparently produced an extended agreement with her trainer about Procietta's virtues. "Yet, I agree . . ." More from Mrs. Hawthorne. Then, "Here it is in a nutshell," Henley said when the woman took a breath. "It's become clear that dear Procietta will not do as well as we had so fervently hoped at the graded stakes level." Mrs. Hawthorne loudly objected, her voice carrying on the warming air.

Harper, having dealt with owners most of her adult life, understood precisely what the conversation was all about. She watched the office manager glance their way as she left the barn, shaking her head.

"Please, listen to me, Mrs. Hawthorne, this is why you hired me." He nodded some more, scowling then jumped in when he could. "Yes, we could do that. I am able to enter her, but I have looked at her times, watched her workouts, and Mrs. Hawthorne, it is my humble opinion that sweet Procietta will have her heart broken in those races." Henley paused, searching the heavens, his eyes rolling. "Yes, I do know you adore her. And because of this, I know you don't want to see her heart break race after race."

Harper made her way down the shedrow more slowly. Henley was, effectively, dismissing a horse who had injured herself. A chip was often fixable, yet Henley was sending her home. She thought back to Marshall's comment. Well, at least he wasn't sending Procietta home in a body bag.

"Perhaps look at it this way," he said diplomatically, though with an impatient frown. He was looking around as if his mind was not really on his words. No doubt, he'd made this little speech before. "You live in the South. You love Procietta, I have witnessed your devotion myself. Yes," he agreed with something Mrs. Hawthorne had drawled. "There are lovely, lovely tracks in your Southern states. We will send her to you right away and recommend a trainer in your area, once she has recovered from her tiny surgery." He paused. "Yes, I assure you, quite routine." He listened and rubbed his bald head, tugging on Minerva's leash with irritation.

Aliana passed Harper and smiled shyly, leading the big, dappled gray to his stall. He swung easily alongside her, his ears pricked. Harper momentarily admired the tucked up, fit young colt. Plainly, he would not be sent home.

"Think of it. You can watch your beloved filly win in races she was meant to run," Henley continued, selling his dismissal of a filly who was not measuring up. "She will do well. I have no doubt about it. And you will be on hand to stride into the winner's circle with her."

There was a prolonged silence on Henley's end. He nodded and surveyed the barn, again rolling his eyes with impatience. He began walking toward his office, lugging Minerva along, glancing again around the barn to see who might be overhearing the conversation. Harper turned toward the stall, hearing him resume his end of the conversation as he walked away.

"We will arrange everything, Mrs. Hawthorne. Do not trouble yourself." He walked briskly toward the door, "Yes, we shall talk soon." He hung up, punching his phone in anger and muttering to himself, as he and Minerva entered his office. He slammed the door.

Harper finished up her chores and headed to her own office to meet Marshall, Tim, and JD, thinking about what a despicable man Henley was turning out to be. She'd seen his type before. If horses he trained weren't headed to the big races, he dismissed them. If such a horse needed veterinary care, they were heading home. There was always another client with deep pockets and a promising juvenile to step in and take over the empty stall.

She sped home, impatient to examine the evidence and hopefully find something she could use to take Henley down.

Shortly, she turned into Eden Hill and sped past century old oaks lining the drive, headed around to the office building where she parked and jumped out, hurrying into the building and skirting around the foyer's high marble counter. She was more anxious than ever to review the material from Henley's office.

Behind the counter Pepper, as usual, waved a yellow wad of calls for her to return. "Insurance, stallion bookings, feed bills . . .," she called as Harper grabbed them, entering her office and depositing them all on her desk. She picked up the printouts and headed to the glassed-in conference room where Marshall and Tim already sat. Only JD was missing. She took a seat across from the men just as Pepper popped her head in and asked if anyone needed anything, returning with bottles of water. She went out and came back with a tray full of cheese, crackers, olives, nuts, rolled salami, plus a fruit tray. She grinned. "Leftovers from the meeting Mary had with prospective clients."

Harper smiled. Mary Edvers and her nicking chops were in high demand. She plucked a green grape and called up the photos she'd taken on her phone, handing El Karta's radiograph to Tim, along with the few others she'd snagged. A day ago, she'd asked Pepper to print out the file folder photos she'd taken, and she handed those to Marshall.

Tim's warm brown eyes squinted at the x-rays as Marshall flipped through the printouts, sipping water and munching almonds.

JD walked in, his blue oxford cloth shirt rolled to his forearms and a serious look on his face. He sat next to Harper and gave a kiss to the cheek she presented while not taking her eyes off the photos on her phone. She finished and handed it to JD, who grabbed a water and studied the array.

"Let's get to it," Harper said, all business. It was time to find out exactly what was going on at Barn 41.

Chapter 12

Tim spoke first. He held up El Karta's radiograph and all eyes were trained on the colt's left front leg. "What you've got here is, in all probability, a high suspensory ligament injury—just what you thought, Harper. It doesn't show up on a radiograph, but the symptoms you mentioned and what you've got here tells me that's pretty likely what's going on." He leaned forward holding the radiograph out so everyone could see it. "Here, see this?" He pointed to the back of the upper part of the cannon bone. "Can you see this little sliver of bone that's broken off?"

Harper and Marshall leaned forward, squinting. It was very slight and hard to see.

Tim nodded. "Right, it's as thin as an eggshell, so you might not pick it up. But that's what tells me it's probably a suspensory issue." He sat back and put the paper down. "I'd need an ultrasound to be sure. Suspensory injuries are tricky." He picked up the few other printouts Harper had given him. "And you've got some very small hairline fractures in the others." He dropped them in disgust. "Continuing the sort of training regimen you've discussed with me isn't what I would recommend," he said, "if that's what's going on."

Harper felt her pent-up anger surge to the surface. "Yes, that's what's going on. That's exactly what's going on." It looked like Henley was heading toward breaking down a bunch of Lowen client babies. Running them into the ground and losing some—well, to trainers like Henley, that was the game.

And the not-so-great prospects—the ones who didn't pan out, like Procietta—he'd get rid of them one way or another. Suddenly Mrs. Hawthorne's filly seemed one of the lucky ones.

Tim frowned and Marshall looked disgusted. "Just what I'd heard about the guy," the trainer said. "It's all about the money. And his ego."

The money made sense, given the debts Aubrey had racked up.

Harper pointed to El Karta's radiograph, laying on the table beside Tim. "I saw Manuel, the assistant trainer, at El Karta's stall with a syringe. What would he shoot the colt up with to make him train?" And race, she thought, her anger continuing to mount.

Tim was quick to respond. "In all likelihood, steroids injected at the site."

Marshall glared around the table and spoke to Harper. "You have to report this," he said.

Harper knew he was right. The racing commission would do an investigation. All she had to do was call the tip line. She could do it anonymously.

Tim again spoke. "There's another thing," he said, frowning. "I called Stella, the broodmare manager over at Lowen about the fetus they lost." He paused. "They picked up prostaglandin and dexomethasome in the necropsy." They all knew prostaglandin, what you short-cycled a mare with to get her in heat. "Thing is," he continued, "you administer both when a fetus is less than thirty days along . . . and the mare will lose it."

They stared at Tim. "Yeah, she was close to thirty days, but that's what killed the fetus."

"So no insurance," Marshall chimed in.

"Nope," Tim agreed. "Somebody either made a bad mistake or had some other reason for doing it. That was going to be a big-time foal, too."

"Stella's not stupid," Marshall said and Tim nodded. "So why?" to which Tim shrugged his shoulders.

Everyone stared at the food in silence, but no one ate.

"Something's going on," Marshall said, stating the obvious. He stared a hole through Harper. "You need to report this right away."

JD hadn't said a thing during the whole discussion. He'd been studying the printouts Harper handed him, while taking in all that was said around the table. Harper glanced his way. His jaw was set hard—a sure sign he was displeased. Her blue eyes narrowed as she turned back to Marshall and Tim.

But it was JD who spoke first. Setting the printouts to the side, his stare was penetrating. "Harper can't report this."

Everyone was silent for a moment, trying to take that in.

"What the hell?" Marshall said, raising his arms in anger. "Why the hell not?" One of the things he hated in the racing game were trainers who ran their horses into the ground. It broke his heart and made him furious, always had.

JD spoke. "Miguel Figarosa had a bunch of drugs stashed in a hideaway in his apartment. Illegal drugs, performance-enhancing drugs." He turned to Tim. "And prostaglandin. And chlorhexidine, and insulin . . ."

Tim nodded. Those last three were legal, but they could also kill a horse. "And who is this guy, Figarosa?" Tim asked. Marshall, too, seemed confused. Harper realized neither of them knew about the groom who'd been tortured and beaten to death just before Aubrey was . . . murdered. A lump formed in her throat thinking about it.

Harper considered the drugs. Under immense pressure, oversight in testing had been ramped up, which had cleaned up a lot of drug abuse on the track. She put her elbows on the table and let her forehead rest on her open palms, recalling the hard lesson she'd learned about PED use on the track. Chemists could change one component in a performance enhancing drug, rendering it effective but not detectable. She looked up, searching the faces around the table. Even with testing, they all knew the dark truth—cheaters always found a way.

JD filled them both in on Figarosa. Marshall became even more furious and Tim looked stricken.

Harper looked at her husband. "That's more reason for me to report it. Or you," she said. "You found the drugs."

Marshall, Tim, and Harper all stared a hole through JD.

"The Feds tapped Figarosa's phone." He picked up the printouts and turned to Harper. "You only got a few pages here, but it's clear Minetti has a big stake in a lot of Lowen's horses. Some he owns outright, some he's the major investor in." He paused, consulting the papers again. "Or at least he's listed that way." He looked around the table. "Including, it seems, Aviragus." He looked up, his green eyes steely. "Minetti is deeply involved." He handed the sheets over to Marshall. "And take a look at the training schedules."

Marshall ignored the papers, so JD pushed them over. "What they found in Figarosa's place allowed the Feds to extend surveillance on Aubrey, Minetti, and Henley Smythe."

Harper blanched at Aubrey's name.

Marshall picked up the papers reluctantly and paged through them.

"The Feds said Figarosa was turning state's evidence." He paused. "So somebody took him out of the picture," JD said, his voice serious. “We can’t interfere with anything at the barn or the farm.” He focused on Harper. “So no reporting. We have to stay out of it.”

Harper shook her head. “There’s no way I’m staying out of this,” she said angrily. She glared at her husband.

JD paused a moment, his eyes softening. “You don’t have a choice.”

The hell I don’t, she thought.

Marshall spoke up, looking at Harper, waving the sheets he’d been looking at. “It looks like Henley hardly ever trains on the big track, it’s mostly the Polytrack.”

Harper nodded.

Marshall looked down at the papers, frowning. “Which means he either likes the surface or he’s trying to do something on the times.” He looked from Tim to JD. “On the Polytrack, the trainers can clock their own times.” He shrugged in his ochre-colored chamois shirt and straightened his shoulders. “On the big track, there’s a Keeneland clocker so you can’t fudge anything.”

Harper considered it. Official times were posted at Keeneland and on Equibase, so the only reason she could think of to avoid the upper track was to hide times, maybe somehow lengthen the odds on horses who might be faster and end up in the money. There would be no reason at all to train primarily on the Polytrack in terms of racing surfaces—Lowen client horses ran on turf, dirt, and synthetic tracks—she’d checked. It had to be about the odds.

And about the money. Another thing to follow up on.

“The Feds want Minetti,” JD broke in, returning them to the subject of keeping their noses out of Barn 41’s business. “He’s got his fingers in a lot of things, not just the horses. The

Feds see this as their chance to nab him on something that will stick." JD ran a big hand over his eyes.

Harper noticed how fatigued he looked. The situation was taking a toll on them all. Still, that was no reason to let down, especially not now.

JD folded his hands on the table, looked down at them a moment, then continued. "Look, I'm feeling frustrated, too. You're all right, the situation should be reported." He looked from person to person. "You know I've never been one to sit on things, so the collar the Feds put around my neck—it's tough."

Marshall nodded and looked to Harper. Her face gave nothing away.

JD spoke directly to her. "You know I could crack this case wide open if given the lead. But I can't buck the Feds, not openly."

Harper perked up at the word "openly." "Ok, yeah," she said. "So what are you going to do about it?"

"Anything necessary to keep you safe," JD said, staring into her eyes. "But it's got to be circumspect. I can't let Al Walker or the Feds know I've still got my hand in."

"Dicey business," murmured Marshall.

"Exactly," JD said.

Just then a loud conversation outside the conference room disrupted their focus.

Harper saw Mary Edvers in a faded green caftan lumber by with two of her assistants. The breeding consultant glanced through the glass at the foursome, her long black braid pulled forward over her ample bosom. She nodded at Harper and turned back to her crew, jabbering a mile a minute at her assistants and continuing down the hall to her office.

"At present," JD continued, and Harper looked his way, "all the Feds have is that the three know each other. There's nothing tying Minetti, Henley, or Aubrey to anything criminal, or to the drugs Figarosa had stashed. The Feds think he'd gathered them up to use when he turned state's evidence, so he was tortured to find out where they were. And maybe to see what he'd already said and to whom."

"But why you? Why did he come to the precinct asking for you?" Harper asked, unscrewing the top from a water bottle and taking a sip.

JD gazed at his wife. "Because he knew you and Aubrey were close, I think." He paused. "He must have had information that either implicated Aubrey or something that showed Aubrey was in grave danger."

Harper felt a rush of deep sadness. What JD said rang true. Poor Aubrey. He'd been right in the middle of something heartbreaking, altogether outside his capacity to handle, and she hadn't had a clue. She paused. Maybe. Or maybe she'd misread him, and he was knowingly complicit, or worse. She shook her head, trying to clear it. She didn't have a clue which of the possibilities was true.

At any rate, he hadn't asked for her help. And that thought saddened her further.

Marshall got up abruptly, snatched his Stetson and said, "I could give a damn. I'm with Harper. Not do anything about what's going on with Henley? Not at the expense of the horses. No way in hell." He slapped his Stetson on his thigh and stormed out.

All eyes watched Marshall leave and everyone felt his anger.

Then Tim spoke up. "The vet's got to be involved. The radiographs, the drugs . . . I can look into him on my end if you like."

"Tim, stay out of it," JD said, but Harper nodded affirmatively.

Tim continued. "I don't know what the federal surveillance shows but what we have here—and he held up the radiographs—could be proof of hideous training practices, but we don't know when the radiographs were taken so it's impossible to tell if these horses were trained or run while injured." He fingered the radiographs. "And like I said, I'd need an ultrasound to be absolutely sure on El Karta." He glanced around the table, his brown eyes conveying his disappointment. "I wish I could be more definitive, but what's here doesn't scream sure-fire proof of anything."

JD nodded. "Right. Figarosa had the drugs, not Minetti. That's why we can't interfere. They want to get Minetti on the illegal drugs, or maybe Figarosa's death. They just don't have the goods yet."

Or perhaps Aubrey's murder, thought Harper. She was convinced Minetti had to be involved.

Marshall walked back in, his hat literally in hands, and sheepishly returned to his seat. "I'll do whatever is needed," he said. "But I don't apologize." He laid his big hat on the table and sat stone-faced in silence.

"None of them talked about using drugs in the surveillance?" Harper said, picking up the conversation. "Not Minetti? Not Henley?" If they had tabs on that many people, surely someone would have divulged something they could use.

"Not that I know of," JD said, unfolding his hands and placing them flat on them table. "They're cagey in their conversations is what the Feds said."

Harper got that. Minetti had a lot of practice in cagey, that's how he'd stayed out of jail all these years. She turned to JD. She'd heard enough. "You know I'm going to keep working at Barn 41."

"Harper, God no," JD said, "it's much too dangerous." He sighed, staring at his wife. "Listen, I need everyone to keep a very low profile, especially you, Harper. That's the only way I can do my work around the edges."

She glared at him again. "I am going back to Barn 41. Period. Just so we're clear." She got up, ignored her husband, and turned to the vet, conclusively dismissing JD. "Can I talk to you on the way out, Tim? Just for a moment?"

Tim got up, glanced uneasily at JD, then nodded to the two men, and headed for the door, waiting there for Harper.

She turned to her husband again. "I'll see you at home," she said, her eyes hard as stone.

"Whatever, Harper," JD replied, waving at her dismissively. "You're beyond infuriating," he muttered, shaking his head.

Marshall looked from Harper to JD, his big, dark eyes filled with sadness. He got up and whispered to her, "Harper, please," but she batted a hand at him and turned to the vet. She exited with Tim and didn't glance back.

Marshall watched her stiffened back stride away. "I get it JD," he said, turning to him. "I wish she'd stay out of it, too." The trainer folded his arms across his chest. "She needs to listen to you, she's putting herself in danger. Again. And Lord knows we saw enough of that when Paris died."

JD spread his hands and looked disgusted. "She's got her own mind. She'll do what she wants. Always has." He glanced toward the foyer. "We'll keep an eye on her. Both of us."

Marshall nodded. He was used to that. He'd been doing it since Harper's parents had died. He walked to JD and laid a big hand on his shoulder. "We'll get through this together. Just like we always have."

Outside the conference room Harper and Tim walked past Pepper who picked up on the mood and didn't say a word.

The two exited the building and Harper walked Tim to his car.

"So if I wanted to keep El Karta from training, is there anything I can give him?" she asked as Tim opened his car door. At her question, he stopped and turned to her. "That's the protocol right, just rest?" she continued. "Something to sideline him but not harm him?" Harper didn't think there was a good answer to that, but she had to ask.

Tim's usually kind brown eyes took on a hard cast. "Yes, he'd need rest, no training. And for sure no racing. Then rehab, maybe swimming, shock wave perhaps, some people try stem cells. Then reintroduce him gradually to training." He said it all very professionally, not like the friend he'd become. "On that other thing. Harper, you know I can't advise you on that. If you give the horse something to sideline him, by definition you're harming him. I'd never advise anybody on how to do that."

Harper nodded and looked down, ashamed. "I know," she murmured. "I just don't want him to injure himself horribly because they won't rest him."

She glanced up, searching Tim's face. The vet relaxed and looked more like himself. "Well, he won't break down, if that's what you're worried about. At least not from what I saw."

"What about long term? If they keep pounding him?"

"Could injure himself further, sure. He's already compensating, putting more pressure on the other leg. Could be a weak point for him going forward." Tim was thoughtful for a moment. "Worse case, it could tear badly. It could end his career." He thought a moment more. "Or something worse, of course, depending on the pressure put on the other leg."

Harper knew what his last comment meant—a catastrophic breakdown. She felt her anger rise again. "And the other radiographs?"

"Didn't look bad," Tim said.

"But I didn't get all the documents either," Harper said. "So who knows about the rest of them?"

Tim nodded and patted his car door. "Keep me updated on El Karta." He got in and shut the door

Harper watched him drive off, turning as JD strode out pulling on his Hawk Ridge ballcap, focused forward, jumped in his police unit, and sped away, too.

Whatever, JD, she thought. What-the-hell-ever . . .

She got into her SUV and sat there a moment, picturing Marshall sitting forlornly in the conference room feeling useless. She put her hand on the key and turned it. Can't worry about that now, she thought, steeling herself. So much had happened so fast and not any of it good. Aubrey gone. Aubrey maybe implicated in drugs, in the murder of Figarosa? Henley running the babies into the ground—and he had a whole lot of Lowen and client horses in training. All four strings in various locations around the US, not just at Keeneland, were in danger.

She put the Range Rover into gear and hit the gas.

Chapter 13

Aubrey's visitation was held in the middle of the following week and it was all Harper could have hoped for, though she'd left most of the arrangements to Pepper and Alia, Eden Hill's landscape and flower designer. The setting was grand but subdued and the feeling both formal and a little irreverent, just as Aubrey would have liked it. The Lexington hierarchy showed up in droves and Millie spent the evening primarily in tears with Harper and Harold by her side. The funeral was scheduled for Thursday morning, the day the two-year-olds-would race at Keeneland and the day before Aviragus and Deacon were slated for their head-to-head on the turf course. The weekend and the visitation found JD giving Harper a lot of space. There was a slight chill in the air when they had words, and by the end of the public send off for Aubrey, Harper sorely missed her husband.

So it was with sadness that she stripped off her black visitation dress and jumped into the shower later Wednesday evening. She let the warm water flood over her and stood with her head down for a long time. The water was soothing but did nothing to wash away her grief, yet she couldn't cry. When she was finished, she noticed JD had called and left a message. He said he'd spoken to Rawley, Rood and Riddle, and Park Equine Hospital—the folks Lowen Farms was deeply in debt to—and each of them was willing to set up a payment schedule for Millie. He'd follow up and get in touch with the lawyer and Millie. He closed the message by saying he was at the precinct if Harper needed him. He sounded detached and ended the call abruptly. Harper sat on the bed and wept.

The next morning, she stopped by Memphis' paddock before heading to the funeral and sat on the ground in cool April morning beside him as he grazed, hugging her black coat around her. Every now and then, he'd swing his head her way and she'd put her palm under his mouth for a nuzzle. He sensed her sorrow and moved closer. She sighed and stood, stroking his neck, putting both hands on him and closing her eyes, breathing in his presence and letting her love for him restore her. Finally, she patted his mane and gave his eyelid a kiss when he raised his head for goodbye. She brushed herself off and hobbled out of the paddock on heels.

She headed for the cemetery a bit restored but still missing JD. She wished she hadn't been so caustic in the conference room about continuing her work on the backstretch. There was surely another way to have made her point without causing such hurt. She'd try to patch things up right after the service.

On the way, Harper's phone dinged, showing a text from Sophia thanking Harper for the suggestion to watch El Karta's workout earlier in the week. After her conversation with Tim, Harper had called a vet on the other side of the country, lying, saying she was doing research for a book and asking about a way to sideline a horse from training. She was told she could scratch his eye, mimicking something he might do with a blade of hay. Or, the vet said, she could inflict a puncture wound to his hoof sole or frog as if he had stepped on a nail. It would keep him out of training but could also result in complications later on.

She'd thought about it, but in the end couldn't bring herself to harm El Karta. Instead, she'd suggested Sophia come watch him work before his next race, hoping to point out his lameness. She'd hauled Sophia to the rail away from Henley to watch and after, with surprise in her voice, asked whether or not El Karta looked a little off after his workout. She'd hoped seeing that, Sophia would insist on Henley resting and treating her colt, or better yet pull him from the string altogether. Unfortunately, even with her riding experience all those years ago, Sophia wasn't able to pick up the slight hesitation in the colt's movement. Harper had pressed the issue by pointing it out, but Henley had come over just then and interrupted, saying how fit and ready the colt looked for Thursday's race. After that, Sophia could only see through the lens Henley held up for her. Harper's back-up hope was that El Karta would be scratched due to his poor workout performances but after Henley's comment, it was clear that was not happening. She'd frowned and stared out at the big track recalling JD's mention of performance-enhancing drugs found in Figarosa's apartment. Harper's only option was to hope El Karta held up until the mess at Barn 41 could be resolved.

With these unpleasant thoughts on her mind, Harper parked and walked up the hill to Aubrey's burial site. There were chairs and a polished wooden casket with a bouquet of white lilies on top poised over the burial pit. She knew the minister. He'd presided at her sister Paris' funeral, and was a solemn, respectful man who would give the burial the honor it deserved but not prolong everyone's agony.

The overcast sky portended rain. A large headstone with a polished granite face and a carved white marble statue of a winged horse towered over Aubrey's last resting place.

The small crowd included only family and immediate connections. They stood in a semi-circle in their mourning garb, serious and quiet. Marshall and Surrey were there.

Marshall had his head bowed and held his hat in both hands while Surrey had hooked her arm through his at the elbow. They both were lost in their own sad thoughts and didn't look up as Harper approached. She headed to Millie and took her hand, gazing into her brimming hazel eyes and kissed her cool, rouged cheek. Harold stood behind the black folding chair just behind the widow, but Millie didn't sit. The grieving woman's desperate eyes searched Harper's face as if looking for a way to take away her pain. Harper put her arm around Millie's shoulder, moving next to her as the aging woman leaned on Harper as if the weight of her grief was too much to bear. The other attendees stood in an arc around the casket with the minister in his black hat and suit standing to the left of the headstone in full view of Millie and Harper.

Harper didn't see JD, but it seemed everyone else was present. Except Sophia, which struck Harper as odd. In her text, Sophia had excused herself, deciding to watch her colt race rather than attend the funeral and be a support for Millie. Even Marshall had sent his assistant trainer to Keeneland to get Eden Hill's juveniles set for their races, including Meadow Flower. Harper sighed, knowing that people processed their grief differently. But Sophia not showing up for a grieving friend as deeply in pain as Millie seemed to Harper heartless.

She nodded to the minister, and he began the service by soberly thanking everyone for coming, then opening his Bible.

Harper felt hands on her shoulder and JD's presence without having to look. She leaned back, resting against him though not letting go of Millie who sobbed as the minister spoke words of comfort. Harper stroked Millie's lacquered orange hair and held her more tightly, tears welling up in her own eyes as the service continued.

Those around the casket clutched each other, several in tears, as the minister spoke about how much Aubrey had meant to them all, and how much he'd changed the racing industry. Aubrey had been a central figure both personally and professionally and, if eccentric, had touched many lives.

The service ended shortly after that and Millie went forward to unsteadily lay over the casket for a brief moment clutching the brass railing, then lifted her head, and kissed her husband goodbye. She stood there for long moments as around her everyone remained respectfully silent. Then Millie turned, tears streaming down her face, and held out her arms for Harper who moved to her side. Harold came up to help Millie as she turned away from a man she'd devoted her entire adult life to. She shook her head as the minister approached, unable to utter a word. Her eyes pleaded with Harold, and Harper understood Millie would be unable to stand and receive consolation from the people who'd also loved her husband. She nodded and gave Millie a large, gentle hug, sending her down the hill with Harold and into her Mercedes.

JD was suddenly by her side. She felt his two hands on her cheek as he raised her eyes to his. Harper found a deep softness in his green eyes which were usually so piercing. She broke down then, falling against JD, grieving for Aubrey, for herself, and for her lost sister, a grief she knew she'd always carry with her. She sobbed as the subdued attendees filed by, most of them understanding the depth of Harper's pain and not wanting to disturb it. Marshall murmured to JD that he'd take his car home and Surrey stood by looking forlorn and helpless. The minister stopped for a moment, too, laying a comforting hand on Harper's shoulder as JD held her, his big arms gathering in her grief as if it was his own.

The rain began to fall, a gentle shower as was fitting. Harper and JD walked to the Range Rover and JD drove them both home. As Surrey had done during Harper's ordeal bringing her sister's murderer to justice, JD tucked Harper in on the couch, wrapping her grandmother's quilt around her. Kelso lay just in front of her, keeping vigil, as JD made a fire, though the day was not cold. He brought tea and later some soup, but Harper wouldn't eat. She spent the day and evening curled there, her head on JD's shoulder for hours until the sun blessedly set and left the earth in comforting darkness.

Chapter 14

Friday dawned sunny and warm, the previous day's shower lasting only a short time and not interfering with the juvenile races. El Karta had again prevailed in his race and Fleet Light did well against his competitors. Meadow Flower ran down the front runner in a late stretch run, proving she had some tactical skills to go along with her drive to win. Cassandra was pleased and bubbled over on the phone to Marshall about what a gem she was.

But for Harper, there was no joy in any of it. Her sadness had deepened through the afternoon, even after Marshall's jubilant call, leaving her depleted emotionally. The only way she'd gotten through the day was JD's presence and quiet care. He had never had many words to say, but the ones he had were potent.

In the morning, he'd opened her eyes with two kisses and held her as she'd come fully awake.

She sat up and stretched, glancing out the bedroom window at the sun glinting off the far pond. She turned to her husband. Something slid into place, looking at his expression, those green eyes she'd known all her life.

He'd been through so much in Afghanistan, she knew, so much death and horror, so many nightmarish battles . . . she knew because of his nightmares, because of his hypervigilance. He'd lived through hell and guided men in impossible missions, ones that won him medals he kept at a distance, stored in dark boxes in the attic. But of all he did, mostly he was, as he'd always been, devoted to her—to loving her, to keeping her safe. She knew that. She bent and lightly brushed his lips with hers.

She smiled softly, something lifting in her. Feeling lighter and more herself than she had through the few last days, she kissed JD's full lips more deeply and snuggled back under his arm. What had eased the unbearably heavy grief she didn't completely understand, but she made her peace with not knowing how or the totality of why. JD sensed the change and smiled, turning to kiss her, grateful to have his wife back and fully present.

Quite a while later they rose, showered, and dressed, all at a leisurely pace. The Maker's Mark Mile would not be run till the afternoon, so they relished the time to themselves, savoring every moment of physical and emotional reconnection. In the midst of a waffle and bacon breakfast cooked and served by JD, Harper got a call from Harold saying Millie was again not leaving the house. She hadn't showered or eaten, either. Harper had Harold put her on the phone and in no uncertain terms, told her she'd be going to the Maker's Mark and sitting with the Eden Hill group. If Harold called again, Harper said, to say she wasn't going, Harper vowed she'd come over herself and bodily carry the widow to the car. Millie had sniffed and in a small voice, agreed.

Everyone from Eden Hill connected to Deacon was at Keeneland that afternoon, sitting in the crowded grandstand among the murmuring racegoers. The afternoon was fair and sunny and Keeneland had experienced a fine day of racing already, but the Maker's Mark Mile, with its large purse, was the calling card of the day.

JD hustled down the row beneath the deep-green grandstand's second tier and patted the seat to his right for Surrey, both of them seated to Harper's left, leaving a space for Marshall so he could be close to Harper and share the excitement of Deacon's first race on grass. Lucas, the stallion manager and his wife Alia, Eden Hill's landscape wizard, sat in front of them. Even John Henry, the old groom with a deeply lined face, who loved Deacon as much as the colt loved him, had agreed to come, and sat right behind Harper. He was as uncomfortable as he could be, feeling much more at home with the horses, so Harper leaned back and patted his knee then laid a gentle hand on Millie's shoulder, seated just to her right.

In front of them, the turf course gleamed in the sun just inside the dirt track, green and lush, as the assistant starters came on the field to help load the horses. The race was nearing and Harper could feel the crowd's excitement building. The murmuring had become louder, and everyone began moving to find their seats.

Sophia hopped up the steps and sat next to Millie, crowing about El Karta's win the day before, oblivious to the widow's continuing grief. Millie shrugged her old friend off, casting a glaring eye at her, having finally taken her measure. She turned a devastated countenance to Harper who seemed her lifeline at the moment and leaned on her shoulder refusing to look at Sophia. Sophia's gray eyes turned to Harper in question, but Harper merely shrugged her shoulders, disgusted with the woman, and pointed across the way to where Henley sat with his crew, Minetti's noble profile standing out beside the trainer. Sophia seemed not to understand but rose and took a seat between Minetti and Henley, glancing Harper's way, a question lingering in her expression.

So much for the rich and clueless. Harper caught the look that passed between Minetti and Sophia out of the corner of her eye. She turned to them. The look had been brief, but there. Did they know each other? She studied them. In the next moment she reconsidered, as the pair's attention went elsewhere—Minetti's to the track, Sophia's to her binoculars. Harper considered that maybe she was making something out of nothing.

"We're gonna see here in a minute how Mr. Badass likes the grass," Lucas said, turning in his seat in front of her laughing, his arm on his chair back. Harper faked a scowl at the stallion manager, hit him on the shoulder and resumed her excitement about the upcoming race.

Around them, the last of the racegoers mounted the steps, chatting excitedly. There were a lot of folks in attendance. An early race in the season, at 300,000 dollars, the Maker's Mark Mile was a big race for turf horses so the grandstand would have been well-populated normally, but most folks understood this could turn out to be a match race between Aviragus and Deacon. The Eden Hill colt's connections had been slapped on the back on the way to their seats by any number of well-wishers, and a murmur was presently going through the crowd as the ten horses began to walk into the sunlight, picking up their pony horses as they, one by one, made their way to the starting gate.

Marshall jumped up the stairs, bumped by everyone in the Eden Hill row and plopped down next to Harper, turning to her but patting his wife's arm. Surrey rolled her eyes and looked at JD with amusement. "As if I mattered," she said in good humor.

"Loads of Grade 1 winners in this race," Marshall panted to Harper. "Lotta class," he added breathlessly, having just watched them all get saddled. He'd given Cassandra her lastminute instructions about Deacon, which amounted to—more or less—let the colt do whatever the hell he pleased, and then he threw her up in the saddle and hoped for the best. She'd grinned down at him, bent, and patted the huge black colt's neck, and walked forward into whatever destiny lay before them.

Harper smiled at Marshall. He was so hopeful. Some horses did well on both turf and dirt, but most of them stuck to what they were bred to do. Aviragus could handle both surfaces. They'd see today if that was also true of their big, black—and beloved—menace.

Harper turned to Millie who had collapsed into Harper's right shoulder, not bothering to even glance at the track. Harper's heart went out to her and she wondered if she'd made the right decision insisting the widow come, after all they'd just buried Aubrey the day before. Maybe the memories at Keeneland were too much for her at the moment. She hugged the grieving woman and turned her attention to the track, glancing over at Henley who was staring a hole through her. She felt unnerved but forced a smile in his direction.

Aviragus emerged, majestic and gleaming, calmly walking to his pony horse just before Deacon was to enter the big stage. They'd pulled side-by-side post positions, which made the match-up even more intense. Aviragus was a regal colt, and in total control of himself. He surveyed the other horses, gazed at the stands, and dismissed them both as irrelevant. As he walked to the gate, the nobility of his breeding was as clear as the name he bore. His muscles glided beneath his radiant, deep bronze coat and it was obvious from his carriage that he was completely aware of who he was and why he was there. He loaded in the gate, post position 5, and all eyes were on him.

Deacon seemed to sense the hoopla surrounding the big bay and had refused to walk forward until he damned well wanted to. Once he emerged into the light, a roar went up from the crowd and it fell over Deacon like a wonderous shower of adulation beneath which he drew himself up to his enormous height, arching his neck and prancing, his huge muscles rippling beneath a brilliant, steely black coat. Harper turned to Marshall who beamed and stared with his mouth slightly open. Deacon seemed to be born for this very moment. He pranced to one side of the pony horse, then gathered himself and reared, rising into the air on his massive hindquarters, Cassandra leaning forward and laughing. The colt was putting on a show and Harper grinned at his audacity. She knew he was playing to the crowd, who again roared their love for a colt that had shaken them to their core in the last year with his antics and huge wins. All of Kentucky loved Deacon, and he was showing them why.

He loaded nicely in the sixth position, and the last four went in soon after.

"Safe trip," whispered Harper, as she always did.

In another moment, the bell sounded and the stall doors clanged open. Everyone jumped to their feet, craning to see the start and how the colts came out of the gate, how they took their first few strides, and who'd take the lead.

The field broke sharply, Aviragus coming out with guns blazing, getting three huge jumps and surging into the lead.

But Deacon did not break alertly as he normally did. He had a poor start, in fact, the first of his career. Harper felt alarm and glanced at Marshall who seemed confused. The cheering of the crowd dropped to a shocked murmuring as Deacon then labored through the first hundred yards, bringing up the rear for the first time in his life. Harper's heart sank. She glanced around at JD, who looked her way and shrugged. No one could figure out what had just happened. Harper glanced down at Millie, who seemed perplexed at everyone on their feet but her, and she unsteadily rose, craning around Lucas' big body to watch the race unfold.

Across the way, Henley was again staring at Harper, and when she glanced his way, he smiled. It was a smug smile. Harper looked back to the track.

She focused on listening to the announcer. The first quarter mile were honest fractions, not blazing. Aviragus moved easily, settling in, comfortable on the lead. Behind him, there was a three-way shuffle for second place among horses who'd never been off the board in a G-1 turf race. As they rounded the first turn, Deacon still labored behind the pack, as five horses in front of him vied for position.

No one had expected Deacon to perform less than spectacularly.

"Maybe he just doesn't like grass," Harper muttered to Marshall, who had his eyes trained on the first turn and didn't reply. He looked distressed and confused.

Just like the rest of them.

They rounded into the backstretch and the three horses in second place all challenged Aviragus, coming up on him on the rail and to his right. The four leaders left the five pack behind as the daylight between the frontrunners and bunched pack increased. Behind them all, Deacon continued to labor.

Aviragus seemed comfortable. He could run on the lead or run when challenged it seemed. He was a tactical horse; he'd proved that in Europe. Good on turf or dirt, too. Versatile. A horse to be reckoned with.

Harper glanced again at Marshall who seemed increasingly distressed. Now he was shaking his head. She turned to Millie who appeared to be gazing in the track's direction but blankly, not seeing a thing. Harper turned to John Henry behind her and took in a sharp breath. John Henry was smiling.

"John Henry?" she whispered. He looked down at her still smiling, and said quietly amid the perplexed and agitated crowd, "Just watch." He turned his eyes back to the track.

Harper put her binoculars up to her eyes and searched the track on the far side, finding Aviragus first. He didn't appear to be expending himself at all. She swept the binoculars over the five behind the leaders. They were bunched and running hard, and then startled, she saw coming up on the outside a black streak.

Deacon!

She turned once more to John Henry who gazed down at her, calm and smiling. "Just watch," he said again, nodding toward the racetrack.

As they neared the far turn, Harper found him, Cassandra bent over Harper's black colt staying with him as he raged past the five packed runners, ears pricked, eyes flashing, streaming by them without effort. Deacon's stride was enormous, his body as if made of pure air flowing effortlessly forward just above the earth which seemed as insubstantial to him as ether.

He switched leads rounding the far turn ahead of the pack and shot into the lane like a comet, his tail flying, his whole being stretched impossibly out and gaining with each second, pounding the turf as if it was there simply to propel him into a future only he envisioned.

Then he was into the stretch with his ears pinned, his neck extended, his body an elongated black arrow of focused purpose. He flew by the three contending with Aviragus and then it was, as it was always going to be, just the two of them.

Deacon had never had a horse ahead of him in the stretch. He rolled his eye at Aviragus, and the big bay colt rolled his right back. They took the measure of each other in a moment more primitive than training could touch, their bodies brute force locked in war, their minds absent any purpose but conquest and everyone in attendance could see it.

The crowd was utterly silent, stunned.

Deacon pounded forward and Aviragus matched him. Their hooves battered the track, their great lungs heaved, their hearts swelled with purpose. They matched each other stride for stride, each one lengthening beyond what seemed possible to match the other. They roared toward the finish line, nearly one being, so perfectly matched to one another they seemed.

Neither jockey had their sticks out. Both had abandoned their jobs to be present in this moment, aboard as mere spectators to two warriors in a battle of wills that had nothing to do with anyone but each other, an ancient battle where the only measure was greatness of spirit, the only outcome—dominance.

They were into the deep stretch, both continually taking the measure of each other then turning their attention to the wire, enemies in a battle bred into them from their dawning, pouring themselves forward, every ounce of their breeding and being serving insurmountable power, an outcome that exceeded them, theirs for the taking.

And then Deacon turned to Aviragus in the middle of his stride and Harper would swear later, saluted the big colt.

And then he kicked effortlessly, impossibly, away, his hooves blurred fury, flying down the last furlong in a joyous, ever-expanding lead that had nothing to do with muscles or training or breeding or physicality. He ran as if he was simply a gift to the world that day, a gift of grace and glory, of spirit and speed, and only a few thousand people would bear witness in person to such a gift as was given.

When he crossed the finish line going away, merely grazing the earth with his hooves, there was not a murmur. Even the announcer was speechless. And then the roar began and got louder and louder until there was no other sound than the spectator's praise of Deacon. In praise of who he was and what he had given them.

There was no savagery that day. There was only a great gift.

Harper felt a soft hand on her shoulder and turned to see John Henry gazing into her eyes. He smiled and nodded, then left. She watched him leave, her heart caught in her throat, then she turned to Millie who seemed somehow buoyed by Deacon's performance. Millie smiled and whispered, "I sure wish the ole coot had been here to see that." Harper smiled, too, and leaned to her ear. "He was, Millie. You know he was." She patted Millie's arm and held onto her as JD came up behind and leaned down to kiss the top of her head. He walked to the aisle to wait for them. He'd give them some time to take it all in.

Around them all the crowd was still shouting its exuberant praise. No one had seen anything like the race they'd just witnessed. They'd all come for that, and no one that day left disappointed.

In short order, Surrey got everyone moving, and they all headed down to the turf for the trophy presentation.

As she passed Sophia and Henley, she stopped a moment and spoke to Henley.

"Aviragus is an incredible racehorse."

Henley looked grief stricken. But Minetti leaned around him, a wolf grin on his face. "Yes, but you have a beast there, Ms. Hill. A beast. And I'll give you top dollar for him."

Harper scowled at him and turned to help Millie down the stairs.

Once on the turf for the award ceremony, they all waited a bit for the trophy presentation to be set up. Cassandra was on the ground next to Deacon, with Marshall and Harper standing together in front of her. They had a moment to catch their breath and try to understand what had just occurred. The two of them talked with Cassandra as Deacon towered over them all, surveying his domain with disdain, as usual.

"What happened out of the gate?" Marshall said to Cassandra with real concern.

Cassandra laughed, and laid an affectionate hand on Deacon's neck, just behind her and off to the side. She seemed not to want to lose contact with him.

"I'll tell ya this," she said, glancing at Deacon and shaking her head then turning back. "He had that race in his pocket from the first jump."

Marshall looked abashed and planted one leg in front of the other, pulling on his black Stetson. He trusted Cassandra but seemed totally confused as he had most of the race.

"Yeah," Cassandra said. "He hung back because he wanted to." She giggled. "Well, you did say let him do whatever the hell he wanted to . . ." She grinned at Marshall, who frowned. Cassandra was one of the best judges of pace in the game. But still. "I swear," she continued, "he knew exactly what he was doing from the get-go. He put on a show and I let him. Plenty in the tank. Pull-en-ty, if I needed it. He could have taken the lead anytime he wanted to."

Harper nodded. That sounded just like him. Marshall seemed relieved, looked at the grass and shook his head, smiling.

The three of them chuckled and took a moment to look at Deacon who turned his huge amber eye at them. It seemed he understood everything they were saying.

"God, I love this colt," Cassandra said, gazing at him, and they all laughed. "He was literally toying with Aviragus. Literally."

Harper sobered. That was likely true. She gazed at Deacon, mentally scolding him. Karma, buddy. She shot a clear message his way. Then she glanced around. Marshall was beaming, Cassandra was laughing, Surrey looked smitten as she always did by Deacon, Lucas was puffed up and proud, and Alia looked demur and pleased, and even Millie looked revived. John Henry was nowhere to be found. Of course, she thought. He was probably heading back at the farm, preparing for Deacon's return.

She turned to her husband, letting JD's arms encircle her. Then she moved to Deacon, planting a huge kiss on his enormous cheek as he bent to her and the photographer snapped a photo for the ages. "Thank you," she whispered. "Thank you," she said again into his enormous heart.

Chapter 15

Harper escorted Millie to her limo. The widow lumbered forward, Harold's looming presence on her left to steady her. She seemed to have aged years in the past week. The crowd surged around them, chatting and gesturing, no one able to let go of the high the race they'd just witnessed had given them. Jubilant spirits surrounded the trio as the colorfully clad racegoers toasted, counted their money, and high-fived each other on their way to their cars.

Millie's eyes were trained mostly on the ground, her frizzled head bent, her hands clutching the orange and blue scarf around her neck. Every now and then, she'd stop, take a breath, and then haltingly move on.

Harper caught Harold's eye and smiled sadly. They arrived at the limo and Harold opened the door, leaning into the cooler to retrieve Millie's martini shaker but she waved him away with a wrinkled hand. She looked around at the crowd, seeming a bit disoriented, glanced down at her purse and began rummaging through it. Both Harper and Harold were patient, giving Millie space and time to say goodbye in whatever way she needed to a racetrack she'd spent a lifetime attending with Aubrey.

Presently she drew out a wadded-up piece of paper and wordlessly stared at it for a moment. She looked up to Harper, her hazel eyes troubled.

"'Member that mare lost her baby few weeks ago?" she said. "The good one?" She looked down at the crumpled paper, held it out to Harper and nodded at it. "Got this nailed to the door that day."

Harper uncrumpled the paper to see the reproduction of a Theodore Gericault's lithograph. It was titled "Dead Horse" and pictured the body of a horse prone on the ground circled by predatory birds. A disturbing image and one obviously meant to send a message.

Harper stopped breathing for a moment, staring at the image, a famous one. She looked up at Millie, then back to the paper, understanding it was a warning. And sent by someone who knew the art world well. Her next thought was one word: Minetti. She smoothed out the paper in her hands. It had to be Minetti. It was exactly his M.O. Intimidation. Invisibility. Death.

"Millie, who did Aubrey borrow money from?"

Millie wouldn't answer.

"It was Minetti, wasn't it?" Still, Millie was silent. Could she really be that scared of him?

Millie looked to Harold, tears again streaming down her face. She briefly turned back to Harper, the running mascara causing Millie's bloated face to look clownlike. "I ain't givin' up the farm," she said through her tears. "You get that bastard. Get him for Aubrey." With that she stuck her elbow out and Harold helped her into the black limo.

Harper watched them go. She folded the paper and stuck it in her pocket as they turned the corner and vanished out of sight.

Once home, she showed the image to JD, and told him about how Millie had indirectly confirmed Minetti was behind it all.

"I agree—seems to implicate him," JD said, "but I doubt he'd leave fingerprints or any way to trace its origin." He handed the image back to Harper. "If it was Minetti, he'd be scrupulously careful. But I'll look into it. Criminals always made mistakes."

Harper nodded, feeling deflated and exhausted, even after Deacon's stunning performance.

He put his arm around her, inhaling her scent. "There is only so much one human being can endure," he murmured. "And you are already way over the limit on that one."

The next morning, Harper showed up at Keeneland early. Henley didn't arrive until the workouts were nearly over, and when he did, he seemed just as morose as he had the day before at Deacon's win. Harper supposed Manuel was handling workout duties, and they were on the big track for once. She watched Henley, head down, trudge into his office and shut the door. Harper followed. Maybe in his vulnerable state, he'd say something she could use.

She knocked softly but got no answer, so she cracked the door and peered into the dim office. There were no lights on, and dust motes swirled in what little sunlight the window admitted.

Henley sat at his desk, stone-faced, staring. He ran a hand over his head then put both hands to his eyes and leaned on his elbows. Harper knocked again and entered causing Henley to glance up. Immediately his hands dropped to the desk and held them in a rather tight grip.

"What?"

Harper went to the desk and sat in the metal chair. "I just wanted to say, again, what a performance Aviragus put on yesterday."

Henley snorted. "Are you trying to humiliate me further?" His shoulders slumped and he gazed at his desktop. "A race he should have won . . .." He muttered, more to himself than to Harper. "Aviragus broken like that, and in front of thousands . . ." his voice trailed off. Then he caught himself and with eyes on fire, he looked up. "*Clearly* he should have won. That idiot jockey, taking him to the lead in a mile race?" Henley shook his head in disgust. "That man will never ride another race—not for me, not for anyone," he vowed. "I'll ruin him for what he did . . . " his voice trailed off again as he picked up a pencil and began to tap in agitation. "Whatever it takes," he said under his breath.

Harper watched the trainer. She knew how it felt to lose, and Aviragus had been soundly beaten. But not because of the jockey. She'd been serious, though, in praising the colt. He had a huge heart and will to win. She looked forward to seeing him and Deacon go head-to-head again. And she had something up her sleeve that just might set the stage for a rematch.

"There is the Saratoga Stakes in August," Harper said, trying to get Henley's attention. "Mile and an eighth." She paused, waiting to see if he'd react. "Large purse at a million." She smiled, that had done it. Henley's head snapped at the purse amount. She drove the last nail in. "It's also a win-you're-in for the Breeder's Cup."

At that Henley also smiled. "Yes, the Saratoga," he said, brightening. "I'd been considering it already." He sat back and squared his shoulders a bit. "Yes, a bloody grand idea." His lips curled in a superior smile. "It will be our second head-to-head, then. A match race." He thumped the desk with certainty. "I look forward to it. There will be redemption on the first

Saturday in August." He nodded forcefully as if that sealed the deal.

Secretly Harper smiled, knowing there was no way Aviragus would ever beat Deacon. "Your colt really is a one-in-a million runner," she said. "It will be a wonderful match-up."

Henley opened his computer, checking his emails. His mood seemed to have lifted somewhat. "Yes," he said, not looking at Harper, "yes he is." He glanced her way, picking up his phone. "Was there something else?"

Harper leaned over and flicked Henley's desk lamp on, which he seemed not to mind. "I noticed Stuart Minetti was at the race with you," she began, noting the sour look that flitted across Henley's face.

He quickly recovered and assumed a noncommittal expression. "He's the owner of Fleet Light. He was my guest." Henley consulted the time. "In fact, he's due here shortly."

"We met briefly in New York," Harper said, wanting to continue the conversation. "We both moved in the art world back then." She stopped. How she was going to get Henley to talk more about Minetti eluded her. She crossed a leg over one knee, noticing it bounced a bit. Henley wasn't the only one agitated.

Henley nodded. "He has a lot of art money to invest. We have him in a number of runners." Henley paused, as if he'd said too much.

Here we go, though Harper. Was the "we" he and Aubrey? Harper tried to look curious. "Oh, so he's part owner in many of Lowen's horses?"

Henley's eyes narrowed and he leaned forward a bit. "We keep our client's particulars quite private, as—in your position—I'm sure you understand." He glared at Harper.

There was a forceful knock at the door and in walked Stuart Minetti, dressed in khakis and a black polo shirt. A huge gold watch dangled from his wrist and his black leather belt shown as highly as his tasseled, leather loafers. His silver hair was thick and swept back from a high forehead and his dark brown eyes were mere slits as he took in Harper. He might have stepped right off the pages of GQ.

"So nice to see you again, Miss Hill," he said. "Or is it Ms.?" He pressed his hands together in studied nonchalance.

"It's Harper."

He consulted his watch. "Would you excuse us, then, Harper?" He glanced Henley's way. "We have an appointment." He looked her way again and a chill went up Harper's spine. "Especially following that mysteriously fabulous performance you colt turned in yesterday."

Harper smiled, mumbling. "Thank you," and looked down, wondering if he was intimating they'd cheated. The man's presence was unnerving. And ominous.

Minetti smiled. He knew the effect he had on people and used it to his advantage. "My offer, of course, to buy the colt, still stands."

"He isn't for sale," Harper snapped, rising from her seat. He was a head taller than Harper, yet she made herself give him a penetrating stare. "Not at any price."

He smiled again and stepped aside, gesturing to the door. "Well, you may reconsider." He tipped himself forward and looked at the door, then back to Harper. "So nice to see you again after New York. I do hope we run into each other more often." His eyes looked menacing. "Perhaps quite soon?"

Not if I can help it, Harper thought, and exited with as much dignity as she could muster. I will not let that man intimidate me, she said, shooting him a look as she went by.

I've handled worse than you and I'm still standing. She left and felt the door click shut behind her.

As she exited the office, she heard the alarm. Glancing up she saw Manuel racing toward her and she ran to meet him, nearly colliding partway down the shedrow. His face looked panicked. "Come! El Karta, he down on the track! Come, the vet, he there with!" Manuel shot past her and into Henley's office, and Harper broke into a dead run heading for the track, hearing the alarm the outrider had sounded getting louder as she drew closer, fear coursing through her.

She met the rest of the set walking up the hill, and as she looked from rider to rider, her own panic increased. Each one looked blankly, sadly forward. There was no light banter today. Harper sped past them down the hill and in the early morning light, she saw the ambulance on the track, all the other riders halted, the alarm still ringing in her ears, and the big black colt down. Not good. He was still down, which meant the vet couldn't get him up to enter the ambulance. She whipped her head around and saw Henley yelling into his phone, lumbering with all his might toward the track.

"Yes, Mis Creighton, it appears he has injured himself," Henley panted into the phone as he passed Harper. She broke again into a run, speeding past Henley and arriving at the rail, just as the colt tried to rise, and fell back, his eyes wild. She'd seen so many breakdowns. Too many. Her heart broke as she looked at the big colt who had won both races he'd entered, even injured. She simply could not look at another snapped bone, and yet she knew she had to see what happened to the colt she'd tried so hard to protect. She forced herself to remain planted.

The vet rose, his face serious, at Henley's arrival. Henley turned away, his expression as solemn as his exercise rider's. He knew what he saw. On the track, El Karta began thrashing, the colt not understanding why he was in such pain. His instincts kicked in and he tried to rise, to run, to escape the pain.

He made no sound. Prey animals survived by not alerting the predators.

Henley glanced her way and waved her back up the hill, his face contorted in anger. I'll be damned if I'm leaving, she thought, tears welling in her eyes. She stayed where she was, leaning on the rail, forcing herself to watch the spirited colt try again and again to rise. Even the attendants turned away, so heartbreaking were El Karta's attempts. His body was broken, but his spirit would not accept it. How he bore that much pain and panic in silence, she didn't know.

As the colt grew even more agitated, his head thrashing, the vet called his assistant and took the syringe, his face a mask of lost hope. He plunged it into El Karta's neck and turned to Henley. "Make the damn call!" he shouted; his voice full of fury.

Harper already knew the outcome. The vet would have given the shot in a way that made sure there was no air in the syringe if El Karta was going to make it, but he'd plunged it into the colt's neck with no regard for that.

The vet rose before Henley, screaming "He snapped the right cannon bone. Make the damned call!"

Harper sobbed. Henley turned away, still on the phone with Sophia, as the colt seemed to calm a bit from the shot, then again panicked and began to thrash. His big body was lathered in sweat, his legs churning, the whites of his eyes telling everyone he had no idea what was happening.

Henley turned back, the phone at his side, and nodded to the vet who quickly received the second syringe from the attendant standing by. Harper turned away and made herself leave. She'd seen what she needed to and could not watch another racehorse, doing everything asked of him willingly, even injured, being killed on the track.

And one she'd tried so very hard to save.

No more, Harper vowed silently, walking all alone to the barn.

Her phone rang on the way up the hill. Through blurry eyes, she saw the call was from Sophia. The last person she wanted to talk to. If the woman only had eyes, she might have seen the harm Henley was doing. If she'd not been blinded by the trainer's flattery and seduced by winning, she might have saved the colt she professed to love so much. Harper pocketed her phone, and in a few moments got into her SUV and drove home.

Chapter 16

Harper couldn't go back to the barn for a week. She rode Memphis, she consoled Millie, she raged at JD who held her until it passed. She'd finally listened to Sophia's message filled with screams and fury. Her beloved colt was dead. The horse that would take her to the Triple Crown, the horse that would put her on the map as an owner, and on and on she went. Harper listened to the entire message and her disgust grew. The colt did not deserve that owner, an owner whose love for him revolved around what he could do for her. She listened to the message over and over, allowing it to give rise to her own wrath. She welcomed her anger. Those two, she thought—Henley and Sophia. They did not deserve that colt. And yes, she felt culpable. Enormously culpable. She could have ignored JD and called the racing commission's tip line. She could have thumbed her nose at the Feds. She could have exposed herself and told Henley she knew El Karta was injured, insist he not be trained, she could have . . . done so many things. Yes, horses did break down and yes, there were catastrophic accidents. But this was not that. Already injured on his left leg, he'd no doubt compensated as Tim had said, putting more weight on the right under Henley's blistering training program . . . Harper had seen too many hairline fractures not treated and too many times this was the outcome. This was no accident, this was simple—greed and heartlessness. Hard gallops, breezes, races for an injured two-year-old? Harper could not get the image of El Karta down on the track out of her mind.

She'd finally, after a mighty effort, calmed herself. She would not discard her anger; she would use it. The next morning, she swept her blond hair into a ponytail, settled a Lowen Farms ballcap on her head and in the middle of an early May downpour, made her way to Barn 41.

Henley was standing at Aviragus' stall with Minetti when she arrived. The trainer looked furious as Harper rounded the corner and headed up the shedrow. She'd missed training so now all that was left it looked like, was sweeping up since every stall she passed had leg wraps, full water, and hay nets. She glanced around. The rain had stopped, and a few horses were out being hand-walked or grazed just beyond the cool down track. All the grooms she could see were quiet, had their heads down, and eyes averted from the shedrow.

"You're frigging barmy if you think that's ever going to happen!" Henley yelled, giving Harper a good idea about why the grooms were keeping a low profile.

Minetti looked around, seeing Harper. All at once, he seemed uninterested in Henley's outburst, breaking into an inviting smile, and opening his arms as he approached her.

"So very nice to see you again," Minetti said, leaving a fuming Henley in his wake and slotting one hand comfortably in his navy-blue pants pocket when Harper didn't respond to his open armed invitation. His keen eyes surveyed her in an unnerving way, blatant and sexual, finally settling on her face.

"Musn't scowl, Ms. Hill, it ruins the appeal." He shook his head in mock seriousness.

Behind him Henley stroked Aviragus' neck as the colt leaned out of his stall to accept the trainer's attention. When Henley looked her way, he appeared close to tears but that look hardened taking in Minetti's back and then Harper. He turned back to Aviragus.

Aliana came between them and put Miss Somers in her stall, then keeping her head down scurried off to the feed room.

Minetti turned to his left a bit, gesturing toward Aviragus. "Not worth much, after all, now, is he?" he said dismissively. "Not after your colt made a fool of him in front of all those people." He stroked his thick silvery hair back from his forehead then shrugged, resuming his wolfish smile. "But that's the game, now, isn't it? On top of the world one moment, and then the next . . . nothing but buried hopes." He scrutinized Harper to see her reaction.

An obvious reference to Aubrey's recent funeral, Harper thought, a chill running over her. "Yes," she said, forcing a smile. "That's it in a nutshell." She composed herself, moving to the bay filly who stuck her head out of her stall to take in the conversation. The horse looked from left to right, then extended her mouth to the hay net and grabbed some alfalfa. Harper inhaled the smell of wheat straw bedding mixed with liniment and smiled at the filly. We'll see who's in control here, she thought, her hand lightly running over the filly's soft cheek, ignoring Minetti for the moment. Finally, she turned back to him.

"What brings you so far from home?" she said with feigned interest, moving to rub the bay's forehead as she munched and turned a soft brown eye their way. No use pretending they didn't know each other any longer.

He smiled indulgently and gestured behind him. "Had to check out this 'phenomenal trainer' as Aubrey described him." His forehead furrowed a bit as his eyes narrowed. "Can't say I'm too impressed at the moment."

Henley stomped past him, glaring, and headed to his office. “Stay away from the colt,” he commanded, looking straight ahead. Minetti laughed. It was a laugh Harper had heard countless times in the art world. One that sent the message that the artist, the painting, the curator, the gallery . . . was of no consequence.

Minetti moved closer to Harper, and though tempted by revulsion to retreat, she stood her ground and looked up into his dead eyes. “I have interests to protect here,” he said. “And I shall remain until I see that they are.”

Harper had the distinct impression his words were a threat. A threat to her.

He backed away, shot his cuff, and gazed at his watch. “Must be off, my dear,” he said, reassuming his smiling demeanor and staring into Harper’s eyes. “But I’m quite sure we shall see each other again.” And with that, he strode casually by her not waiting for a reply.

Harper stared after him. The grooms, with Henley in his office and Minetti striding off, began speaking to each other in rapid Spanish. She glanced around, curious about where the assistant trainer was during all this, but she didn’t see Manuel.

She fetched a broom, wondering what the blowup at Aviragus’ stall had been all about.

That evening, she talked JD into visiting Millie. The woman’s normal sassiness had left at Aubrey’s death, and she needed her grit, cockiness, and business savvy back if she was going to hang on to Lowen Farms. JD and Harper agreed they’d do what they could to make that happen.

The three of them sat in Aubrey's study, JD and Harper on the couch, Millie behind Aubrey's desk. She gazed around at the walls, taking in Aubrey's art collection, sipping her martini, and tapping her cigarette in the hand-blown glass ashtray to her right.

Harper was secretly glad to see her back to a semblance of her old routine. Drinking and smoking wasn't the healthiest lifestyle, but it was more like the Millie of old and that was a good thing. Harper allowed her gaze to follow Millie's as she surveyed the walls in the diffused light cast by overhead, dimmed chandeliers. She sat forward and scrutinized the early Franz Kline to the left of Millie, glanced to the right of it, patted JD's leg, and rose to inspect the painting more closely. JD sat back and sipped his craft beer, watching his wife do her thing.

"Millie, wasn't there a Karel Appel here next to the Kline?" She turned to the seated woman. Millie didn't look her way. "Aubrey sold it or something. Maybe sent it to the City."

"The fish? I thought he'd never sell it, he loved that painting."

Millie nodded, sipping. "And yet the ole coot did get rid of it, sure enough."

"Who was the buyer?" she asked.

Millie turned. "Who do you think? That damned Minetti. Still haven't seen a cent for it, neither."

Harper looked at JD who sat forward, his green eyes slits, then back to Millie. "Aubrey gave Minetti the painting against what he owed him," Harper said. It wasn't a question. The painting could have been worth a lot—one of Appel's paintings had sold for over a million dollars.

"Yeah, the asshole's been squeezing us," she admitted.

"And sending you a message with that mare," JD said, rising. He walked over to Millie and lifted her out of her chair.

She picked up her ashtray, her tent dress shifting around her as JD led her to a chair opposite the couch. Harper went to join her husband.

"Millie, it's time to let us in," he said. Harper looked over and saw cop eyes. She smiled at Millie and as the widow ground out her smoke, she took her hand.

Bad cop, good cop, Harper thought, looking into Millie's swimming eyes. Not her first martini of the day, it seemed. "Aubrey's legacy is Lowen Farms," she said stroking Millie's hand. "We know that. We loved Aubrey, too, and we love you. We're here to help you hang onto all this." She gestured around with her free hand. "But you've got to let us in, Millie," she finished, her blue eyes not moving from Millie's.

Millie sighed, planted her empty martini glass on the side table, and shrugged. "Well, there's no telling what the hell happened . . . I looked at the books, I asked Aubrey, but he was a tight-assed mother about that first loan. I don't know it was Minetti, to be honest," she finished. "Could've been." She slumped a bit in the chair and patted her hair, which didn't move. "Could be there was no loan at all, who the hell knows with him?" She ran her hand across her lap at the few ashes there. Then she seemed to sober a bit. "Aubrey decided, all of a damned sudden, he was in charge, sold them paintings, bought 'em, gave 'em away—wasn't up to me." She turned serious. "Was never up to me."

Harper and JD looked at each other. Around them the pulled shades over tall windows leant a serious cast to the atmosphere, already in low light. The paintings on the walls stood out colorfully in stark contrast to the dull mood of the three in the room.

"Can we look at the books?" JD said, and Millie nodded. "I'll have Harold get 'em for you."

Harper was frustrated. Things seemed at a standstill and Millie wasn't helping with any of it. Was the loan from Minetti or not? Was there even a loan at all? Aubrey had run up some huge bills, but there was no proof that there was an actual loan before that. And Minetti could have bought the painting or been gifted it, that would be like Aubrey to do. And who beat the hell out of Figarosa? Who killed Aubrey? Who got to the Lowen's big-time mare? Was it Henley? He had the access, but unlikely the money for a loan. He'd have to be working with someone. Was it someone not in the picture at all? And what about Sophia and Minetti?—they'd shared a look at the race that day, Harper was pretty certain of it. Was she mixed up in all this, too? Harper considered it. Sophia was a slippery one, seemed the picture of elegance and refinement when they'd first met, and devoted to her colt. But when push came to shove, she'd shown her true colors . . . could she be behind all this?

JD and Harper left shortly after that, the farm account books in hand, but no closer to an answer to any of the questions.

Chapter 17

The next morning, Harper arrived at Barn 41 on time and on edge. She needed to break through the seeming impenetrable confusion around what was actually going on in Henley's barn. As she turned the corner, she glanced at Aviragus being led out of his stall for training, again wondering what the argument between Henley and Minetti had been the day before. Beyond the colt, Harper saw Sophia standing at what had been El Karta's stall, staring at the new inhabitant, a 2-year-old, bright-eyed, full-bodied colt contentedly munching hay, seeming comfortable and settled in.

As she approached, Sophia turned to her, her gray eyes devastated, her complexion sallow. "Is there a difference between wishing someone dead and doing something about it?" she hissed, pointing to the new colt in her beloved El Karta's stall. "Well . . . is there?" she said, her fury evident. Not waiting for a reply, she stomped off.

Did she mean the new colt? Harper wondered. Or Henley? Harper watched the flowery-dressed Sophia adjusting a big-brimmed black hat as she swayed decidedly toward Henley's office. She pounded the door and stood there, arms folded.

Fear switched through Harper and she took off after the woman. What if she did mean to harm Henley? She clearly blamed him—as she should—for El Karta's death.

Harper arrived and Sophia glared at her. "And he's a coward to boot, I see," she spat, nodding at the still-closed door. She gave the door one more good rap, stood there with hands balled into fists, then huffed disgustedly and headed for her car.

Harper watched her go a minute, relieved, then tried the door, which swung open without protest. She walked in on Henley intent on his computer screen. He glanced up, frowned at her, and muttered "You're up on Fleet Light today," and turned back to his task, waving her off with a dismissive hand.

As Harper turned to go, Henley glanced up and watched her exit. He closed the computer, gathered his keys and stopwatch then gazed around for anything else he'd need to watch the workout. He shuffled some papers, and picked up a pencil, drumming it on the desktop as he stared at the closed door.

Harper stood a moment outside Henley's office her excitement building about getting a feel for Fleet Light on the training track. She'd check the whiteboard for the workout and grab her gear. She looked up. Striding towards the office was the tall exercise rider Harper tried to avoid. He doubled as a groom and had been the one who'd spied her with El Karta on the cool down track checking his lameness. He drew near, and again Harper noticed how small his head was in relationship to his lanky body—much too tall for a jockey, which is likely why he rode exercise—and the two beady, birdlike eyes that now darted toward Henley's office door.

"Get in here, where the hell have you been?" she heard Henley yell as the rider opened the door. Harper headed off to pick up her chest guard, helmet, and stick. "Shut the door and sit," finished the trainer and with that, the door clicked shut.

Harper bent her leg and Aliana threw her up into Fleet Light's tiny saddle. The colt tossed his head and side-stepped, ready to go. She gathered the reins, checked her stirrups, ran her hand along the top of his black mane and patted his neck. As she settled into the saddle, knees bent, the rest of the set walked up behind her and they all headed down the hill to the track, Harper relaxing into the easy camaraderie among the riders. These were the unsung heroes of the racing world, the ones who taught the babies, worked out head cases, and brought along horses who'd been injured. Most exercise riders loved the horses they rode, some so much that when they raced, the riders were too nervous to watch and proud as parents when they won.

Harper scanned the track as the day's pale bluish light settled over the horses and riders, and the scent of warm horseflesh drifted faintly on the slight breeze.

Henley caught up with her as she neared the Polytrack. "Start him off easy and bring him home strong," he instructed. "Pick it up at every pole."

She nodded, accepting the trainer's breeze instructions, checking her helmet as they headed onto the track and stopped along the near rail, waiting their turn. To her right, she saw the lanky rider head toward her and turned away. She focused ahead and shortly moved Fleet Light forward for their workout with the others in her set. The small-headed man pulled in behind Henley's horses as they all moved into an easy trot for warm-ups. Harper rose above Fleet Light, her hands back for the trot then, with the others, she moved him into a jog. Soon she broke off and set about her work, asking the colt for a gallop, focusing ahead between his alert ears as he smoothly picked up speed, his hooves quickening. He felt good beneath her, eager and responsive, his body like liquid. She balanced over him, still and quiet, then feeling him coil beneath her, asked for more as she moved her hands up his neck at the rail, picking it up at the pole, as instructed. The colt felt good, exuberant, ready to run, energy unspooling as they hit the next pole and breezed a bit faster.

She drank in the pleasure of Fleet Light's speed, his willingness to listen to her every cue. Then suddenly her hands felt the colt's distraction, a slight shudder up the reins, and then up on her right came the beady-eyed rider closing in on them, much too close. She glanced his way, gave him a loud, "Back off!" but he kept coming, pushing Fleet Light further toward the rail, putting them both in danger.

Harper's instincts kicked in and she bridged the reins, crouched lower over the colt's center of gravity, moved her hands further up his neck, and pumped her elbows urging him forward. He shot ahead and Harper then eased him off the rail, glancing behind her to see the idiot grinning and slapping his filly's neck. When they were clear, she slowed Fleet Light, stood in the irons, and tucked her stick under her arm. What the hell was that, she wondered, gathering Fleet Light into a trot, rising and falling gently over him. She glanced around, and saw the outrider call the guy over, then launch into a stern lecture—the pin-head dutifully hung his head, nodding. The guy needed more than a talking to—he needed to get off the track altogether.

She could have been hurt, badly hurt, and the colt, too. She settled into the saddle as Fleet Light came to a walk.

Well, she shuddered, maybe that was the plan. She tucked her stick into the back of her waistband. Yes, she thought, running a hand down the colt's neck, she'd narrowly missed breaking a few bones. They headed to the exit, and Harper shot Henley a hard look. He shot one right back at her.

Did he want her gone that bad?

"Nice going out there," Jose said, pulling up on her right aboard his colt as the set walked up the dirt hill to the barn. The two colts moved easily side by side, Fleet Light settling down under Harper's calm assurance, the low clop of the young horses sounding faintly as they continued up to the barn.

"Edgar has always been an asshole, but that one . . ." Jose shook his head. "You got a good head," he said. "Made a nice call." He glanced at Fleet Light. "Saved this boy, too." He nodded and walked on ahead.

Once at the barn, she untacked Fleet Light, looking into his bright, alert brown eyes, liking him more and more. A sensitive colt, he'd understood everything she'd asked of him, which—as Jose had said—saved them both from harm. "Good boy," she murmured, rubbing his white blaze affectionately.

Henley strode by, pulling on his beard, motioning her angrily into his office. Harper handed Fleet Light off to Aliana for his bath and headed into Henley's office.

"Are you daft?" he yelled, his face red, as she entered the office. He loomed behind his desk, his arms wide in disbelief. "Blimey, did I not tell you to breeze the colt, and did I not give you precise instructions?" He poked his finger at her and sat heavily in his chair.

Harper listened to his onslaught, her anger building. Was he seriously blaming her for Fleet Light charging out of danger? Did he not see what his idiot rider did, did he not, in all likelihood, orchestrate it? His tirade was so outlandish, she couldn't respond.

"Do you not have one word to say for yourself?" Henley continued, banging on the table, agitated and angry. "We'll not know until tomorrow if the colt was—quite miraculously—unhurt by your incompetence."

Harper found her voice. "You cannot be serious," she spat at him, still standing. "I kept the colt *out* of danger." She took a step back and sent daggers. It was one thing to not want her around, but Henley had moved into new territory with this one. She couldn't tell JD, of course, but she'd be damned if she was going to let him get away with trying to hurt her—and whatever the hell else he was up to. She took in a deep breath, adjusted her attitude, and tried to look at least compliant.

"I'll check on him tomorrow, no worries," she said into his frown. "And you need to get Edgar off your babies. He's going to hurt somebody." But it's not going to be me, she thought. I've got that imbecile's number.

Henley waved her out of his office without another word, and popped his computer open, dismissing her, but still agitated. In truth, he realized, he was angry with Edgar for not getting the damned job done. Accidents do happen, he mused, something he had been counting on. Jesus, he thought, he'd never get rid of the maggot. He sighed. Ah well, better the devil you know than a lunatic with clown hair. He'd figure out how to get rid of her some other way.

The Lowen books revealed nothing Harper and JD didn't already know. Aubrey had run up debts and Millie was now saddled with the repayments JD had arranged. Of course, there could be a multitude of things off the books, but as for now, the accounts were a dead end.

She'd talked to Tim about the Lowen's' vet, but he hadn't come up with anything, either. So that left who? Who could she tap into that might share something to break open whatever was going on at Barn 41? She'd tried Aliana. Maybe try her again? Or maybe Manuel? The assistant trainer had seemed uneasy, even sad, at El Karta's stall that day administering what was likely a steroid shot as well as the bute. She'd see if she could corner him when Henley wasn't around. Surely the trainer would need to visit his other strings at some point.

Unfortunately, the next day yielded no opportunities to speak to Manuel or Aliana. Everyone was focused and intent on their jobs. Since El Karta's death, a subdued atmosphere had settled over the barn, and the light Latin music seemed the only convivial presence. Harper drew hot walking duty, so she trudged around the track, trying to keep her eyes open for any developments. The same dull routine continued through the end of the week and Harper found nothing of interest to pursue.

But the following week, she sensed things might be about to change. They were well into May and the racing season was heating up. The 2-year-old races were getting longer, and Fleet Light and Meadow were both holding up well. Henley apparently felt things had settled enough for him to travel, and Harper learned he was leaving shortly to visit strings in the other Lowen locations.

It was good Henley was leaving, not just because getting him out of the picture would give her more maneuvering room but because Harper knew she'd already spent much too much time at Barn 41. They'd gotten all the Eden Hill foals on the ground but were still in breeding season, and JD and Marshall continued to pick up the slack. Harper was doing what she could catching up after her backstretch work, but most of the work still fell to the two men. The situation had to resolve soon or she'd have to abandon Keeneland altogether. Eden Hill was her responsibility and she'd been shirking it of late though no one was complaining about the extra load.

Harper was thinking these thoughts as she parked the Range Rover and jumped out on Keeneland's backstretch. It was 4:50 in the morning, and she'd been asked to take Fleet Light out again. He'd been fine after their near-collision and had continued training with alacrity. The colt was learning fast, good in the starting gate, good changing leads into the turns, and he'd had a bit of experience with dirt in the face and had taken it well. Minetti, she was told, was buoyant. She relished the thought of taking the man down and maybe bringing the precocious baby to Marshall, who she knew would take care of him.

She hopped aboard and did a nice, easy jog on the colt, got him bathed and was cooling him down in the blue morning light with the rest of the set who'd gone out first. Manuel stood at the edge of the cool down track, nodding at the hot walkers, consulting the notes he'd made on how the first string felt to the exercise riders. She looked up and smiled at the assistant trainer as she passed him, grateful for the soft shade provided by the leafed-out oak. It was cool in the morning, but exercising a racehorse, even at a jog, was a workout. She'd just finished the cool down and was heading Fleet Light to a bit of grazing when she spied Minetti rounding the corner and heading to Aviragus' stall. She moved the bay colt off a bit, trying to avoid his owner seeing him.

Minetti motioned to Manuel and nodded his head at Aviragus. The assistant walked over a bit reluctantly, holding his pad of notes at his side. There ensued a conversation that saw Manuel taking a step back from the stall and shaking his head vigorously. Minetti narrowed his eyes and spoke in a low tone, so Harper couldn't pick up the conversation, but it was apparent that Manuel was not liking what he heard. It was the same reaction Henley had when Minetti had confronted him at the colt's stall. What the hell was Minetti up to?

The assistant trainer turned toward the colt as the big bay stuck his head out of the stall, pinned his ears at Minetti and took a bite at his blazer cuff. Minetti leaned back on the deep green Dutch stall doors and took a swipe at the big colt. Manuel stepped between them just as Harper's phone went off, sending Fleet Light a few jumpy steps to the left.

JD. She answered it before the next ring, keeping her eyes on Fleet Light and then on the argument occurring at Aviragus' stall. The colt held his head high, which was high indeed, towering over Minetti and it looked like Manuel was doing little to stop Aviragus' antics.

"Learned something interesting," JD said after Harper answered the phone.

"Hold on a sec," Harper said as Minetti sauntered away, Manuel staring after him. The assistant trainer raised a calm hand to the colt's neck, but Aviragus would not take his eyes off Minetti's form. He finally turned back to Manuel who stroked the colt's crooked blaze.

"Okay, what's up?" Harper asked.

"Got some information from the Feds."

Harper perked up.

"Minetti put in a call to Millie last week."

"Millie?" repeated Harper, "what for?"

"Condolences is what the Feds said. Asked to meet up with Millie to convey them in person."

Harper thought that was odd. It was May, a bit late for condolences. Minetti wasn't at the funeral, either, so why now? "That's strange timing," she said, walking to her left as Fleet Light moved to a new patch of grass and the other hot walkers led their charges out to graze.

"Very odd," agreed JD. "And I'd like to know what the meeting was all about."

Right. What could he say in person he couldn't on the phone? "Yeah, and why didn't Millie mention it when we were over?"

The day was warming and the low conversation among the Hispanic grooms grazing their horses seemed oddly comforting to her. She smiled and nodded to Aliana and the others as the big, dappled gray and two colts settled into their grazing. Harper checked the time. Fleet Light had had enough grass, so she moved him toward his stall. She had to wrap his legs and check again for any heat, so she told JD they'd talk about this more at home.

She passed Manuel on the way, still at Aviragus' stall. He looked down as she passed, but briefly turned his dark eyes her way. Troubled eyes. Sad eyes, Harper thought. She'd talk to him just as soon as she got the bay colt settled.

Fleet Light was fine after she checked him once more and got his stall wraps on, but when she looked for Manuel, she didn't see him. She rapped on the office door, but no one answered. The conversation would have to wait until the next day. Disappointed, she waved to Aliana and headed for her SUV.

All the way home, Harper thought about Millie and Minetti. If he had made an initial loan to Aubrey, maybe he was pressing her for payment—she said he'd been squeezing her. But why didn't he mention that on the phone? And Millie hadn't actually confirmed that there was a loan, plus there was nothing on the books. But she had tearfully made the comment about “getting him for Aubrey” at Keeneland that day when she’d handed Harper the disturbing image of a dead horse. So there was something there, something Millie knew. Something Millie knew and wasn’t saying.

Chapter 18

Harper begged off Barn 41 the next morning, intending to talk with Millie about her meeting with Minetti. The only time the widow could meet was early, so Harper agreed to talk with her at Lowen's yearling barn, intending to get to the truth about what Minetti was up to. She was unhappy about putting off talking with Manuel, but this seemed important.

She drove to Lowen Farms mulling over Aubrey's recent decision to take in client yearlings to prep for the September Keeneland sale. He'd done that around the time he'd also decided to take on client two-year olds for Henley to train. Seems he was doing his best to generate additional revenue. It saddened Harper that Aubrey had moved the farm toward a commercial enterprise to fix the financial mess he'd gotten them into. That wasn't his vision, she knew, and it wasn't the legacy he wanted to leave.

Harper found Millie inside the barn, standing in the aisle behind Lowen's conformation expert as he watched a nice yearling hand-walked down the aisle, turn and head back to the group. "Nice, square hip going away," murmured the man as his assistant made notes.

Harper approached Millie and chatted a moment about how well the yearling looked. It seemed Aubrey's idea was a good one. They watched the young "would be" racehorses as, one by one they were brought out, inspected, and returned to their stalls.

The assistant said, "Djeddah's up next," and the groom walked down the row and got out the chestnut colt holding him sideways in the aisle for inspection. The conformation expert had the colt walk away and then toward him.

"Put a screw in that right knee," the expert said to his assistant. "Rocks out a bit, put him on the list." He nodded and the groom opened the blue and white painted half door and put the yearling back in his stall.

Millie turned to Harper. "Now that man," she said, pointing to the expert, "was a damned good hire." She looked much more together and in charge than she had the previous weeks. She stuffed her hands in her aqua pantsuit and looked into Harper's eyes.

Harper brought up the meeting with Minetti.

Millie glanced at the bay being brought out, studying the yearling in profile before his inspection walk began. "I've known that dirty dog forever," Millie said, keeping her eye on the colt. "Known him a helluva lot longer than Aubrey, in fact," she said, glancing Harper's way. "He owned a few of the clubs I sang at back in the day, up there in Harlem."

Really, thought Harper, this was news. So Millie and Minetti went way back. She watched the widow who seemed focused on appraising the horses herself and how sound the expert's evaluations were.

"Millie, we can't talk about this here," Harper said, her frustration mounting. "This is important, and I need you to focus." And I need some answers, she added to herself.

"Whatever the hell for?" Millie said, turning to her with a slight smile. "Stuart and me, we got together and had a few drinks, is all. He's a busy man, just wanted to tell me how damned sorry he was about Aubrey."

Millie's attitude made no sense. One minute it's, "Get him for Aubrey," and the next she's having drinks with the man? Harper's tone turned skeptical. "Millie there is more to it than that."

Millie shrugged her shoulders and pulled her cigarettes out of her pocket. Harper seized her arm and guided her out of the barn and into the brightening light. Millie protested, turning to the assistant, yelling, "Have him call me!" and lit up. Harper huffed disgustedly at her as they left the barn, Lowen's royal blue and white colors gracing the barn's exterior behind them.

"Millie, get in the car," Harper said and she strode with her to the Range Rover, opened the passenger side, plucked the cigarette out of Millie's fingers, and ground it out.

"Climb in," she ordered but Millie simply stared at her, standing her ground.

"What the hell makes you think I can get up in this thing on my own?" she said.

Harper helped her in and Millie stared out the window, ignoring Harper once she sat in the driver's seat. Harper started the car and Millie huffed, folding her hands in her lap, and staring a hole through the driver.

"Kidnapping, now you've stooped to that," she said, and gazed out the window.

Harper ignored her and drove off the property, turning into Eden Hill's drive a while later and heading for the lay-up barn. She parked, got Millie out and walked over to the bronze statue of Rayo Del Corazon, one of her mother's favorite broodmares and the statue she'd had multiple serious talks beside. She led Millie to the bench and motioned her to sit.

Inside the barn, injured horses whinnied to each other and stuck their heads out of their stalls to peer at the newcomers through the open door. A Panamanian groom got one of the horses out and hand-walked her into the bright day, the hollow sound of her hooves on the walkway drifting toward them. The groom nodded to Harper and Millie and went about his business, turning the horse down the lane, glancing at the time on his phone, making sure he hand-walked the mare the requisite number of minutes.

"Millie, enough is enough," Harper said, as the groom and mare made their way down the road. "Your husband is dead. The farm is in jeopardy. You said Minetti is 'squeezing you' and Henley is up to something. I can't help you with any of it until you come clean with me."

Harper hoped her sharp glare would let Millie know how serious she was. Millie was not leaving the bench until she had answers, that was all there was to it.

Millie sighed and gazed at the holly bush beside the barn. "Okay," she said, turning to Harper, her eyes clear and focused. "I'm gonna tell it to you straight. That damned Minetti. I'm the one introduced him to Aubrey and I God-damned wish I'd never laid eyes on him. He ruined everything." She looked away. "Every damned thing."

Harper blanched. "Why ever would you bring that man in, Millie? Of all people!" Harper was confounded at Millie's apparent stupidity. "If you knew him in the City, you know how truly evil the man is!"

Millie narrowed her eyes at Harper. "Who the hell else did I know with enough bucks to bail us out and keep it quiet?" She huffed and folded her arms. "We got a reputation. You think Aubrey wanted them debts he run up plastered all over Lexington?"

Harper thought about that. Minetti had the art world connection that would have appealed to Aubrey. And the man did like the ponies. She looked at Millie who sat staring ahead with arms folded. And it seemed Minetti and Millie went way back, so Harper understood the choice. Up to a point. Anyone who knew Minetti, or knew of him, and had any sense at all would stay as far away as possible from him. But then, Harper considered, it didn't appear that Millie and Aubrey had a lot of options if they wanted to keep the situation quiet. Especially given the amount of debt they were in.

"Why did he want to meet with you, Millie?" Harper asked, bringing her back to where they'd begun. "Was it the loan? It wasn't for condolence. It's a bit late for that."

The sweet scent of hay from the barn wafted their way, and Harper tried to inhale enough of it to stem her impatience.

"He squeezed me, like I said," Millie offered. "Wants money. That's all he cares about. Said Aubrey owed him, and I'd damned well better pay up." She pulled out a smoke and lit up. Harper didn't stop her.

Millie took a long, slow drag and exhaled. "Stuart was always into drugs. Always launderin' money through them clubs. Always had his fingers in everything." She drew another drag, exhaling as she spoke. "I know he's givin' them horses dope." She shook her head. "And I'm pretty dang sure that character Henley is in on it. And Figarosa, too—I think he was the guy got the drugs from Stuart and gave 'em to Henley."

"Do you have proof of that?" Harper asked, trying to quell her excitement. Finally, something concrete.

Millie looked at her, squinting as the smoke curled up in front of her right eye. "Course not, you idiot. Think Stuart stayed outta jail all these years by being an imbecile?" She shook her head and tapped her ash to the side of the bench. "Naw, there's nothin'." Her eyes narrowed in anger. "And that good-for-nothin' . . . squeezin' me and I ask him for papers, proof, something he can show tellin' me Aubrey borrowed anything from his ass?" She shook her head again. "Nothing! He just sits there with his scotch and soda and smiles. Like I'm gonna pay him a damned cent when he can't give me one piece a paper to say it's legit?" Her hazel eyes flashed with anger. "Hell no, I told him. *Hell* no!"

"What about the drugs?" Harper asked. "What makes you think he's drugging the horses?" She corrected herself. "Or having Henley do it?"

Millie looked at her skeptically. "Have you met the man? How the hell do you run so many damned winners—and big winners—without cheatin'?" She huffed and ground out her smoke, pulling another one out and lighting it. Another long drag. "You don't. You cheat. They're like two damned devil peas in a pod."

Harper deflated. "So you don't have any proof?" Dead end. Another one.

The Panamanian groom brought the mare back to the barn and opened the end stall door. He glanced out the shedrow to where the two women were sitting, his dark eyes curious, as the mare walked in and began munching her hay. Harper smiled his way and gave him a thumbs up. He smiled back and headed into the storeroom.

Around them the day was warming, and a light breeze played through Harper's hair. She tugged on her Eden Hill ballcap and tucked up a few stray blond hairs. The breeze felt good, and the light twitter from the holly bush was a reminder that spring, and maybe renewal, was somehow well underway though the present state-of-affairs suggested otherwise.

"Millie, have you got anything? Anything at all we can actually use?"

The widow grimaced and seemed thoughtful. She stared straight ahead into the layup barn as the groom came out of the storage room with bandages and Betadine.

"I'm gonna tell you what happened." Millie turned to Harper, her body rigid with conviction. "Minetti's got his fingers in nearly every horse we own. He and Henley just want winners, just money. With Henley it's ego. Aubrey found out and by God, it got him killed." She turned away. "And no, I don't have the goods." She looked at Harper. "But I tell ya, Minetti's callin' the shots. Always has." She looked away and smoked, having nothing more to say.

"So you think Aubrey wasn't aware of what was going on?" Harper asked. How could he not be aware? She stared at Millie, wondering how much she could trust what the widow was saying was true.

Millie spoke. "You know, to be honest, I really can't say. Don't think so, but he got away from me the last couple a years . . ." She seemed to withdraw into herself then, into some sorrow Harper couldn't touch even if she wanted to. "But I bet that Figarosa character got himself into some deep doo-doo with Minetti, and that got him killed, too." She looked hard at Harper. "He's the worst person I ever met in my life." She took a good pull on her cigarette. "And believe me, I've met folks would chill you right down to the bone."

Harper felt deflated. It seemed every turn she made ended up at a dead end. There had to be something. But where she was going to find it completely eluded her.

"Why don't you get that hunk of a husband to pick up the scum bag and smoke him? He's good at that. Put the squeeze on that asshole Minetti like he's puttin' the squeeze on me." She raised an eyebrow at Harper.

Harper stood and stretched. She wasn't going to get anything she could use from Millie, that was clear. She held out her hand to the widow who flicked her cigarette into the grass. Harper scowled and ground it out, picked it up, then lifted Millie off the bench. "Can't do that, Millie, you know that. Without any shred of evidence, JD can't haul Minetti in on anything." Besides, she thought, the Feds wouldn't allow it anyway. She sighed and headed for the Range Rover. "We'll just have to keep looking."

Chapter 19

That evening, Harper reluctantly brought up the subject of giving up on Barn 41 to JD. She felt she'd taken advantage of Marshall and her husband for too long and though it pained her to consider letting Aubrey's murderer go free and Henley's abuse of horses go unpunished, she couldn't think of an alternative.

She and JD sat in their cozy family room surrounded by photos of much-loved racehorses and the early days of Eden Hill, including her beloved Grandpa and her Grandma Eden, both of whom had moved from Virginia three generations ago to start the stud. Harper glanced from photos of Marshall with coal black hair, to her sister Paris show jumping, to the family smiling from ear to ear in many winner's circles—everyone looked young and pleased with themselves. She and JD snuggled in, set for a night of watching a horse movie on cable. Mind numbing distraction was on the agenda for the evening. Harper settled under JD's arm and gathered a handful of buttered popcorn from the bowl on his lap.

As JD flipped through the available movie choices, Harper mumbled through a mouthful of popcorn. "I'm giving it one more week at the barn and then, well . . . that's it." She sounded as forlorn as she felt. "I'm calling it quits."

JD stopped scrolling through movies and looked down at his wife. He stared at her a few moments in silence. "That's not really what you want," he said softly, pulling her close and kissing her temple.

She leaned into him and sighed. “But you and Marshall have other responsibilities. And I haven’t made enough progress to keep asking this of you.”

JD drew back and tilted her face up to his.

“We’ve got this,” he said, “Really. Marshall and I are handling things. And I know how much Aubrey meant to you.”

Harper nodded. “It’s not just Aubrey, it’s what he’s built,” she said. “He has a legacy, one he was proud of. I get that.”

“Then stay. The only way to preserve that is to bring Aubrey’s killer to justice.”

Harper sat back against the cushions and touched her husband’s arm. “I know.” She thought a moment. “And I know you’re frustrated.” Harper had seen how hard it was for JD to tiptoe around an investigation that rightfully belonged to him. Working under the radar was definitely not his style.

“Yeah. Frustrated is an understatement,” he complained. Then, “But weirdly, the idea of you getting out of the line of fire—what I thought I wanted from the beginning—isn’t bringing me any happiness either.”

Harper nodded. She knew they both need to keep working this case if they hoped to get to the bottom of who killed Aubrey.

“Don’t leave the barn,” he said, finally. “Marshall and I can manage.”

Harper took a deep breath, feeling conflicted yet understanding JD was right. Still, she thought, there were practical concerns. Eden Hill and Hawk Ridge were two of the major farms in Lexington. After the death of their farm manager, Harper had taken over most of his duties and not replaced him. It was her job to see to both farms—not Marshall and JD’s.

She thought it over a few moments, deciding to forego the movie and talk specifics about how they'd manage if she did stay at Keeneland until the matter was settled. But in the next moment, JD's beeper went off. He unclipped it from his belt and frowned then sighed. "Jesus," he said. He turned to Harper. "The movie will have to wait. Needed at the station."

Harper nodded; it was not an unusual occurrence. She stretched and put her arms around his neck. They'd talk about it all later. "I love you," she said. "Go, I'll think about the barn." JD leaned closer and parted his lips for a kiss. Good Lord, she thought, aroused. He better go quickly. "Go on," she said, smiling.

After he left, Harper settled back into the soft couch, her hand on the place JD had left, still warm. She gathered the popcorn bowl from the table in front of her, and crunched a few kernels, scrolling through the movies. Might as well enjoy a night of doing nothing, not a pleasure she afforded herself often.

Halfway through a movie about a young, troubled girl foisted off on the father she never knew who, what a surprise, owned a horse ranch, her phone rang. Harper plucked it from her shirt pocket and glanced at the number.

Aliana.

She'd never called Harper, not since the day Harper had put her number in the Hispanic groom's phone, hoping the young woman would muster the courage to call her about Miguel Figarosa or the goings on at Henley's barn.

She answered it, her pulse quickening. "Aliana, what is it?"

Harper heard Aliana's muffled, urgent voice, "Come! Manuel—and the colt! You *must* come!" and she hung up.

Harper felt a flush of fear. What colt? Fleet Light? One of the others? Aviragus? Aliana had sounded terrified—either a colt or Manuel was in danger. Or both. She jumped up, not thinking further, and raced to the Range Rover.

The night was a darkening amethyst as she sped down Eden Hill's long drive lined with towering trees, passing under the wrought iron Eden Hill entry, and out onto the road. She put in a call to JD, which went to voicemail. She left a forceful message for him to get to Barn 41 immediately. She couldn't get Aliana's terrified voice out of her mind. Next was a call to JD's boss, Al Walker, but that, too, went to voicemail and she left the same message there. She threw the phone on the seat next to her, disgusted but determined. She'd handle whatever happened at the barn herself if it came to that. She'd handled her sister's killer; she could handle whatever the hell Minetti and Henley Smythe threw her way.

She peered impatiently through the purpling twilight, the trees a green blur beside her, the rising moon casting its faint, mysterious glow over the highway. She picked up her phone and put in a call to the police dispatcher, telling her she needed to get in touch with JD. She was told he and Walker had been dispatched to a domestic violence call turned bad and were out of range. "Then send a message to JD's beeper!" she yelled, frustrated beyond belief. She pocketed her phone and bore down on Keeneland, making her way to the barn's parking lot and throwing the SUV into park. She leapt out and saw Aliana at the barn entrance waiting for her. She heard Manuel's string of angry Spanish coming from the shedrow, loud even at this distance. The horses were agitated, calling anxiously to each other.

"What's happened? What are you doing here?" Harper said, grasping Aliana's shoulders and looking into her still-terrified brown eyes.

The young woman was shaking, her round face an anxious mask. "Manuel. He insists to come. No want to come alone!" she cried and looked toward the barn as the screams from Manuel continued. "Hurry!" Aliana whispered, and shoved Harper toward the barn.

She took off running and as she rounded into Barn 41's aisle, the few lights on cast an eerie glow on the scene. She saw the horses first, heads high, the whites of eyes showing, pushing on their closed half-doors. Some churned their bedding, some kicked the stall walls, and the ones close to Manuel let out a couple of high-pitched squeals.

Then she saw the bat.

She ran forward toward a man about her height, dressed in jeans and a blue work shirt, his back turned. In the low light, he faced Manuel who was still screaming something unintelligible at him, bending and grabbing for the bat. The man moved it out of the way, then let it comfortably rest on his right shoulder.

They were at Aviragus' stall and the huge colt's head was extended, ears pinned, teeth bared at the man. His jagged blaze looked like lightning. But the man with the bat was out of range.

He laughed at Manuel's attempts to disarm him. "Try that again, Spic," he said, "I'll bust your head wide open." Again Manuel lunged at him, but the man sidestepped and avoided contact. He held the bat out before him and gazed at it. "Let's see how she swings," he said, taking a few light strokes, preparing to use it on the trainer.

Just then, Manuel looked up and saw Harper fast approaching. The man turned his head and narrowed his eyes. He had dark brown hair cut short under a dirty ballcap, flat-blue tattoos crawling around his neck and up his face ending between his eyes in a snake head, a cruel, thin-lipped mouth, and weak chin. He smiled at Harper as if she was of no account and turned back to Manuel, taking a practice swing, and then pulling the bat back and whipping it at Manuel, cracking him in the ribs.

The assistant trainer's eyes went wide for a second, then he doubled over, screaming, and collapsed in a heap at the attacker's feet, just outside the colt's stall. The man looked at Aviragus, then back at Harper who was bearing down on him. He turned to her, planting his feet wide and drew the bat back for a second blow.

Gasping and in pain, Manuel grabbed the man's right leg, startling him just as Harper leapt, leveling a sharp, hard jab to his jaw, and crashing into his thin chest. He staggered to regain his balance, his small eyes filled with hatred now, not humor. He turned, raised the bat, and brought it down hard over Manuel's back. The trainer collapsed, pooled in moonlight, air rushing from his lungs in a cry of anguish more animal than human. He rolled on his side, peering up at his attacker, his eyes going in and out of focus.

As the man grinned down at Manuel, Harper jumped on his back, trying for a choke hold, but the man was strong. He kicked Manuel in the stomach and grabbed Harper's arm at his throat, simultaneously whirling around to dislodge her and raising the bat with his right arm. Manuel was gasping as the pain seared through him, hardly able to breathe through damaged ribs. He writhed on the ground.

Harper heard the man's grunt as she hung on and he continued to thrash about to get her off his back. "Go to hell, bitch!" he screamed. An odor of foul sweat rose from him, making Harper turn her head as she hung on more tenaciously.

Harper felt like she was riding a bronco but stayed on him, glancing to her right and seeing the colt's menace growing. He reared in his stall as around them all, other horses stomped and kicked, picking up the atmosphere of fear and fury. Their own fear increased, and Harper knew they could easily harm themselves if she couldn't get the man with the bat under control soon.

In the distance, she heard a faint siren just as the man threw her into the concrete wall beside the colt's stall. Aviragus lunged at the man, his eyes wild, but the man only had eyes for Harper.

He held the bat in both hands, the snakehead between his eyes staring at Harper, then lifting the weapon, swung it back for a blow as he leaned in and extended his left arm, pointing a finger at Harper's head and leering. Aviragus lunged further out of his stall, his blaze alight, teeth parted in fury and in the next second, he attacked.

Harper had flattened herself as best she could against the upper Dutch door, and saw the colt go for the man's face. Her attacker screamed, dropped the bat, his hands flying to his nose, blood gushing from between his fingers. He looked at Harper, his eyes horrified, disbelief registered before pain.

Harper snagged the bat just as JD rounded into barn, gun drawn, and yelled at her. "Get back!" he commanded, rushing forward, Aliana right behind him. "Get a towel," he said to Aliana seeing the blood. He holstered his weapon, whipped out his handcuffs, and leaned over the man who had sunk to his knees. Blood streamed down his face, soaking his blue work shirt, his hands not moving from his nose. "Bit my damned nose off!" he screamed, a wild eye turning to JD, then to Aviragus whose mouth was stained with blood, ears still pinned.

JD glanced at Harper who gave him a shaky thumbs up, and dialed 911, bending to Manuel whose dark face was contorted in pain. Aliana rushed up, handed a towel to JD and kneeled beside the trainer who gazed up at her, alternately closing his eyes and then staring into Aliana's. He labored to breathe, holding his left side, his face twisted in pain, moonlight wavering over the two of them. Aliana took his other elbow and tried to help him to his feet, but any movement caused the searing pain to increase. He shook his head and gasped.

With JD's arrival, the scene quickly came under control, Aliana attending to Manuel, and JD towering over the bloody tattooed man who had sunk to his knees. The horses slowly calmed, some still circled their stalls, but the squeals had diminished, replaced by snorts. A few stuck their heads out of their half-stalls and swung their heads toward the commotion, which had now all but ceased.

JD hooked the handcuffs on his belt and removed the man's hands to inspect the wound. Aviragus had, indeed, ravaged his nose. It hung by a bit of skin, the rest a gaping, bloody hole, the cartilage appearing white as a Safeway chicken. He closed the wound, resetting the nose and placed the towel over it, glancing up at Harper.

"Ambulance?"

"On their way," Harper replied—she'd requested two. She stood and leaned on the bat, trying to regain her composure. JD told the man to hold the towel and rose, keeping an eye on him. The man nodded and held the towel against his face, squeezing his eyes shut.

Once the ambulances arrived, they quickly loaded the unknown assailant and Manuel separately and sped off into the now-dark night. JD pocketed the man's wallet and grasped Harper in a fierce embrace. "I'm sorry I was late," he murmured. "I'm so damned sorry—if anything had happened to you . . . "

Harper clung to him, her breath still coming fast. She relaxed and after a few moments pulled away. "Your timing was perfect," she said to reassure him she was okay.

JD glanced in the general direction of the parking lot, fingering the pocket with the assailant's wallet.

"Go on," Harper said. "Run the perp down." She knew he wanted to get to the station to find out all he could about the man who'd attacked them, obviously intent on hurting—possibly killing—Aviragus.

JD nodded and fairly ran to his unit, anxious to follow up on the information as soon as possible. He sped off into the inky night.

Harper and Aliana got to work settling the horses, making sure none were hurt, saving the big bay colt for last.

Aviragus had calmed and was getting a drink when Harper came to clean him up. A faint hint of red tinged his bucket and when he swung his head around, she saw all the blood had washed away. She stepped into his stall, and the big bay shifted his weight, turning to face her, his large dark eyes gazing steadily at her. He nodded his head and she moved to his neck, patting it lightly and checking him over to make sure he, too, hadn't hurt himself in the commotion. Satisfied that he was fine, and thankful that the horses had escaped harm, she cleaned and refilled the colt's water bucket, sent Aliana on her way, and headed home. They'd see tomorrow if the horses had registered any damage that hadn't yet showed up, emotional or otherwise. She sighed. The grooms and exercise riders would work anything emotional, and the vet would handle the rest, if it showed. They'd be fine.

Harper corrected herself. They'd better be fine.

Chapter 20

Over the next few days, Harper tried to make herself indispensable to Manuel. Henley had planned to rush home when he got the news about the attack, but since the horses were fine and Manuel was taped up with bruised ribs and only one broken, Henley decided to continue making rounds of the additional U.S. Lowen training locations since he'd skipped the first scheduled trip altogether. Harper breathed a sigh of relief. She had some time to work on Manuel. She already had Aliana's trust, now she needed to somehow gain the assistant trainer's trust, as well.

The man with the damaged nose was Raybone aka "Sonny Boy" Seddon. He was a local thug with a long sheet and a bad rep at the low-end bars. The docs had done a cartilage graft, using his rib, and sewn his nose back in place, though he'd have serious scars and a puffed-up racoon face for quite a while.

Millie had received the news of his identification with one comment. "Let me know when your hunk of a husband hauls in that Sonny Boy SOB, and we'll talk," she said and hung up.

JD questioned Seddon in the hospital but got very little. And the Feds were giving the detective a hard time. Though JD understood federal investigations sometimes took several years to complete, the agents' insistence on control, on hampering his every move, left him cold. Their obvious disdain for local law enforcement also rubbed him raw. He'd done his work under the radar but doing things that way in what should have been his investigation was sitting less and less well. Even though he was a man used to the chain of command, he had a difficult time playing by their rules.

Mostly, he made his own rules.

He'd made his peace with that. He and Harper would continue to work the case together. He'd protect her. They didn't need to discuss it. He knew she understood why he was giving her room to move in Henley and Minetti's circle. They shared information and would continue until one or the other of them broke the case and brought Aubrey's killer to justice. The dark goings on at Barn 41 was central to that, and JD trusted that once things cracked, all the bad guys would be exposed. JD hoped they wouldn't see it coming. He'd enjoy taking Minetti and Henley Smythe by surprise. Especially Minetti. He'd seen his type many times before—the smooth, smug, behind-the-scenes guy who thought he couldn't be touched.

Well, JD thought, that was about to change.

He delayed an official interrogation of Seddon until he'd negotiated with the federal agents, looked more deeply into Sonny Boy's background, and the perp got out of the hospital, moving straight into custody.

The Feds continued putting up a fight, but essentially they had nothing, so they eventually agreed to let JD take the lead as long as they were in on the action. They'd be a party to any and all questioning but insisted Seddon not be informed of their presence. Since they were taking a back seat, they would make the most of it, stressing to JD that they did not want Minetti—if he was, in fact, fingered by Sonny Boy—to know they were onto him. But they wouldn't give JD total control, either.

JD remained steady and focused on the possibility of finally having a witness who could identify Minetti and provide just the damning evidence needed to take him into custody. Provided they could prove he'd hired Seddon and provided they could prove he wanted Aviragus dead. The only reason for a bat in the circumstances Seddon was arrested in was to break the colt's leg, make it look like a stall accident resulting in euthanization, and collect the insurance money. Horses did legitimately have such injuries, and Seddon probably had not anticipated Manuel's presence. Getting him to flip on Minetti on an insurance fraud charge would be nice start to what hopefully would amount to other charges, depending on what he could crack open—drugs, money laundering . . . murder.

JD didn't fool himself. They were a very long way from the goal line, but the game had turned to their advantage. At least JD hoped that was the case.

The agents and JD set up the interrogation room and agreed the detective would be the one speaking to Sonny Boy. The two federal agents, dark suits and all, would watch from behind the two-way mirror.

The room was a dull green like the rest of the station, with a metal table complete with handcuff rail, one shaded light set in the ceiling, and two metal chairs. The room was clean and empty so there would be no distractions. The interview would be recorded.

Sonny Boy entered with one guard, his hands cuffed in front of him, dressed in the ubiquitous jumpsuit, his face swollen and bandaged. JD had told the guard to uncuff Seddon and leave, so in a moment, Sonny Boy sat at the table alone, rubbing his neck and the dull blue, undulating tattoos wrapped around it. Above the bandage, one eye was swollen shut and his entire appearance screamed pain. On the right side of his neck, the one facing the two-way mirror, a snake rose from its coils and wound its way up his hairline, curling above his eye and ending between his eyebrows. His countenance breathed malevolence, nonchalance, and a strange sort of comfortable familiarity with the surroundings. His weren't particularly well-done tattoos, JD noted, standing in the dark room with the two Federal agents.

The two men had little to say to him, which was fine with JD. They were frustrated with their lack of progress and not too interested in the local law enforcement's ability to make headway where they hadn't.

One of them was a fit, dark-skinned man and the other was shorter with a pug nose and a body like a square block. They'd all spoken before the interview had been arranged and had agreed with JD that watching the perp a while before the questioning began might be an okay idea.

Sonny Boy, though, was giving them nothing. Seated, his white bandages prominent, both his eyes dark purple and sickening yellow, he hummed a bit, glanced at the two-way mirror from time to time and once, giving a salute. His one open eye seemed alight with amusement. He appeared at complete ease and in no hurry, as if he'd been through the drill enough to make it almost a part of his life routine.

JD entered the room, carrying a file folder and seated himself across from Seddon. They stared in silence at each other for a few moments, then JD folded his hands on the file folder, tempted to wince at Seddon's appearance, and began.

"So you want to tell me what you were doing at the barn, at night, at a prized colt's stall, with a baseball bat?"

Sonny Boy wiggled a bit in his seat, raising himself more upright. He was shorter than JD, but had a taut, lean body beneath the jumpsuit. "Sure I do," he said, his eye staring at JD frankly. "Got a call from a buddy, says I can make some quick, good cash, if I go take a look at this colt over at Keeneland that's up for sale. Take a look and tell him what I think." He sat back, his hands wide, his mouth a thin line. "Was he worth the big bucks or not? That's it." He smiled and tried to lean forward a bit in mock earnestness but stopped short. His head must be pounding. "You see I'm a student of horse flesh. I got the eye." He touched his eyebrow, drawing attention to the snake. "Can spot a winner a mile away." Seddon attempted a smile, and again sat back in the chair. "So my particular talent is often requested."

JD listened in silence, his face dispassionate. Seddon's "particular talent" ran to most things illegal from the background JD had looked into.

"You're saying you were asked to evaluate a colt who everyone knows has won major races all over Europe and whose value is no secret to anyone."

Seddon nodded. The snake undulated. The one eye stared.

"A colt who is not for sale."

Seddon spoke. "Not what I was told. Got paid good, too."

"So there you were on Keeneland's backstretch to evaluate a world-class colt who is not for sale. With a bat."

JD had considered the bat, thinking Seddon might be behind Aubrey's death, too. The blows Aubrey had sustained were consistent with such a weapon. Figarosa's torture pointed to someone more sophisticated in extracting information than Sonny Boy, but JD couldn't rule him out altogether for both murders.

But who had hired him?

"Well sure I took my bat. I wuz there at night, who knows who I might encounter?" He smirked. "Gotta protect myself." He turned to the two-way mirror. "Right? We all got that right, ain't we?"

Sonny Boy's wallet had contained a racing license, so he was not doing anything illegal by being on the backstretch. How he got a license was a totally different question, an avenue JD was not going down. Bigger fish to fry.

"An as it turns out," Sonny Boy declared, "I was damned right to bring my bat. That Spic attacked me . . ." He held up his hand, pointing to his face. "And have you seen my God-damned nose?" He nodded vehemently. "Yeah, I got a right to sue, ask me." He sat back and crossed his arms. "Damned colt. Somebody oughtta break his legs," he said with a slight grin.

"So who was this guy who gave you the job?"

Seddon let his finger play over the tattoos on his neck, taking his time to answer, thinking. "Funny thing is, he's outta the country, Canada I think." He grinned. "Up there in the Boundary Waters fishin', last I heard." He turned serious. "They got no service up there where he's at, so I cain't put you two in touch. Sure am sorry about that."

"His name? We can have the authorities go in after him."

Seddon shook his head. "Naw, I ain't givin' you that. You can roast me all you want, but I ain't one a them types." He was quiet a moment, then he seemed to have a bright idea. "But I'll tell ya whut. Minute he come outta them woods, I'll have him give you a call."

JD hadn't moved an inch the entire interrogation. He'd stilled himself deep inside, listening with a sixth sense he had for the entrance that would split the perp wide open. But Sonny Boy seemed very well schooled in evasion and JD hadn't found that opening yet.

"Who did your friend say was interested in buying the colt?"

Seddon drew his brows together as if in deep thought. He pursed his lips, his one eye squinted as he seemed struggling to remember. "I think it wuz Risotto," he said and thought some more. "Yeah, that was it. Risotto," he said with conviction.

JD waited.

Seddon then shook his head. "Naw, that cain't be right." He looked up at JD, feigning embarrassment. "Risotto, that would be rice, right?" He smirked again.

"Minetti? Stuart Minetti?" JD said, running a hand through his thick hair. If Seddon thought he'd wear down JD, he was wrong.

Sonny Boy seemed confused. "Who?" He leaned forward, hunched a bit, and winced. "Never heard of the guy." He gazed around. "Can I get a drink or somethin'? Answerin' all these questions has got me a bit parched."

JD's phone went off, signaling a text. *In here, now* it read, so JD rose and entered the dark room with the two federal agents.

"Cut him loose," ordered the dark-skinned man.

"You've got to be kidding," JD said. "He had a bat, he was at the colt's stall. What the hell do you think he was going to do?"

The dark man said, "He never laid a hand—or the bat—on the colt. And by the trainer's own admission, he made a move on Seddon."

Pug nose spoke up. "And then, of course, your wife jumped on his back."

The two agents exchanged a look.

"You can't be serious," JD said. "I've got him. Just give me a little more time."

"You've got nothing," the dark-skinned agent said. "You know it, we know it . . ." he thumbed toward the interrogation room. "And for sure Seddon knows it." He shook his head as if JD had just confirmed the local police force's incompetence. "Cut the guy loose. If you keep pressing this, Minetti's going to find out and we cannot have him alerted to our interest in any way."

"Do it now," the taller agent ordered.

So JD did, not showing the agents how much it pained him, how much it went against his nature, not wanting to give them an ounce of satisfaction. He told Sonny Boy not to leave town. Seddon, nodded and saluted him, saying, "Yes, sir, *detective,*" then sauntered out the doors, inhaled raggedly, and walked to the bus station smiling.

Harper went about her chores at the barn the next morning, sticking close to Manuel. She wanted to help, yes, but she also wondered why he'd gone to the barn the night of the attack and why he hadn't wanted to go alone. She hoped he would finally be able to talk openly to her after the events and the role she and JD had played. She kept her mouth shut as the workouts and care for the horses got underway and stuck by Manuel, trying to be of use and not spook him.

The horses went to their workouts, returned, were bathed and hot-walked, groomed and grazed, then awaited their mid-day feeding. Harper helped the assistant trainer give instructions to the riders and asked each rider how the horse felt post workout, taking notes for him on his yellow pad. The colts and fillies seemed none the worse for wear after the ordeal, perhaps because Seddon's malevolent energy was absent. Once all the horses were finished, the times noted, the leg wraps in place, hay distributed, water replenished, horses groomed, and set out for a little grazing, there was time to talk.

"Mind if I hit the track kitchen with you?" Harper said as Manuel closed the computer after sending Henley a report, intending to head over for lunch. He nodded. The trainer had seemed to relax in her presence as the morning unfolded, so Harper felt the time was right to see if he felt comfortable enough to be honest with her.

At the one-story track kitchen, they stood in line for food with other backstretch workers, awaiting their turn to order. Trainers, riders, guests, and a few owners and vets laughed and talked as the line inched forward. Most everyone had on t-shirts and jeans, and a large number of logoed ballcaps graced heads. Manuel ordered from the smiling woman clad in a black apron and a Keeneland ballcap pushed back on her head. She got to work on Manuel's ham and cheese sandwich, his "usual" she said, while Harper ordered the BLT. They picked up Cokes and chips then headed to the Formica table by the windows looking out on the parking lot. The track kitchen was nothing fancy, just a work-a-day setting for those who spent their days around racing. Most of the lunch crowd knew each other so it was filled with easy banter.

Men and a smattering of women sat and talked, elbows on the tables, stuffing their faces. A murmur of Spanish and English filled the room as Harper and Manuel walked to their four-top and sat on the green cushioned metal chairs.

She opened her bag of chips as Manuel studied his sandwich and took a bite, his liquid brown eyes softening with pleasure.

"Thank you," he said and took a gulp of Coke. "The work, it good today." He smiled at Harper, relaxed for the first time since the attack. Unlike Aliana, his face was well-defined, with a slight cleft in his chin, a square jaw and large brown eyes. He seemed a pleasant, straightforward guy who, Harper had seen, had a hard time concealing his emotions.

Never one to engage in small talk, which irritated Harper no end, she broached what had happened at Aviragus' stall.

"I'm glad I can help," she said, munching a crunchy piece of bacon, "and I'm really glad Aliana called me the other night."

Manuel nodded, popping a fruit cup sliced peach in his mouth. "Sí, sí, and the husband, the policeman." He shook his head, suddenly serious, as if he was thinking about what might have occurred had they not shown up.

"Why did you come that night? You're not on night check." Henley's barn didn't have a groom living on site as did some trainers, so each night, someone had to come back to check on the horses. At Barn 41, that task was assigned to a groom, not Manuel.

The trainer from two barns over passed with his brown tray loaded with the daily special and mentioned how well Manuel's horses looked in their morning workout. Manuel smiled and accepted the compliment, and the young man went on to join his table. The clatter of plates being cleared and trays stacked mixed with a few hearty laughs.

When the assistant trainer turned back to Harper, he was again serious. "I come every night," he said softly. He paused and put down his sandwich. "Since El Karta, I come."

Harper felt the sadness emanating from him. Her own sorrow welled up, and she nodded.

Manuel continued so Harper remained silent. "I bring Aliana, she help."

"She said you were frightened to come alone."

"Sí, the bad things. . ." Manuel didn't elaborate. Then, "I am also doing things . . .," he said, "the bad things." He stopped, looked out the window, his expression crestfallen.

"To El Karta," Harper said and he nodded. She reached her hand across the table, fighting her own devastation over the colt's death. "Manuel, I know people say 'the past is the past' and it's best to put it behind you." She paused until the young trainer looked at her. "What you did was wrong, we both know that. And if you've drugged horses, it's also illegal. You have a right to your shame and your sadness. But you can't change what you've done," she said gently. "What matters is what you do now."

He nodded, but she sensed he was not convinced this was true.

"Did you drug the horses?" she asked, and Manuel again bobbed his head, not meeting her eyes.

"Who tells you to drug them?" she said, pressing him, watching emotions flicker over his face in a sad reverie—a flurry of confusion, fear, and sadness. He pulled his hand away from hers, grabbed the napkin from beside his plate, and glanced around the dining room, his eyes dropping to the green painted floor.

"No," he whispered. "I cannot. No, they say hurt for my mother." He looked into Harper's eyes, pleading. "She live with me. She old."

"Is someone threatening you, Manuel?" Harper leaned over the table a bit, keeping her voice low.

Mutely, Manuel nodded, looking at his plate.

The trainer's response did not surprise Harper. He didn't appear the type of guy to comply with illegal drugging without coercion. Was it Henley? Minetti? Both of them?

"Stuart Minetti?" she asked. "He is not a good man, Manuel, I know that."

The young man brushed his hands on his thighs, agitated. "No. Henley, too. They bad men. They use the drugs and make the babies run." Manuel looked devastated. "The others, the same."

"Manuel, will you speak with my husband? We can protect you."

He vigorously shook his head no, not waiting for her to finish.

"We can't let them hurt any more horses, Manuel. Please."

Manuel would not discuss it further. He put his napkin on the plate, gulped the last of his Coke, and stood, clutching his tray. "We go. See to the babies."

Harper stayed seated, staring at him. "At least tell me where the drugs are. I'll keep you out of it."

He sat down heavily, his tray clattering on the table. "*No sé*. Miguel, he had." He shook his head, batted a hand at her. "I no talk more. The babies they be okay. No more El Karta. No more," he said, his eyes brimming. He stood again and walked his tray to the end of the counter where his aproned friend took it, and all the while he stared at the floor.

Even in grief, Harper thought watching his slumped form, Manuel was a kind, sweet soul.

Chapter 21

She could ask JD to bring Manuel in for questioning. She turned that thought over in her mind on the way home. He'd divulged information that JD could use. But the idea of sweating the trainer, fearful already of the threats to his mother, seemed to hold little hope of gaining any real information. She'd have to think about of how to protect Manuel's mother and then perhaps get his cooperation. It was a delicate business, especially with the Feds involved.

She called JD and shared what Manuel had said to her, and he agreed they'd have to find a way to protect the mother without the Feds getting wind of it or find another way to nail Henley and Minetti on drugging the horses and who knows what else. Hauling Manuel into the station in his terrorized state would not prove useful.

The threats to Manuel's mother sounded more like Minetti than Henley, but she relished nailing them both.

That evening, JD insisted they head to the Florence Cafe, an upscale restaurant they'd frequented in their youth. They both needed a break and their old hangout seemed just the place. They could talk about plans for Manuel's mother over dinner.

Back then as now, like the track kitchen, the Florence Café had been a place where local horse people gathered. But unlike its early days, the restaurant was now as stylish as any in Lexington. JD had made reservations for seven o'clock and right on time they walked through the etched glass doors, JD in his charcoal jacket and gray pants and Harper in her jeans, heels, and a mocha silk shirt. As they were escorted to their table, they passed Minetti and Sophia in a raised booth. Harper registered surprise as Minetti beckoned them over amid the low murmur of dinner patrons and soft background music.

So, she'd been right at Keeneland that day. Minetti and Sophia did know each other, and by the look of things, they knew one another well. Minetti smiled, the cordial host. He was dressed in a brilliant white shirt and expensively cut navy jacket. "Join us, please," Minetti said, flicking his index finger at Sophia to move to the left to make room for the couple. "Please, I insist," he said, looking at the maître'd and asking for the wine list. "We've just arrived and had our drinks." He lifted his empty rocks glass, his gold cufflinks glimmering in the low light.

Sophia looked as if she wanted to crawl in a hole. Her black hair was swept up in a French twist which she patted and fiddled with. "Yes, please," she said finally, if reluctantly.

JD glanced at Harper and made a decision. "Thanks, sure," he said, extending his hand. "Don't think we've formally met."

Minetti's brown eyes sparkled with delight. "Detective," he said, nodding. He glanced at Harper. "Good to finally have a chance to catch up. We've missed you in New York."

Harper tried to smile, though her back teeth ground a bit. She looked at Sophia, who was now smoothing her floral skirt. Seemed the woman had a closet full of flowers. Her gray eyes appeared worried.

"So you two know each other," Harper said, allowing JD to slide in first. The last place she wanted to be was next to Minetti. Or Sophia, for that matter.

"Oh yes, we're good friends," Minetti said.

"From the City," Sophia chimed in, regaining her elegant composure.

The waiter came and Minetti ordered an appetizer and a bottle of white wine. He didn't consult anyone on the choices.

He turned to JD, as the waiter lit the table's candles, adjusted everyone's place settings, and headed to the kitchen. "I hear you think I have something to do with that attack at the barn the other night." His eyes were piercing, his posture relaxed. He put elbows on the table, tenting his fingers and didn't take his eyes off JD. A slight, self-satisfied smile played over his lips.

JD did not take the bait. His face showed nothing, his green eyes sharp and direct. Under the table he laid a light hand on Harper's thigh which she interpreted as a signal to not show any reaction.

"Did you?" JD said quietly, just above the muted clatter of plates and dinner table talk.

Harper looked at her husband and then turned her gaze to Minetti, interested in how he'd handle someone as used to wielding power as he was. For her part, Sophia seemed more interested in her water glass.

Minetti's slight smile widened. A match worth contending with, he seemed to be thinking. He turned to Sophia, taking her hand, then turned back to JD. His silver hair gleamed in the soft light. "I assure you," he said, "I was otherwise engaged." He kissed Sophia's hand and gazed up into her eyes, his profile sharply cut. "Quite engaged," he murmured as Sophia looked mortified and withdrew her hand.

Minetti turned to the couple. "It would be unlike me to be involved in such nefarious business." He paused for effect.

"Such notions are a distraction to you finding the actual culprit."

Harper blurted out, "We'll see about that," and instantly regretted it. She felt JD pat her thigh and turned to see his calm, cool eyes.

"What makes you think you were a suspect?" JD said.

Minetti responded, his hand gesturing to the busy, gaily clad dining room. "There are no secrets in Lexington," he noted, his gaze returning to JD. "Being raised here, I would have thought you aware of that."

The appetizer arrived. The waiter efficiently distributed plates and small forks to extract the escargot. He turned to his assistant for the wine, opened it and poured a sip for Minetti who sniffed, swirled, tasted, and nodded. The waiter then poured for them all and left.

Minetti turned graciously to Harper, lifting his glass in a mock toast. "You may inquire all you wish," he said, clicking her glass which sat untouched on the white tablecloth. "But you will find nothing." His tone was assured, again self-satisfied. "This is because there is, in fact, nothing to find." He smiled, then turned to JD, his countenance darkening. "I suggest you look a little closer to home for the true culprit," he said.

Harper looked at JD, but her husband had kept his gaze on Minetti. "Elaborate, please."

"Shall we order the entrées?" asked Minetti, again the gracious host.

"Would you care to have a chat at the station?" JD said flatly.

Minetti chuckled. "Oh, yes," he said glibly. "In the room with your famed two-way mirror? I wonder who lurks behind it. No, I think not." He beckoned the waiter with a raised finger.

The young man came over, hands clasped behind him and waited for instructions.

Harper rose and looked at JD. "I'm not feeling so well," she said, turning to Minetti, "suddenly." She nodded at Sophia and raised an eyebrow at JD who got the message and rose, too.

"So sorry," Sophia said, extending her rock-laden hand, finding her voice. "I hope you're not coming down with something." Her lovely, plucked brows furrowed softly, the picture of concern.

Harper exited the booth followed by JD and glared at Minetti. "I'm coming down with something all right," she said with conviction. "And nailing you is precisely the remedy I need."

Minetti laughed as JD tipped his head to him. "We'll see each other again. Hopefully quite soon," the detective said and escorted his fuming wife to the exit.

Harper glanced back at the couple as they neared the doors. Minetti and Sophia had their heads together and both were smiling.

"Dead end after dead end after dead end," Harper complained as they sped through the darkness broken by a waxing moon and a canopy of stars. Her stomach growled. "I need to eat something," she finished, glancing at JD's profile. His high cheekbones stood out in the glimmering light, his full lips pursed in thoughtfulness.

"We're getting there," he said, reaching over and touching her cheek, putting together the little they'd learned in the last few days. "Manuel is threatened. And he admitted they're using drugs on the horses . . . we'll crack that open. Minetti is aware I'm looking at him for the barn attack." He glanced at Harper. "My money is on him also knowing the Feds are involved. That comment about the two-way mirror was pointed." He turned back to the road. "And let's not forget Sonny Boy. Clearly, he spoke to Minetti."

They rode on in silence, thinking about the threads they'd both been pulling. At present they seemed disparate, disconnected. Harper sighed. After a short time, JD put his blinker on and turned into Eden Hill's long drive, the oaks looming over them like dark sentinels. "The bat, too," he said. "Somebody's obviously after the insurance on Aviragus. And Minetti holds a very large interest in the colt."

Harper nodded. "Exactly. No other reason for Seddon to be at the colt's stall that late with a weapon. He likely didn't expect Manuel."

JD smiled and turned to Harper. "Or you."

Harper was thoughtful, picking at a hangnail as they drove up the long curving drive. The progress was not fast enough for her. Sure, they'd gathered bits and pieces, as JD had said. But nothing was hanging together. There was no central focus for all the separate parts. She glanced at her husband. They were both relentless, they made a good team, she thought. And it was great that JD had finally given up pressing her to leave the investigation. They always worked better together and all hands on deck were needed if they hoped to solve Aubrey's murder, save Lowen Farms, bring down Minetti and, she fervently hoped, Henley Smythe. JD had been just as great as Marshall at picking up the slack she continued to leave at Eden Hill. He'd been right. As hard as it was to burden them, she had to see it through at Barn 41. After the attack, she'd vowed to stay on until she found Aubrey's killer and cleaned up the operation for Millie. But all she was running into was frustration.

"What do you think Minetti meant by looking 'closer to home?'" she asked her husband. The comment rankled her. Was Minetti trying to deflect attention from himself? He was clever, that would be right in his wheelhouse. And what about him and Sophia, and the tête-à-tête she'd just witnessed? And Manuel lumping Henley in with Minetti—two "bad" men? She turned to JD as they neared the circle in front of the house.

"Let's say he was telling the truth," she said as JD put the Range Rover in park and turned off the engine. "Just for the sake of argument. Who could he be talking about?"

Around the house came Kelso, barreling toward the SUV and parking his hind end on the gravel, wagging his tail.

Harper opened the door and they both exited. The moon's eerie silver light cast shadows as they mounted the steps to the porch and JD stuck the key in the lock. He shook his head as they entered, Kelso barging in after them.

"I have no idea."

"The only one around other than us is Millie, and the last thing in the world she'd want to do is hurt Aubrey."

JD nodded and bent to ruffle Kelso's big head as Harper turned off the porch light. They stood in darkness amid the flickering star and moonlight filtering through windows. Kelso looked up at JD in the dim light and thumped his tail.

They made their way to the kitchen for food, as much in the dark about who was behind it all as the night swirling around them.

Chapter 22

Minetti's "close to home" comment still nagged Harper the next morning. In fact, the comment troubled her so much, she found herself pacing the bedroom hardwood, whipping up the plantation blinds and staring out over the pond sparkling in sunlight broken by koi swirling the surface now and then. She sipped her coffee and fumed, alone at the window, JD having left some time ago. She should be at the barn, she chided, not moving from the spot. She should be getting something—anything—done that might wipe that God-awful smug expression from Stuart Minetti's face.

Instead, she had called Lowen Farms and made arrangements to again meet Millie, the only "closer to home" person she could think of. She planned to grill her till she was done to see whether or not the widow was involved. Minetti, damn him, he better not have gotten her goat and led her down another blind alley, she thought, as she pulled on her jeans and a cotton shirt.

Henley had flown in late the night before, so he'd be at workouts and she probably wouldn't be able to speak privately to Manuel anyway. Still, she felt conflicted, hoping Minetti wasn't leading her around by the nose as he'd done with so many people over so many years.

She agreed to meet Millie at Lowen's yearling exercise center, where Harold said she'd be when Harper had phoned to set up the appointment. Giving Millie the benefit of doubt for the moment, Harper was glad the widow seemed to be taking an increasing interest in the farm's business. With a barnful of client yearlings prepping for the upcoming Keeneland sale, it was important to make sure the training went well.

She pulled up and parked, looking over the late May plantings in bloom by the royal blue and white barn housing the yearlings. Along the walkway, soft pink peonies were in full flower ringed by low lime-green sweet potato vine, and surrounding it all was a carpet of thick, lush greening grass mowed in stripes. A statue of Minted Prospect stood to the right of the barn, across the walkway from the pastel garden. The coloring in the bright day was positively cheerful.

Harper parked and headed around the barn to the exercise facility. Aubrey had installed a circular, automated performance trainer a few years back, and it proved a good investment for conditioning and rehab. The yearlings each had their own section with interior, dividing flaps, and when the system was running, the yearling manager could control the speed so the youngsters could build muscle and get some cardio in, six at a time.

As she rounded the barn, she saw the wash stall with grooms spraying down the horses who'd just completed their exercise. Sunlight glittered off the misting spray as three deep bays, and a wet copper chestnut raised their heads, their manes and tails soaked, their bodies glistening. Harper stood for a moment admiring the beauty of the animals she, Marshall, and so many others, devoted their lives to.

After a moment, she turned and headed to the yearling manager conversing with Millie, who stood like a large tent, her arm around her substantial heft holding up her left elbow, which rhythmically brought her cigarette to her lips. She didn't bother to turn her head on the exhale to avoid the manager and Harper noted the young woman took a step back as Millie spoke.

"Well, it's about damned time, honey," she said, as Harper approached, the smoke drifting in her direction. She poked her cigarette at the manager. "Meet Shelley. Aubrey hired her when he got that hair-brained notion to take in all these damned yearlings to prep." She waved her cigarette in a wide arc, including the ones getting bathed, the ones being loaded into the exerciser, and the barn. She threw the cigarette down, scowled, and ground it out. "Damned fool idea," she mumbled, then looked up at Shelley and smiled. "Sorry, kiddo, no insult meant. The horses look just like they oughtta."

Harper glanced at the two Thoroughbreds tied to the still machine waiting to be loaded. They looked fit, already nearly 16 hands, alert and curious. Millie was right. Shelley was doing a good job.

The yearling manager tugged on her ballcap and tried not to look miffed. She was tall and rail thin with scraggly brown hair pulled into a very short ponytail sticking out the back end of the Lowen ballcap. She was definitely not going for the glamourous horse trainer look. She nodded Harper's way.

"Measuring and weighing the others," she said in a pronounced Australian accent, "best be off." She nodded again then trotted off toward the barn, leaving Millie and Harper standing before the machine as the final two horses were loaded in.

Millie pulled out another smoke and lit up. Harper was surprised the woman could breathe with her continual chain smoking. She reached over and rubbed Millie's back a brief moment, trying to make a connection so they could have a frank talk.

"And why the hell aren't you over at Keeneland figurin' out what the hell went on out there with Aviragus?" Millie said, squinting an eye at Harper. She blew out a stream and made circles with the smoke.

So much for the connection idea.

The horses started off at the walk, the sun gleaming off their shiny coats, their heads bobbing gently as the machine began to circle them. Shelley's assistant stood at the exerciser door keeping a watchful eye on the young ones.

"You'll never guess who JD and I ran into at the Florence Café last night," Harper began, sticking her hands in her back pockets.

Millie turned to her, lifting an eyebrow.

"Stuart Minetti," Harper said. Millie huffed and looked back at the horses.

"With Sophia Creighton." She side-eyed Millie.

"Well, I'll be damned," Millie said, very surprised. She ashed her smoke on the grass and considered the horses. "Well, I'll be God-damned," she said again, shaking her head.

"They invited us to join them."

Millie didn't respond.

"And Minetti said something really interesting." Before he pissed me off and we had to leave, Harper didn't add.

"Oh, yeah?" Millie said, still not looking at Harper. "Like what? Like he set up that little episode at the barn the other night? Killin' my colt for the insurance?" She snorted. "A damned baseball bat." She looked at Harper, her eyes severe. "What is he, a Neanderthal?"

"He pleaded innocent."

Millie snorted again.

"Said we should look 'closer to home' for the real culprit."

Harper watched Millie closely. The widow turned her eyes skyward and took a deep breath, inflating her tent dress. She shrugged her shoulders then curved a finger of orange hair around her ear, a gesture she seemed fond of.

"What the hell did he mean by that?" she said, staring at the exerciser as the yearlings moved into the trot. Then venom crept into her voice, startling Harper. "Was the asshole pointing a finger at me?" She kept her eyes averted.

The grooms walked past the women, handling their rinsed and glimmering horses with ease, the yearlings' muffled hooves heading to the barn on the thick carpet of grass. The scent of warm horseflesh drifted their way.

Harper considered Millie. She'd wanted to talk to her in person to see her reaction to Minetti's comment. She did seem insulted by the accusation. But why wouldn't Millie look at her?

Instead of answering right away, Harper let Millie's question hang in the air. Hers was a good question. Was Minetti, in fact, pointing a finger at Millie?

The widow sighed and took a drag, then flicked the cigarette toward the exercising horses as one big colt made a run through his front flap and circled the machine, causing a bit of chaos for the others. The assistant hit the off button and the machine slowed gradually to a halt. He turned to the two women, both still gazing in his direction. "That's exactly why I gotta get in and teach these babies what to do in there!" He laughed, lifted his ballcap, and shook his head. "There's always gonna be one." He replaced the hat, opened the door, unhooked the first horse, clipped on his lead, and gave the colt to a groom who'd seen the charging yearling and hoofed it over.

That's right, Harper agreed. There does have to be one. One person responsible for all the chaos associated with Lowen Farms. She looked at Millie. She'd been so sure it was Minetti. The Feds' involvement, the fact that he was a terrible, terrible man who'd done terrible things . . . And Henley. Well, he *was* guilty as sin—the drugs, the mindless drilling of babies. She paused a moment, thinking through it all. Minetti. Millie. She'd been so convinced of Millie's love for her husband and sorrow over his loss that she'd never seriously considered her involvement. She studied Millie's profile. Shrewd Millie.

Could she have been wrong?

"You got nothin to say?" asked the widow, her eyes locking with Harper's. "You think Minetti's fingering me for this?" Her eyes shot arrows. "Aubrey's dead, for Christ sake, and I got a shitload of debt to unload. You think I'd kill my own God-damned husband and put myself in a mess like I got?" She turned sad and looked down, her shoulders slumped. "A guy give me the best years of my life?"

Harper felt the truth of Millie's sudden sorrow and put an arm around her shoulder. The older woman rested against her for a moment, staring at the dewy grass sparkling in the sun. Again, Harper thought of how deeply Millie had loved her husband, their long colorful life together, and the farm they'd worked so hard to build. Her devotion was singular, her sorrow deep and penetrating.

Still, Harper thought, looking at Millie's powdered and rouged cheek. Could she have been wrong?

Having missed Keeneland barn duties in the morning, she spent the rest of her day in her Eden Hill office tending to her actual responsibilities, which that day amounted to signing checks, reviewing Marshall's and Tim's reports, looking over syndicate contracts and stallion booking applications for the next season, plus assorted other tasks that fell to her on a daily basis. She loved it, truth be told. She loved her family's legacy, and the place she and JD had made for themselves in a world they'd both grown up in. She loved it because she loved the horses, loved to see them at the height of their abilities flying down the racetrack. As long as the playing field was level.

She sobered. The presence of Henley Smythe, among others, would always jeopardize that, as cheaters did in any field of athletic competition—animal or human. But to her, horse racing was different. Humans could do whatever they wanted to themselves and suffer the consequences. In her mind, they deserved what they got.

But the horses. Humans were their caretakers, their guardians. Anyone who conducted business as if that weren't the case was not fit to be in the game. Just as Aubrey had been Millie's devotion, the horses were Harper's.

Thinking of this put her in mind of how much she missed her family. Except for the half-sister she'd yet to meet, all her blood relatives were gone, Eden Hill's success was solely hers to continue, hers and JD's. She sighed and finished up her business, missing her sister most of all. She glanced around the office, still filled with Paris' presence. It had been her sister's office until her murder. Then it had passed to Harper as had the entire legacy of Eden Hill Stud.

Well, she thought, chiding herself, no sense going down that road. She'd spent enough time in grief—first her parents, then her grandparents, then Paris. She clicked through the files on her computer, scanning the racing schedule. Focus. She refused to indulge herself. She couldn't afford that, not at this juncture. Get the day's business finished then turn a laser eye on Aubrey's murder. And the rest of it.

Her head popped up at the soft knock at the door. Pepper stood there quietly. How long she'd been there, Harper couldn't guess.

"Got another round of calls," she paused, looking at the wad of yellow notes in her hand. "from the folks you haven't called back." She held them out. "Yet." She smiled, and then entered the office and sat in front of Harper.

Pepper was a pixie, slight and lively, in her mid-20s, her dark bob always curled perfectly at her jaw. She gazed at Harper.

She was indispensable to the stud and to Harper's well-being. She could read her boss like a book.

"I'd get you a sandwich, but I know you wouldn't touch it," she said, setting the yellow call-backs on the desk. "Why don't you take some time off, Harper, you're running yourself into the ground."

Harper looked at the open computer screen filled with work, then surveyed her desk loaded with files and notes and return calls to make. "Yeah, right," she said, surveying the mess.

"Like one hour," responded Pepper. "Get out of here, go do one thing just for yourself." She snapped her fingers in front of Harper's face. "Hey, this way," she said, laughing, pointing her finger at herself. "I mean it. You're circling the drain, lady."

Harper smiled, nodding. She knew Pepper was right. She needed a break, she was feeling as exhausted as she was frustrated with the lack of progress. Minetti's smugness ate at her. Millie's obfuscation confounded her. Manuel's reluctance, while understandable, saddened and further infuriated her.

And Henley Smythe was somebody she'd like to sock in the jaw just as she had that low-life Sonny Boy Seddon.

She closed the computer and nodded. "Yeah okay, you're right." She shook a finger at Pepper. "One hour. I'll take one hour."

"And no riding Memphis," Pepper added. "Get off the property." She got up and headed for the door, turned back and grinned. "Get out of here, that's an order." Then she went to her desk behind the high marble counter.

Harper saluted her on the way out, and headed for the Range Rover, intending to do exactly what she'd agreed to. But just as she passed the house and started down the drive, her phone chirped. A call from Sophia. Harper stared at her phone, her distaste pronounced. What could she want? The ringing continued and Harper gave in, answering it.

Chapter 23

"It isn't what you think," Sophia blurted. When Harper didn't respond, she added, "It's not what it looks like."

"*It* being?" Harper said.

"My relationship with Stuart," Sophia said with force. "And so much else. Oh please, Harper, do let me explain. Can we meet?"

Harper considered it. The woman's reaction to El Karta's death disgusted her. And yet, Harper realized she needed some opening to move forward. She had no idea what Sophia might be cooking up, but maybe, just maybe, she could turn the conversation to her own ends. She agreed to meet, said the only time she could do it was within the next hour at her home. Sophia said she was tied up for the next hour but could make it over there just after that. Harper again agreed.

She backed the Range Rover a short distance up the drive, turned around, and pulled into the circle in front of the house then made for Grandpa's barn over Cedar Creek. She drove because she wanted to hide the SUV in case Pepper decided to head out.

If she couldn't get off the property, she'd find her restoration in Memphis.

Oh, hell, she thought, throwing the car into park at the barn. She was the boss. She could do whatever the hell she pleased. She jumped out, got Memphis' lead rope, and headed to his private pasture finding his head bent to the grass, standing at the edge of the enclosure. His black head rose as she climbed over the five-slat fence and strode toward him. He eyed the lead rope and bent again to his grass.

Harper put a boot just under his chin and he sighed, raised his head, and allowed Harper to slip the halter on. They left the pasture, the sun's heat easing in the late afternoon. She lay a hand on the colt's neck as they walked, feeling his warmth. She began to relax, coming into his presence, and as Harper took in a deep, slow breath she found the colt did the same. He swung his big head her way and nuzzled her shoulder.

"Good boy," she murmured, the gratitude she felt for him welling up, a balm to her anxiety and frustration.

She walked with him to the round pen and undid the halter, pointing to the rail and sending him around the circle at a walk. He looked good—relaxed, his joints moving fluidly. Harper lifted her arm slightly, increasing her energy and Memphis moved to the trot. She checked him out again and was glad to see his movement was even and effortless. She took a step back, lowered her energy, looked at his hindquarters and Memphis turned to face her, slowing to walk as Harper sent him the other way. She put him through his paces—walk, trot, canter, and then she stepped back and became still. Memphis stopped, turned to her, his ears pricked forward and when she beckoned, he walked to her and stood, awaiting her next command.

Harper reached a hand up and rubbed his head, put his halter back on, and left the round pen for the large arena just to the side of Grandpa's barn. There she tied the halter under his chin, flipping the make-shift reins over his head, grabbed a hunk of mane, and swung herself up on the colt's back. She settled in and stretched her legs out long, clicking to him to go forward.

Harper loved to feel the colt's big body beneath her, her long legs embracing him, his willingness to move at any pace Harper set with her seat. They moved as one, and Harper felt no need to work the colt or to do anything at all except exist in one moment of union as it moved into the next. She inhaled the green grass, her colt's earthy scent, and the slight curl of dirt as Memphis' hooves made a path weaving through poles set a bit over four feet apart, good for helping his bend. She closed her eyes then and just let Memphis take the lead, go wherever his big heart desired. He wandered around at a slow trot as the breeze ruffled his black mane, then moved into a canter. After a time, feeling much more restored and centered, Harper and Memphis left the arena and she deposited him back in his pasture. He turned a deep brown eye to her, the blue horizontal pupil making his familiarity seem suddenly alien. Harper smiled, kissed his eyelid, and patted him on the rump, sending him off to graze.

She turned and headed to house to wait for Sophia's arrival and whatever the woman had in store to say.

When Sophia arrived twenty minutes later, Harper was ready.

She escorted Sophia to the study, signaling that this was a business meeting, not a social one. Harper opened the door and walked in, glancing at her family's history in racing lining the walls in winners' circle photos, shining silver bits and a few stallion name plates from the halters of Eden Hill's most successful runners and sires. She circled her father's huge rosewood desk and planted herself in the chair, gesturing with a hand for Sophia to take a seat in one of the two club chairs before her. She glanced out the window to see the day's light had turned a soft blue-violet as the sun began its descent, flooding the far grass expanse with dimming light as the sun moved behind a cloud. She turned back to Sophia to see her gray eyes troubled. The woman sat forward, the picture of earnestness in a bright coral dress. Harper again took note of her elegance and beauty, diamonds glinting at her ears and the large gold and diamond bracelet on her arm.

"Say what you came to say, Sophia," she said.

The woman nodded and sat back, appearing anxious. "Your comment at the restaurant, I want you to know you're wrong about Stuart." She waited a moment and when Harper didn't respond, she went on. "I've known him a long time. In the City. He's a philanthropist, Harper, he does so much good for the art community."

Harper looked down, fingering her grandfather's ivory horse carving.

"You may have known him long ago, but he changed. Since I've known him, he's been nothing but a gentleman of the arts. A patron."

Harper scoffed and squinted at her. Was she serious? "You do know Minetti is responsible for El Karta's death, right?"

When Sophia scowled and shook her head, Harper said, "He supplied the drugs. He's been trafficking in drugs for decades, Sophia."

"That is not the man I know," the woman firmly responded. "When Millie asked Stuart to invest in all those horses—"

Harper cut her off. "Wait, Millie asked Stuart? Not Aubrey?" Millie had said she'd introduced the two, but had not indicated that she'd initiated the buy-ins.

Sophia nodded. "Oh yes, I'm certain of that because when Millie told me to bring El Karta into training, she mentioned she'd gotten Stuart to purchase shares in many of her own horses. It was Henley's presence, she said, that convinced him. Millie thought it would be a good idea for El Karta, as well."

"So, Millie lured you in by telling you your 'friend' Minetti was already on board? Is that what you're telling me?"

Sophia nodded again.

Harper picked up the engraved letter opener and turned it over and over, thinking. Millie had not divulged any of this. She looked up at Sophia. Of course, that's assuming Sophia was on the up-and-up. She stared into the gray eyes, which seemed frank. Sophia blinked but appeared sincere. So Minetti had duped the heiress in to believing he was a patron of the arts.

Harper studied the engraving on the letter opener. How could she convince Sophia that Minetti was not a "gentleman" of the arts or of anything else? Her thought turned to Millie. The widow's story was starting to seem a bit thin.

The doorbell chimed, startling Harper. She glanced at the time. She wasn't expecting anyone. She rose, excused herself and once at the door, peered out the vertical window.

Stuart Minetti stood on the porch, his hands clasped comfortably in front of him. Harper turned to see Sophia exiting the study and heading her way, the coral dress swirling at the hem. Harper glared at the woman, who arrived at her side. "Let him in, Harper," Sophia said. "You need to hear him out."

Harper opened the door reluctantly, frowning at the tall, immaculately groomed man awaiting her invitation.

Instead, she stepped out onto the porch and gestured to an Adirondack chair to the right, Sophia following, seeming a bit confused. She pulled the door shut and took a chair next to Minetti while Harper leaned on the white porch rail. Harper crossed her arms and didn't say a word as a large truck filled with feed sped by beyond the gravel circle drive.

Minetti ran a light hand over his swept back silver hair and turned to Sophia. "I told you she wouldn't listen to the truth. Yet you insisted." He turned back to Harper.

In his off-white silk shirt and light gray pants, he looked out of place in the green painted rustic chair.

Sophia spoke up, also staring at Harper. "She's beginning to," she said, turning to Minetti. "Though you're right to say she's not easily convinced."

Minetti spread his hands wide and focused on Harper. "The truth is, Millie got me involved. Millie's responsible for that groom's death and the death of her own husband. She's trying to implicate me because . . . frankly, I displaced her."

Harper uncrossed her arms and rested her hands on the porch rail, elbows bent. "Explain that."

"When I came into the picture and invested heavily and secured Sophia's involvement, Aubrey came to depend on me for advice. Business advice. Millie was jealous."

Harper considered that. Millie had repeatedly mentioned that Aubrey had cut her out the last few years. Still, it was hard to believe anything Minetti said held water.

"And?"

Minetti glanced at Sophia and back to Harper. "And . . . I have a reputation. An unearned, fallacious one. One I've worked years to set right." Here he glanced back at Sophia and took her hand. "Millie is taking advantage of that."

"You threatened me," Harper said flatly, remembering the malice in his voice that day at the barn when he hissed about his "interests" and "seeing more of her." His tone had been malevolent.

"I did nothing of the sort," Minetti asserted. "I have a lot of money invested in Lowen Farms. There is a very large debt. I have interests to protect." He stared at Harper. "And I will protect them." The malevolence crept back into his voice.

Or was it merely conviction? Harper now wondered.

Minetti put his elbows on the chair arms. "You would do the same," he said.

Beside him, Sophia nodded, glancing at him and back at Harper. "What we've told you is the truth."

Minetti rose, bringing Sophia to her feet in the process. "We'll leave it to you to verify what we've said." He paused. "Millie is a vindictive, conniving woman beneath that bumbling exterior. You'd do well to heed my words."

"Do you have even a shred of evidence for any of this?" Harper said, not moving from her position.

Minetti's countenance grew haughty. "It is hardly up to me to provide evidence. Sophia and I are attempting to aid you and your husband in an investigation he—and you—are obviously making little headway in." He and Sophia stood silently side by side.

Harper wasn't buying it. Minetti might have duped Sophia, but Harper saw right through him. Accusing Millie was an attempt to deflect attention from himself. Millie was a shrewd businesswoman, but capable of murder? Of the husband she'd devoted her life to?

The three stared at each other for another long minute, the tension rising.

Minetti spoke. "The evening Millie and I had drinks, she spoke about the debt. I can tell you, nearly verbatim, what she said. She insisted the farm produce winners and mentioned she'd 'botched it' with El Karta breaking down. Millie effectively admitted responsibility for his death."

Harper glanced at Sophia who held a hand up to her mouth, shocked and stricken.

Minetti ignored her, continuing. "She then lamented Aubrey hiring Henley, calling him 'that Limey SOB' and again emphasizing the need to raise money from the horses. She indicated that if the horses could not be made to win, and here I am quoting, 'we need to get the money in some other way.'"

Minetti pointed a finger Harper's way, "Then she said, and this is also a quote, 'Do you catch my drift?'" He paused a moment. "Is that blunt enough for you?"

Harper was not impressed. "So you say."

Minetti lost patience. Exasperated, he spoke through tight lips. "I can see we're wasting our time here." He glanced at Sophia, who was still speechless after Minetti's El Karta comment, and signaled they were through. "Why don't you convey what we've told you to your hot-shot husband?" Minetti spat, as he escorted Sophia to the steps. "Maybe he can do his damned job and arrest the real culprit before somebody else gets killed."

And with that, Minetti and Sophia strode off the porch, and each one sped off down the long drive leaving Harper confused.

"To hell with the Feds!" JD declared, storming through the front door a while later, slamming it. He strode into the living room, his eyes blazing.

Harper was still trying to puzzle through Minetti's visit and was sitting in front of the fireplace, Kelso at her side. At the outburst, the golden retriever jumped up, meeting JD at the edge of the living room, and wagged his big tail, gazing up at the detective shyly as if he wasn't quite sure what to expect from him.

JD ruffled his head and after a few moments walked into the room more calmly to sink down on the leather couch beside his wife. The day's last rays filtered through the windows and cast a softness over JD's auburn hair and a face set uncharacteristically hard. Harper watched him settle but didn't say anything. Usually, the tables were turned. Usually, Harper was the hothead, JD the calming influence. His normally steady, appraising expression looked like storm clouds.

"Today I was told to completely withdraw from the investigation," he said, staring straight ahead. The two federal agents, dubbed "Muscle Man," and "Pug" by the detective, had decided that JD's participation in bringing Minetti to justice was no longer needed. Al Walker had delivered the news behind closed doors, with some sympathy knowing JD's connection to the Lowen family. But the captain noted in a frustrated tone, he wasn't calling the shots. The two federal agents had been pretty useless anyway was JD's reply, and his boss had nodded. Nonetheless, Walker said, orders were orders.

Harper ran her hand along the back of her husband's neck, gazing out the far window to the tall, leafed-out trees lining one side of the pasture and the mares grazing there quietly in the dusk. They'd been turned out for the night after their dinner and were doing what horses did best, continuing to eat. She massaged JD's muscles lightly. He sighed and looked at her, leaning in for a soft kiss.

"Maybe that's okay," Harper finally said. JD looked up, a question in his eyes. "Now we don't have them breathing down our necks." She knew there was no way on earth JD was giving up the investigation. Maybe this was exactly the release they needed.

JD straightened his big shoulders and stroked Kelso's back. The dog was standing at his side, and now sat, content that the temperature in the room was back to normal.

The detective nodded, considering Harper's words, then smiled. His composure regained, the smile turned into the boyish smirk that had caused many Lexington ladies to swoon back in the day, like the Southern belles they attempted to be.

But Harper turned serious. "Had a visitor just before you got home," she said and filled JD in on Sophia and Minetti's visit.

JD's smirk vanished. "So, Millie," he said. He looked from Kelso to Harper. "You'd thought about that yourself."

Harper nodded. She had, that was true. And she'd checked out the possibility. But it just didn't sit right. Still didn't, even after her talk with Millie and Minetti's visit. Yes, Millie was a behind-the-scenes mover and shaker, the rudder steadying Aubrey's flamboyant ship. They'd been a formidable team. But Millie's grief was real, and very deep—Harper had felt that from the first days in the hospital and so many times since. The widow had leaned on Harper more than once, unable to contend with an overwhelming sadness that was palpable. There just wasn't a way Harper could square how much Millie loved Aubrey, how authentic and pervasive her grief was, with Minetti's story. It didn't make emotional or business sense. The best chance Lowen Farms had of regaining its financial footing and its reputation was if Aubrey was at the helm with his wife doing what she did best. It made no sense at all that she'd orchestrate his death.

Finally her eyes turned to JD and she gave him her full attention. "We can't keep waiting for things to come to us," she said into his clear gaze, having had enough of patience, watching, and waiting. "We need to bring the game to them."

"Yes." JD nodded. "My thought exactly."

Whoever the hell "them" ended up being, Harper thought.

Chapter 24

In the end, they decided to enlist Aliana and Manuel. The next morning, Harper approached Aliana as she sprayed down Miss Somers after the two-year-old's workout.

"Fillies," Aliana murmured, the young bay racehorse shaking her head and glaring as Aliana lightly sprayed her face. The sun glinted off Miss Somers' shining coat and she shied a bit to the side, Aliana settling her as she continued her work.

"She's a nice filly," Harper said, standing at Aliana's side, appraising the well-made runner. Aliana focused the nozzle and ran a harder stream down the filly's neck and along her back, widening it as she rinsed off the filly's ribcage. The groom turned an eye wise beyond her years to Harper. "She a filly," she said as if that about summed it up.

Harper laughed. Yes, you had to prove yourself to fillies, and you could lose a filly's mind and trust in training a heck of a lot quicker than you could a colt. They were, well, they were fillies.

Harper was quiet a moment, taking in the sights, sounds, scents of the life she loved—the soft Latin music punctuated by good-natured, soft laughter; a thin groom hoisting a pile of manure high over the white fence back behind a tall, deep green oak, then turning to see if anyone had witnessed; the horses' whinnies and snorts; the hollow, regular clop of their hooves on the shedrow. A good trainer could tell a lot about the horse from that sound, regular and rhythmic.

This was the heart and soul of racing, this and the breeding shed. This and the double stalled, deep-bedded foaling shed. This and the training track and the slow, gentling way a groom brushed a glowing coat on a body big enough to crush him. Those who came to the track on Derby Day missed what made so many men and women spend their lives, generation after generation, all over the world, doing what she and her family did. It was right here in front of her. There was nothing on the earth as majestic, as intuitive, as fragile as a Thoroughbred. Harper let her eyes take it all in—a life she loved, yes. But a life so often put in jeopardy. Where lots of money was involved, there would always be jeopardy.

Aliana switched off the hose and removed water from Miss Somers coat with a curved rubber scraper, then she and the juvenile started toward the filly's stall.

"Wait a moment," Harper said, and the young groom halted as Miss Somers' head immediately dropped to the short grass. "I need your help."

Aliana looked Miss Somers way, her hand playing along the filly's glistening deep bay withers. She looked like she knew what was coming and glanced down. "Sí, I know this."

"You and Manuel, I need you both."

Aliana glanced toward the Polytrack where Manuel was at his post, standing beside Henley watching the babies move and taking orders.

Harper had one other card to play to bring the two on board. "I have made arrangements for Manuel's mother to come stay at Eden Hill. She'll reside at a little house we have on the river. No one will find her there, I promise you." Harper had asked John Henry if he'd mind having the older Hispanic woman as a guest and he'd, of course, agreed. John Henry would do anything asked of him. "She'll be safe with us," Harper added.

Aliana turned back, her look serious. "Sí, we have talk." Her dark, worried eyes looked into Harper's. "What you want us do, we do." She nodded gravely, murmuring again, "We have talk. We do."

So Aliana and Manuel had already spoken of the need to bring Henley, Seddon, Minetti and possibly Millie, to justice. Good. She'd send a car for Manuel's mother that afternoon. The situation settled, Harper told Aliana what she needed from the two of them.

That evening, after feeding but before Edgar, the pea-headed groom, showed up for night check, JD and Harper pulled into the parking lot by Barn 41. Aliana stood guard at the entrance to the barn's shedrow, glancing behind her as the two walked up. She turned, startled, her brown eyes large and luminous in the moonlight.

"Horses quiet, Manuel in office," she said seriously. Her round face glowed with purpose. Once the small, stocky woman set her mind to something, Harper saw, she did it for all she was worth.

They headed into Henley's office to find Manuel at the unlocked file cabinet—it was long and two-tiered, so potentially a lot of information was stored there. The only light came from the desk lamp, and it was weak. As JD and Harper walked in, Manuel glanced their way then back to the top drawer, which was open.

"Drugs," he said, pointing to the array. JD and Harper looked inside and then at each other in the low light, shadows playing across the room as the three extracted several vials, bottles, syringes, and other paraphernalia and set them out on Henley's desk. JD picked up a vial and studied the label. There was a pharmaceutical company listed at the top, Lowen's vet, the name of the drug, and instructions for use. Notably, there was little listed as caution in the application of the drug.

"We need photos of these," JD said crisply, and Harper pulled out her phone as the other two continued to take the damning evidence out of the cabinet. Most of them were housed together in cardboard cartons. That meant that either they were to be used together or used on a particular horse.

The vet's name was of particular interest, but of course Harper knew that any name could be pasted on a label, it didn't mean the Lowen's vet was dirty. But it also didn't mean he wasn't.

They finished the work, and moved on to the drawer beside it, finding files there with receipts for the drugs and files on horses receiving them. It was risky to have hard copies, but no riskier than having it all on the computer, she supposed.

Minetti's name was nowhere to be found. Nor was Aubrey's.

But Raybone "Sonny Boy" Seddon" was penciled in on several of the files, including the one labeled "Aviragus." JD pulled each of those files out but didn't find the man's name inside. What he did find and shared with Harper, were copies of insurance held on each of the horses. Reading a few of the files, JD noted the insurance premiums had been increased over the last month. That could be because the horses legitimately increased in value due to races won, Beyer speed figures improving, or any other number of things as the juveniles matured over the race season and older horses posted winnings.

But it could also be because Seddon was expert at wielding a bat. They couldn't kill a horse for insurance money if the cause was detectable on the required necropsy. But more than one "stall accident" would also raise suspicion. They took note of the horses whose folders had Sonny Boy's name on them and would look into those later.

"Gracias for my mother," Manuel said to Harper as the two replaced the last of the drugs. Harper put a hand on his shoulder. Manuel closed the file cabinet and squatted to pull out the lower drawer, walking his fingers through the files and looking up at Harper after a few moments, shook his head.

She knelt down next to Manuel, noting how young he was. Wirey, too, and strong. He turned to her, the cleft in his chin shadowed, his brown eyes the color of chestnuts, both kind and worried.

Harper looked through the files as JD opened the lower file to the right of them. She saw nothing of interest. Feed bills, files from other years, and all U.S. locations containing horse specifics—ownership, sales figures, pedigree, racing results, and so on. The cabinet's contents seemed an innocuous compilation of horses who'd been in training over the past five years.

She peered over at JD but he had his head bent to the cabinet in front of him. He pulled out a file and opened it, standing up and taking it over to the light on the desk.

Harper glanced at the time. They needed to wind up things or Edgar, the groom who'd nearly run Fleet Light into the rail, would show up for night check.

"This is interesting," JD said, staring at the file's contents, a collection of scraps of paper with handwriting on them. He looked at Harper. "It's notes Henley must have made. Handwritten and dated. Notes about—" He sorted through a few more scraps and looked up at Harper, holding one up. "This one is about a conversation he had with Aubrey." He resumed reading, flipping through the scraps. "They seem to have started last year. When Henley was in Newmarket . . . Looks like he documented some of what he and Aubrey spoke about." He turned the lamp to one of the smaller pieces. "This one mentions Minetti." He flipped it over and then back. "It's dated last fall. Talks about—" He looked at his wife. "It makes mention of Millie, says 'Millie brought in New York art collector Minetti. Big money.'"

Harper nodded. "Millie as much as admitted that to me, remember? She said she introduced Minetti to Aubrey. So that's not surprising. It makes sense Henley would know him, Minetti has a ton invested."

"Right," JD said, nodding, continuing through the file, "but if Henley mentions anything in here that would connect Millie and Aubrey to Minetti and to drugs, then we'd have something."

Harper glanced at her phone. "We're out of time," she said. "Edgar will be here any minute."

JD nodded but kept reading. Manuel moved to close and lock the file cabinets. "No can see computer," he murmured, glancing over his shoulder.

"JD we need to go. Take the file."

JD closed it, deposited it in the cabinet, and kicked it closed as Manuel moved to lock it. It wouldn't be wise to give away that someone had been in the files. Better to leave things as they were and maybe catch another opportunity.

The three exited Henley's office and made for their vehicles, Harper and JD in the Range Rover and Aliana and Manuel in his truck.

They all sped off into the night with much to contemplate.

Once home, JD paced the kitchen while Harper set out Gus' spicy fried chicken, picked up on the way to the house. She spooned out the sides and set the chicken on a platter.

"These people," JD muttered. "So subtle, so careful." He looked at Harper. "Normally, long before this Minetti would have made a mistake, tipped his hand." He laid his hands on the counter. "Or Henley. Minetti knows the Feds are onto him. He knows I'm on his tail."

"He's had a lot of practice in being careful," Harper said, noting JD's irritation. "In letting others take the fall. That's his MO. Believe me, I watched him do business in New York. He's smart, and that's how he's stayed in business and out of jail." She plunked down plates and circled the countertop to put her arms around her husband's neck, looking up at him. "Don't let him get to you. That's what he does best."

JD nodded. "I'll haul in Seddon in the morning."

JD turned to dinner. He loaded his plate and headed for the wooden booth at the side of the kitchen. "And Aubrey and Minetti will be right behind him."

The prospect of being fired for disobeying an order didn't seem to factor into JD's thinking.

"And the vet," said Harper, joining him in the booth. "don't forget Iggy Renken." The Lowen's longtime vet had a stellar reputation in the horse world. But you never did know, now did you? The year Paris had died, a trusted Eden Hill employee had shot John Henry, drugged and bet on her runners, and tried to burn her stallion barn down. And he'd been with them since her father was alive. She shook her head. No, you never could tell for sure.

"And the company supplying the drugs . . ." JD said. "We absolutely have enough for a search warrant."

"You know the Feds will never allow that. And they won't let you touch Henley or Minetti either," Harper declared. They had to work under the radar, somehow.

"Maybe Seddon," JD said.

They ate in silence, Harper eying her husband over a thigh of crispy chicken. She knew what they really needed wasn't suspect interviews or search warrants. What they needed was to catch the culprits red-handed. Catch Minetti and Henley and Seddon in the act. She paused. And perhaps Millie. She stared at JD. You do what you have to do.

JD stared back, nodding as if he'd heard her.

And so will I. She smiled.

They'd see what tomorrow brought.

Chapter 25

The next morning before dawn Harper headed to Barn 41, anxious to see if JD could prevail in getting search and arrest warrants. She wanted to be there to see Henley receive what was coming to him.

As she rounded the walkway into Henley's domain, he crooked a finger at her, then turned to give a leg up to Edgar on the big, dappled gray. Henley patted the colt's neck and Edgar moved off at a walk just as Harper approached.

Henley had Harper slated to take notes for him as he evaluated the workout. They'd be on the big track, Henley said, shoving a pad of paper her way. Manuel was nowhere to be seen.

They all walked the distance to the main track together and came out onto the dirt oval in front of the deep green race stands just now being lit by the rising sun. To the right of Harper a large bay, neck arched, rider perched above, made his way from shadow into the new sunlight. Far off, Harper saw the pink and light blue sky at the horizon, and closer Keeneland's white and red poles, as the haze on the track began to lift and the other riders and mounts moved into position, setting up for workouts. Horses whinnied and snorted, and the muffled sound of hooves carried on the slight breeze.

Everyone—riders, trainers, horses, outriders, clockers, lookers-on—went about their work in a businesslike manner. The exuberance of race day was absent, replaced by trainers and their assistants littering the stands or down by the rail. Harper climbed the grandstand stairs and took her place next to Henley as the Lowen set assumed perpendicular positions and, when it was time, moved into their work on the track.

She glanced at Henley, her anticipation of his take-down building.

Nothing momentous ensued. Harper took notes as Henley murmured businesslike observations her way, ignoring her presence otherwise. When the set was finished, he waved her back to the barn, grabbed the pad and told her to send Manuel down with the next set. He then turned his attention back to the track, effectively dismissing her.

She trudged up the hill with the set who'd just worked, impatient to hear the police sirens, anticipating watching the shocked look on Henley's face as the cuffs were slapped on.

The rest of the morning went like clockwork and the trainer avoided Harper altogether once he was back at the barn, which suited her just fine. She continued to bide her time, getting more concerned as the morning wore on and no police showed up.

After quite a while, when it became clear that the police were not arriving to haul the trainer in for questioning or search his office, she put in a call to JD and it went, as usual, to voicemail.

Glancing at the time, her worked completed, she entered Henley's office to see what else she might do. Henley scowled at her and said she was done for the day. He waved her off with a dismissive hand, pulled his beard, and turned to his computer.

Disappointed, she decided to head over to Millie's. Harper still harbored uneasiness about her story and hadn't been able to shake it. She glanced at the barn and everyone busy at their tasks, wondering again where the police were as she headed out to her SUV. On the way to Millie's she put in another call to JD, wanting to know if there was a problem getting the warrants, but again got his voicemail. She left a message to call her and focused on what she'd say to Millie.

She pulled in the drive and parked to the left of the Lowen's stucco mansion. An American flag flew to the right of the door. The veranda running the length of the house was studded with three large pots overflowing with yellow and fuchsia late May flowers. Behind them, in the shade of the overhang, a porch swing and three chairs flanked the doorway. Harper climbed the stairs and rang the bell. Harold answered right away, stood back, and welcomed her inside.

"I know I'm not expected," Harper said stepping through the doorway into the large foyer, the terrazzo-tiled floor in marbled gray and white shining before her. Harold's large frame loomed over her. "Thought I'd catch Millie for a chat, is she around?"

"Ms. Lowen is at the mares' barn." He consulted his watch. "If you'll wait in the study, I'll summon her." He started off that way, expecting Harper to follow.

"That's okay, Harold," she said to his wide-shouldered back, "I'll just pop over there, no problem."

Harold turned a troubled face her way. "Mrs. Lowen stressed to me that she not be disturbed."

"It's okay, I know where the barn is," Harper said, wondering why he seemed so serious.

Harold shook his head. "Please, Miss Harper, she was pretty insistent." He smiled. "You know how she gets."

Harper turned toward the door, laughing. "Oh, yes, Harold, I know exactly how she gets. But no worries, I'll catch up with her at the barn."

The more Harold insisted, the more Harper felt inclined to head to the mares' barn. She turned as she opened the door to see Harold staring at the shining floor, a deep frown on his face. Harper hoped she wasn't getting him into trouble.

She jumped in the Range Rover and drove to the barn, passing the Lowen's stallion paddocks where massive horses behind five-slat fencing stood grazing or gazing out over the deep green landscape undulating into the distance. A few stallions took off as she passed, bucking and frolicking like colts. In a few minutes she spied the blue and white painted mares' barn up ahead. A beat up and rusted Chevy pickup stood in front along with Millie's Mercedes. She parked and walked into the bright barn, the smell of fresh hay laced with a barn full of warm mares greeting her. She walked past stalls filled with pregnant moms on either side of the shedrow, some munching hay, some out in their paddocks or dotting the pasture they shared. Up toward the center of the barn on the left was a door to the tack and storage room. Harper heard two voices, so headed that way down the neatly raked shedrow dotted by green alfalfa and orchard grass square bales.

Turning in at the doorway, her mouth dropped open. Standing at a wooden table laden with cardboard boxes filled with vials and bottles were Millie and Raybone "Sonny Boy" Seddon. Harper was speechless. She stood there with one arm pressed against the doorjamb, the other hanging limply at her side. She couldn't seem to move or process the two figures before her, so out of place seemed the pair of them. She looked from one to the other, then to the cardboard container and back up to the two of them, dumfounded.

"Millie?" she finally said, her eyebrows knit in disbelief. Anger also welled in her as the significance of the pair and the cardboard container exactly like the ones they'd found in Henley's office hit her.

Seddon and Millie turned to her at once. Sonny Boy's nose was still bandaged but the wraps were smaller. The menacing snake arching above his eyebrow and ending between his still swollen chartreuse and purple eyes was more threatening than at their first encounter. He smirked, and said "My oh my, lookey who we have here."

Millie's mouth made a little "O" of shock and she stared at Harper as a flush of red moved from her neck up to her substantial cheeks. She shook her head briefly, her orange hair unmoving as a helmet. "What the hell are you doing here?" was all she could finally say, her voice full of confusion and a slight bit of wonder.

The low hum of the refrigerator was the only sound in the white cinder block room. Harper stared at Millie who seemed bewildered while Seddon stood off to the side smirking.

"What the hell am *I* doing here, Millie?" Harper blurted out, looking around, focusing on Seddon, then moving her eyes to Millie. Unbelievable, was the sole thought she could muster. She shook her head, unable to fathom that Minetti had quite possibly been telling the truth. She scowled at the widow. Millie at the center of all the death and mayhem Harper had been working so hard to resolve on the widow's behalf? Harper looked hard at her old friend, barely containing her astonishment and anger.

But even given the scene in front of her, Harper still wondered if Millie could actually have arranged Aubrey's murder. It seemed impossible to conceive that was true, given how real, how deep, her sorrow ran. Still, Harper considered, she'd been initially wrong about Paris' killer as well. How often, she wondered, did we miss a truth that was so obviously right in front of us?

She stared at the cardboard boxes. Was Millie responsible for the drugging, too?

"You are behind all this?"

At that, Seddon strode toward her aggressively. Harper stood her ground. He pushed her into the doorjamb as he fled, a sour, unwashed smell following him into the barn aisle. Harper turned briefly to see him run to his truck, then returned her gaze to Millie, who had placed both hands on the square table and was leaning on it heavily.

"It ain't what you think," she said, looking up at Harper, her eyes full of sorrow that abruptly turned to fire.

"That's exactly what Sophia said when she and Minetti dropped by to give me the news that you are behind it all." Harper walked into the brilliant white room to stand facing Millie across the table. Behind her, a cabinet stood open exposing other carboard containers filled with bottles. She could barely contain her rage.

"You killed your best friend's colt. Did you also hire that low-life Sonny Boy to work over Figarosa?" Harper asked, glancing uneasily at the door then back, her palms wide, feeling so furious her hands shook. "And Aubrey? That's the worst of it, Millie. How *dare* you profess to love and mourn him when you are responsible for his death." She leaned forward, staring daggers into Millie's eyes. "How dare you," she whispered.

Suddenly, a feeling of unease washed over her. Harper turned again to the door just before the sound of running footsteps reached her, followed by Seddon blasting through the doorway, his bat at his shoulder.

"No!" Millie screamed as Seddon, face set hard, whipped back the bat, aiming at Harper's head.

Harper's rage surged and found focus. Ignoring Millie, she lunged at Seddon just as he swung the bat. She ducked hard to the right, lifting her left arm in defense as the bat whipped past her hand, just grazing her fingers. She winced as they bent back sharply and drew her hand in, crouching in pain. In a moment, Seddon was on her, grunting, shoving her to the ground and again raising the bat high overhead, his eyes blazing over the white bandages. Harper staggered up, her legs wobbling, then dropped and rolled to her right as the bat came down on empty air. She struggled to get her shaking legs under her, crouching again to gain her balance. She stood, shaking her left hand out and caught a glimpse of Millie who seemed frozen in place by the table.

Harper and Seddon squared off, staring at each other, then a thin smile crept over the tattooed man's face. His head bobbed as if he listened to a favorite tune as he stepped toward Harper, watching her side-step him then square off again. No words passed between them, but the message was clear.

Seddon was enjoying himself.

Harper studied the man, then her eyes darted to Millie whose expression now included her own building anger. She met Harper's eyes and nodded toward Sonny Boy's back. Harper understood. The widow would attack from the rear if Harper would keep Seddon's attention.

Harper watched Sonny Boy approach, still bobbing his head and smiling, the bat resting on his shoulder as it had at Aviragus' stall that night. He pointed the bat at her, just as

Millie lunged into his back, sending him careening toward Harper, off balance and staggering.

His eye went wide. The snake eyes glared between his brows. Harper knew this was her chance, maybe her only chance. She drew back her right arm and shot a power jab to his nose just as she had at Barn 41. Seddon's nose instantly erupted in a burst of red soaking the bandages. He screamed, and folded into himself, glaring up at Harper with hatred in his eyes. He struggled to rise, fighting the pain, but that was one fight he wasn't going to win.

He dropped the bat and Millie moved to retrieve it, whacking Seddon on the back and screaming, "Get the hell off my property! Get!" Millie's face was a mask of fury and fear. As she looked from Harper to Sonny Boy, her eyes narrowed to slits, tears streaming onto her powdered cheeks.

Harper had never seen this side of the widow. Millie was frightening and focused and yet there was sorrow there, too, regret and heartbreak. Millie lifted the bat for another blow, and Seddon, clutching his bleeding nose, turned, and raced out of the room.

Millie turned on Harper, her face still a mix of fury and sorrow. "You, too, missy! You get on outta here, this is no business a yours!" She sobbed as she said it but wielded the bat with a clear threat.

Harper stood rubbing her hands, checking her fingers. None were broken, but both hands had taken a beating, and both were shaking. She studied Millie, seeing clarity and malicious purpose in her eyes even though the widow's face was wet with tears.

"Go on, girl! I'll club you like a baby seal, don't think I won't," she said with quiet malice, her arms clutching the bat, her tears still streaming.

Harper was confused. Millie had just saved Harper's life and now the widow was threatening her? She cocked her head at Millie, trying to gauge whether the threat was serious. Millie was careening emotionally, lurching from sadness to anger to malevolence.

And yet. Harper stood her ground, looking into the widow's eyes. Yes, there was massive fury there, a strange, purposeful malice towards her. But Harper also saw there was struggle, and sorrow. It was as if Millie fought with herself, self-preservation set against her love for Harper, her knowledge that Harper had always had her back. Maybe, Harper thought, she could work that to shift the balance in her favor.

"Millie, I can help you. Please. Just let me help you," Harper said. The two had known each other for many years, and even though the evidence in front of her looked horrific, Harper still held out hope that somehow the widow was not as culpable as she appeared.

Millie drew herself up, something settling into place in her. "There's nothin' to do, honey." Her mood again shifted, her voice barely a whisper. Her shoulders slumped a moment, then she seemed to gain new energy and again set her shoulders and stared down Harper. "It's just as bad as it damned well seems." Through tears that again brimmed in her eyes, she continued. "An I told you before, I ain't givin' up the farm." She banged the bat on the floor, hard. "I can't. No matter what I gotta do." She glared at Harper and drew in a shuddering breath. "And that includes handlin' you, girl." She pointed the bat at Harper, as tears streamed down her face. "You better go while you still can," she finished softly, but with steel in her voice.

Out in the barn, Harper heard the mares calling to one another. A few kicked the stalls, their agitation reflecting what was going on in the small room.

Harper folded her arms across her chest and planted her feet in a shoulder-wide stance. "I'm not going anywhere, Millie," she replied just as softly and with conviction to match Millie's. "It's over. Put the bat down." The hell with your sorrow, she thought, after all you've done. And, she added, after how hard I've tried to help you. She glanced at the door, a bit of worry fluttering through her.

"He ain't comin' back," Millie said, glancing that way. "That asshole Sonny Boy is one helluva coward." She stared at the door and laid the bat on the table. "An he don't take directions." She looked squarely at Harper. "An he don't work for me."

"Minetti," Harper said, glancing at the drugs being packed in cartons.

"I told him not to hire local talent," she said wearily, seeming to give in. Harper saw there was a part of Millie that would be relieved to finally get it all out in the open.

"But no," Millie continued, "Stuart knew a guy who knew a guy . . ." She shook her head in disgust. She looked into Harper's eyes. "If you ain't goin', you might as well sit," she said, picking up the bat and pointing to the chair. "I'll get you a drink." Millie turned to the refrigerator as Harper seated herself.

"This isn't a social call, Millie. Forget the drink. Tell me what happened." Harper's phone dinged with a text. She checked it. JD. "Heading to Keeneland, Feds took over the raid." She stared at the words, going numb. It took a moment for it all to sink in. So it really was, she thought, finally over, or would be soon—at least where Henley was concerned. After one frustration after another, and now, at last, Henley would face the consequences of his actions. How she wished she could be there to see the look on his face . . . "You okay?" Harper texted back. JD responded. "Got chewed out, but it's all good." Harper let him know she was at Lowen Farms with Millie, that Seddon and his bat had been there, and set her phone down.

Well, she thought, Henley might be getting his due, but there was still Minetti.

She stared out the window to a baby blue, cloudless sky. She turned to her friend.

And Millie.

Across town, JD along with the two federal agents and their crew pulled into Keeneland's backstretch and exited their vehicles at Barn 41's parking lot.

JD's pulse had raced when he picked up Harper's text as he and the others sped toward the racetrack. Seddon at Lowen Farms? He glanced around, agitated, but knowing he'd have to see the raid through. The Feds had made it clear—he'd instituted the raid, and he would be there to take the fall if it turned out a bust. JD wasn't in charge, so he'd have to follow the Feds' lead and trust Harper's strength would see her through until he could get there.

No one drew weapons but they were clad in protective gear. "Pug nose," whose real name was Todd Miller strode forward with his partner, Horace Johnson, right behind. They rounded the barn aisle and surveyed what went on day after day in normal life on the backstretch—the last set's horses arriving at the barn from the big track, stalls being finished up, grooms chatting as they raked, hand-walked, bathed, and groomed the young racehorses. The huge oak was fully leafed out, its leaves turning in the breeze and beginning to cast dappled shadows on the cool down track beneath. The air carried the green, sweet scent of hay as far off, toward the Polytrack, the world's up and coming racehorses honed their skills in the day's light.

JD walked alongside Miller and Johnson, pointing to Henley just now making his way up the hill from the training track beside the long-striding Aviragus, the trainer's head bent to the path in deep thought. He stroked his beard and looked up, seeing the five black-clad officers standing straddle-legged by his office. He stopped open-mouthed, his hand closing around his beard. Around him as he neared the wash rack, all movement had halted with the new arrivals, the grooms gazing from one to the other in question, the horses ignoring it all for the moment, standing like the rest and waiting. Low strains of lively Latin music drifted around them.

Johnson moved forward, pulling out his ID and the warrant, meeting the shocked trainer in front of his big colt's stall.

Henley's eyes were wide in stunned anticipation, and he put a hand out to the steady himself against the deep green door, staring blankly at the motionless grooms and horses. In the next moment, as panic switched through him, his face lost all color, then flushed. His hand went to his cheek, as if feeling for fever.

He looked from Johnson to the others behind him, his eyes narrowing at the sight of JD.

Slowly, realization welled up from the depths and he read the scene precisely. Why those damned drugs were still in the file cabinet was entirely Figarosa's fault, Henley thought morosely then suddenly furious. Him and that damned Minetti. He looked again at JD. That pissant, Minetti. He's to blame for all this, Henley realized, his hatred now finding a laser focus. Him and that incompetent sot Aubrey. He damn well deserved what he got. And in that very instant a flash of understanding arrived and settled in, and with it the self-loathing he knew he'd be contending with for many years in a small cell . . . Henley understood that the fix he was in was his own doing. The only thing Aubrey was good at was digging massive holes of debt. And Henley saw that's what had sucked him in. If he hadn't been so damned swelled up about himself—so convinced only he could save them, so damned self-satisfied . . . He should have told Aubrey he was a barmy prat and to piss off.

Henley felt nothing, his focus mired in self-disgust as Johnson moved behind his frozen form and cuffed him. Henley's next thought was of Aviragus. He glanced back at Aliana holding the big colt at the wash rack as Johnson moved him forward toward the office. Fear and sadness replaced the disgust, but not the anger. He'd never see his colt again. Never. What would happen to his kingmaker?

Henley's body slumped. He looked at the ground as he made his way, Johnson letting go of him and walking by his side. He glanced at the agent's face and found Johnson's dark countenance unreadable.

As Johnson nodded to the other agents who stood with their hands on their belts, Henley stared at them, his eyes moving from one to the next. He wondered at how official it all seemed, knowing he was staring at the loss of his career, his freedom, and his reputation. Then, as if in some form of primitive self-preservation, adrenaline rushed through him and he took off clumsily, his hands locked behind him, moving beyond Johnson as best he could, veering around Miller, and seeing the other agents smiling at him in amusement. Damn them, Henley thought, puffing, making for the parking lot.

JD easily caught him and looked deep into the trainer's flushed face. He did not share the others' amusement at the feeble escape attempt. Nor did the detective feel satisfaction. But he no longer expected that.

His focus was entirely on getting to the end of things at Barn 41. Henley had become an obstacle, but one JD knew he'd have to finish with. He aimed to do it quickly.

He held the trainer and glanced toward Manuel, whose body and expression registered relief. Next to him, Aliana's round face broke into a smile. The other grooms began to move forward with their work, serious and focused. No one spoke.

"You're done, Henley," JD said, looking down at the trainer, his gaze absent emotion. He yanked him toward the office and held out his hand for the keyring. Henley nodded toward his pocket. JD pulled out the keys, unlocked the door, and the crew moved inside.

The minute Johnson and Miller set about collecting evidence, JD announced he was leaving. Hardly looking up from sorting through a carton of drugs, Johnson nodded, dismissing him. JD raced to his unit, feeling as if he'd held his breath the entire raid.

He sped out Keeneland's front gate, hit the siren, and pressed the accelerator nearly to the floor. The presence of Seddon at Lowen Farms alone was enough to cause concern. If Minetti had been telling the truth about the rest of it, Harper was in danger. Weaving dangerously fast through traffic, eyes narrowed, he focused on getting to his wife. Still, it seemed to take an interminable amount of time to reach Lowen Farms.

As he neared, he silenced the siren not wanting to alert anyone and once there, he threw the unit into park, jumped out, and pounded on the stucco mansion's front door. He made short work of getting Harold to divulge where Harper could be found.

Harper stared at Millie, her longtime friend now seated across the table, the woman she'd tried hard to protect and console. The refrigerator's hum and shifting mares outside the open door seemed vain attempts at normalcy. What a fool I've been, Harper thought. Millie was behind it all and she had missed it. She'd ignored her own tiny misgivings and refused to believe Minetti's accusations. She stared into Millie's eyes, bloodshot eyes, but clearer than they'd been in a month.

"What happened?" Harper said, sitting back and folding her hands in her lap. She'd stay there as long as it took to get the whole story. This time, the true one.

Millie moved the vial laden carton to the side and stared at it a moment. She didn't look at Harper as she sighed and then spoke. "I loved the ole coot." She took a slow, shallow breath then spoke again, her voice hushed. "Loved him all them years. Loved him right to the end." She looked at Harper, desolation filling her eyes. "Still love him." She shook her head, staring at the wood-topped table, the orange halo not moving. "I told you he cut me out the last couple a years. That wasn't how we rolled. Not ever. We was always a team." She looked at Harper, her eyes moist. "And a damned good one. You know we were."

As she had through the entire ordeal, Harper could feel the truth of Millie's statements. Which is why the widow's actions made no sense. "If you loved him, why this?" she said, pointing to the drugs. "Why murder the man you say you loved?" She searched Millie's face for answers, finding none.

"I did no such thing!" Millie shouted, sitting back and straightening, shocked at the notion. She gathered herself a moment, then went on. "I told Stuart. Give him a little work-over. It was supposed to be a wake-up call. Just hurt the ole coot a little bit." She leaned forward and made an inch-high gesture with her hand. "So I could step in and nurse him back. Make him see me again." She set her hands on the table and leaned back. Tears rolled down her cheeks. "Make him let me back in."

Harper nodded. Yes, that made some sort of odd, perverted sense.

"And that asshole Sonny Boy fuck-up took it too far . . ." Millie sobbed, wiping the corners of her eyes with her index fingers, mascara cascading down her rouged cheeks. "You know the rest."

"I do, Millie," Harper said. She paused, waiting for Millie to compose herself. "But you are still responsible."

Millie looked up. "That piece of shit did the same thing to that damned Spic groom. Supposed to get information about what he was tellin' the Feds. You know he was turning State's evidence, right? Mr. 'I'm battin' a thousand' took it too damned far an we got nothin."

"What about the drugs, Millie?"

"And the mare he got to? Sending me a message to keep my mouth shut?" Her eyes flashed. "Like he owns me?"

"The drugs, Millie," Harper said. She'd already figured Minetti was responsible for the dead fetus.

"I had a damned good plan. It woulda worked," Millie said, more to herself now than to Harper. "You gotta see. We were in debt. Aubrey had no idea how to get out of this one. So I thought to myself, Minetti's got the drug connections, I'll get us goin' again and get my husband back to boot." She patted the desk with a flat palm in emphasis. "Get on the winning side," she said sniffling and nodding, "Get some bucks, get us outta the red . . ." She focused on Harper. "Wasn't working." She shook her head. "Then Aubrey up an dies on me and your damned colt beat the hell outta our "Kingmaker" an shot that big chunk a change all to hell." She muttered to herself. "Had to keep hold of the farm . . ." She looked up at Harper. "For Aubrey. You see that, right?"

Harper studied Millie, keeping quiet for the moment. The widow had created an impossible situation for herself, and Minetti was at the center of it. She'd get to him in due time.

"The bat, Millie, the bat and Aviragus . . . "

Millie got up and pulled cigarette out of her black pantsuit pocket, lit up, inhaling and sending a narrow stream toward the ceiling. She reseated herself and put her elbows on the table. "What about it?"

"We found some papers with Seddon's name on files saying you increased the insurance on several of your horses. Aviragus was one of them."

"Found what papers?" she shot back, her normal, combative attitude back in place.

"The Feds are raiding Barn 41 as we speak, Millie. The files are in Henley's office. Along with the drugs. He'll be taken into custody. Like I said, it's over."

Millie looked stunned. "Well, I'll be a son-of-a-bitch," she said, shaking her head, ashing her cigarette on the concrete floor, then looking up at Harper. "Henley was keeping a paper trail? That Limey imbecile." Her look went from outrage to disgust. "I told Aubrey. Told him not to bring that idiot over." She took a deep drag. "God-dammit!" she said, exhaling smoke in a forceful stream. In the next moment, Millie looked deep into Harper's eyes, and something shifted. Harper was becoming exhausted by the widow's sudden mood changes—one minute the affable buffoon, the next off on a tangent, followed by sorrow, then a rage prompted by who-knows-what in an internal world only Millie inhabited. So Harper waited. But then the atmosphere turned ominous, and Millie's eyes filled with something Harper recognized, something that made the hair on her arms stand on end.

She'd seen that same look in the eyes of her sister's killer the day he'd tried to murder her.

The widow's eyes went flat, without depth, without emotion, without focus. She turned unseeing to her right, staring at the wall then out the large window into an endless, cloudless blue sky, her left hand creeping over the bat and caressing it, running her fingers up and down the shaft.

Harper sensed danger and began to rise, but Millie turned to her and smiled. It was an eerie smile, one that lifted the facade of a helpless, sorrowful, desperate widow into a malevolence that Harper realized had been present all along, quiescent just below the surface. Yes, Millie had loved her husband and his loss had taken precedence for a time. It seemed, now, that something else had risen to the surface and Harper watched a transformation take place, watched the widow's posture change from defeat to dominance, her chin lift, her eyes bore into Harper's with purpose.

"Millie," Harper whispered, realizing that she was in danger. She'd become an obstacle to be eliminated.

"Yeah, you see it now, honey," she said with menace, nodding. "You gotta roll with them punches, learned that back in Harlem. Funny how death don't seem so bad after you seen enough of it. Just wall off a little part a yourself. You get used to anything, I guess." She picked up the bat, casually looking it over, and planted it on the floor, using it to heft her substantial weight from the chair. As she ground out her smoke, Harper watched her in horror. More swiftly than Harper imagined she could move, Millie went to the door, closed and locked it then turned to Harper.

Harper shook herself out of her stunned immobility as Millie spoke.

"I bet that big guy you got at home'll think a Sonny Boy first," she said, rolling the bat between her hands. She smiled again at Harper, a bit wanly and tilted her head. "Just know this wouldn't a been my first choice, sweetie. I am fond a you." She studied the bat a moment, wrapping her hands around the base and glanced toward Harper.

"Millie, stop. You don't want to do this," Harper said, as if reason could reach the widow. She rose from the chair, collecting herself to rush Millie, but in that moment, Millie moved forward, lifted the bat above her head and brought it down on the table with a blow more ferocious than Harper would have thought possible, splintering the wood with a loud crack.

"You think I don't *wanna* do this?" she roared, all control now abandoned. "Or can't?"

Just then, Harper heard JD call her name out in the barn aisle. Millie and Harper looked at the door and froze.

"In here," Harper screamed, lunging toward the locked door. "In the storage room!"

Millie stepped to her left and blocked Harper, simultaneously swinging the bat at Harper's head. Going for the door, Harper caught the blow, but the bat glanced off the side of her head. Harper's head snapped to the right and she dropped to her knees, her vision going blood red shot through with white. Hearing JD at the door, Harper clutched the bloody gash above her ear.

"Millie's got the bat!" she screamed at her husband.

Millie raised the bat again, and Harper looked up from the floor like a small, wounded animal wincing in anticipation of the blow to come. She held her head with her left hand and reached for Millie just as the door crashed open and a split panel hit Millie square in the shoulder sending her reeling backward.

"God damnit!" she cried, dropping the bat, her eyes ablaze, her right hand grabbing her left arm. "You broke my damn shoulder!"

JD lifted Harper to her feet, looked at the wound, and then moved to the widow, securing Millie's arms behind her with his cuffs, pain be damned, his eyes boring holes.

"Jesus, be careful! My shoulder's broke!" she cried, wrenching her head around. Seeing JD's fierce look, she cowered. "It's just a little ole head wound," she murmured to JD. "You know how they bleed."

JD walked Millie the few steps to the table and pushed her into the chair. "Don't move a muscle," he ordered, running an exasperated hand over his hair.

"I'm okay," Harper said, standing, though she did feel dizzy. "Really." She turned to her husband. "I need to talk to Millie, just for a second." She seated herself across from the widow and JD rifled through cabinets until he found a gauze pad and wet a cloth under the faucet, handing the gauze pad to Harper.

"We need to get you to the hospital," he said sternly, dabbing the wet cloth at the wound. Harper batted his hand away and pressed the gauze on the wound. JD looked at Millie and scowled. "We'll go in my unit, and she can ride in the back."

Outside the window a large hawk circled, wings unmoving, and soared out of sight on an updraft, his flight an effortless melding with his world. The mares out in the barn, agitated at the violence, had all fled to their pastures or paddocks. A heavy silence settled over the trio.

Harper nodded and lifted a finger. "In a minute." She took the wet cloth from JD and wiped the blood from her cheek and neck, then again held the gauze up to the wound, pressing to staunch the blood. She looked at Millie, who sat mutely, though from the look on her face, in some pain.

JD rose and walked to the door, punching in the precinct on his phone but keeping an eye on Millie. He spoke in low tones as Harper felt the room wheel a bit. She laid her arm on the table to steady herself. She watched the woman sitting across from her, allowing her a moment more to calm down.

Then she said, "You can't wiggle out of this, Millie. You must see that." Harper forced herself to focus, her attitude all business. "I need one thing from you." She waited to see Millie's reaction.

Again, the widow's mood shifted. "Can you get the damned cuffs off, for Christ's sake? It's pullin' my shoulder, hurts like a son-of-a-bitch." She glanced at JD who ignored her, then back to Harper, seeing that was not going to happen. "OK, whut?"

Harper felt faint, whether from the loss of blood or the blow, she wasn't sure. But she knew she had to finish it, though her stomach began to churn.

"Federal agents got all the evidence they need on Henley," she said, "and there's some mention of Seddon in

Barn 41's files. And of course, the drugs." She'd gone over this with Millie before the attack and waited to see if the widow could rewind enough to remember where they'd left off.

Millie nodded. "Yeah, and?"

"When JD and I were in Henley's files we didn't find anything at all to implicate Minetti." Harper took a deep breath and let that sink in. "Looks like he's going to get off Scott free on this one just like he's always done." She pulled away the gauze, saw it was soaked with blood, and turned it over to press the clean side against her head. Her blond hair was caked in drying blood, but none of it altered her focus.

JD pulled up a chair and sat down his seat, staring hard at the widow. "He won't do a minute of jail time," JD emphasized, looking with concern at his wife.

"The blasted hell he won't!" shouted Millie, causing Harper to wince. "I got the goods on him, don't you worry." She shook her head with vigor. "If I'm goin' down, he's damned well goin' down with me!"

Harper nodded. She just hoped he wouldn't slither out of this one as he had all the others over the years.

"Oh yessiree, baby," Millie said forcefully, ignoring her shoulder. "Get the damned cuffs off, willya?" she said to JD. "Where the hell am I gonna go?" JD rose and complied, keeping the bat well away from her.

Millie pulled a cigarette out of her pocket, her left arm hanging limply at her side. She poked the cigarette in her mouth, then went for the lighter, flicking it and inhaling deeply. "I got *all* the goods on his slimy ass," she said, her tone self-satisfied. She looked at JD, squinting as the smoke stung her eye.

"I hope so, Millie. I really hope so," Harper said. She looked at her husband, but he sat stone-faced, which Harper realized, was better than what he was likely feeling.

The widow glared at Harper. "You got no idea how bad I can be when I try . . . I got him by the short hairs. He ain't goin nowhere but down." She smiled at Harper.

Harper didn't smile back.

"And you can take that to the damned bank," Millie said as, far off, the sirens wailed.

Epilogue

Harper spent the night in the hospital but was released the next morning, though with a concussion. Millie was good on her word. She provided all the evidence federal agents needed to arrest Minetti on drug manufacturing and distribution as well as murder. He seemed unphased as agents entered his posh New York digs and put him under arrest, but upon hearing about the evidence against him, Minetti's lawyer seemed concerned. The art collector would not see the outside of a prison cell for a very long time. "Sonny Boy" Seddon was apprehended at his favorite low-end bar, hoisting boilermakers and after protesting his innocence at arrest, found he was facing two counts of murder. He clammed up after that and sat morosely in jail being deemed a flight risk and having no funds for bond, anyway. No one stepped in to take up his cause. Millie was also under arrest for her part in Aubrey's death, participating with Minetti in the drug operation, and conspiracy to commit insurance fraud. Henley Smythe was facing a long prison term for illicit drug trafficking, drug use, and conspiracy, among other charges. Only the Lowen vet escaped arrest when it was determined that there had been no veterinarian involved at all since the signatures on the documents were found to be forgeries.

Manuel would testify and was being placed in protective custody along with his mother. He was given immunity for his testimony and so would not face charges for his part in drugging the horses. Aliana bid him a tearful goodbye, but when the assistant trainer leaned in to kiss her, she threw her arms around him and sobbed. Manuel assured her they would see each other again.

Lowen Farms went up for auction. Harper saw Aviragus purchased by a reputable Australian racing syndicate and wondered if she would ever see the big colt again. She hoped so. In a very real way, she felt he was the only horse that might just give Deacon a run for his money.

Most of the other Lowen horses went to local farms or farms on the east and west coasts, and the client horses went back to their owners or to the trainers the owners indicated. Harper prevailed on JD to purchase Fleet Light, though they had to wade through some legalities since his ownership was technically listed as Minetti, and all the Lowen Farms horse assets he'd owned outright had been seized. After JD called in some favors and Minetti's lawyer got the paperwork in order, Fleet Light was moved to Eden Hill and housed down the aisle from Deacon. Lucas immediately fell in love with the affable colt, laughingly saying the stallion barn sorely needed him as ballast to balance out the Devil Boy.

After the Lowen debts were paid and the rest of the holdings disbursed at auction, Harper and JD took a small vacation. They flew to New York for the weekend and visited Harper's old haunts, which amounted to Arcadia Gallery where she got her start in the New York art world, and then to the woman who'd purchased the small SoHo gallery Harper had subsequently owned. It was wonderful to see the gallery thriving and good to reconnect with old friends. No one was shocked at the turn of events about Stuart Minetti. Their last night in New York, after strolling by Harper's old apartment in the East Village, they made their way to their favorite Italian restaurant, a hole in the wall, dimly lit, but with a great wine list and delicious Northern Italian cuisine. They toasted the end of Henley, Minetti, and Seddon. They mourned Aubrey and felt sorrow for Millie. Then they gazed at each other in the low candlelight, toasted to renewal, went to their hotel, packed their bags, and took the red-eye home. When the plane lifted effortlessly into the deep night sky, JD pulled his wife close, settling in, leaving the recent past and its heavy burden far, far below as they made their way over a darkened continent sparkling here and there with brilliant, restorative light.

Also available: *Blood in the Bluegrass, Book One* in Virginia Slachman's *Bluegrass* Series.

Thank you for reading *Betrayed in the Bluegrass.* Please consider telling a friend about it and maybe leaving a review. Both truly help other readers find the book and that helps authors.

All books available on Amazon.com

CPSIA information can be obtained
at www.ICGtesting.com
Printed in the USA
LVHW051923110722
723236LV00003B/408